The Babel Conspiracy

The Babel Conspiracy

a novel

Sylvia Bambola

Heritage Publishing House

Reader Alert

The Babel Conspiracy is a reworked and edited version of *A Vessel of Honor*, an out-of-print novel written three years prior to 9/11. Because it dealt with terrorism and so much has happened, it needed to be updated before going back to press. In the process, I've added new characters and changed the name. And though it remains basically the same story, there are enough different elements in *The Babel Conspiracy* that those who read the earlier version and enjoyed it, should find something new to enjoy in the updated one, as well.

Also by Sylvia Bambola

"Let us build us a city and a tower whose top may reach unto heaven; and let us make us a name." Genesis 11:4

CHAPTER 1

Another Riot.

Trisha Callahan knew something had happened when she woke up to the smell of smoke drifting over her apartment complex. And between gobbling down a piece of buttered toast, and showering and dressing, she gleaned the details of last night's siege from KFOM.

Now, she stood brushing her long, black hair that fell in waves over her slender shoulders and wondered how this could happen. Impatiently, she tossed the brush onto the rattan tray holding an assortment of toiletries then fastened her blue blazer, leaving the top buttons open to reveal a stylish silk blouse.

Riots had been popping out all over the country like pox, but she never thought it could happen here. Not in Everman—a city known for its low crime and friendly inhabitants.

Where are you God?

If my people, which are called by my name, shall humble themselves, and pray . . . .

Hadn't her pastor predicted this? That America would fall unless believers prayed? She couldn't get it out of her mind. It was the reason she rose an hour early every morning before work. So she could *pray*. Well, she had been praying for months now and where was God? Everyday another car bomb; another random killing by a terrorist.

This was not the America she knew. The America she had grown up in. It broke her heart to see what was happening to the country she loved.

She fingered the buffalo-horn cross by her throat.

What more could she do? She grabbed her purse and keys. She had to stop thinking about it and get her mind on work. The boss's secretary had called even before her alarm went off and told her to come in for an early meeting. And Michael Patterson was not a man to be kept waiting.

Even so, she'd try getting more news in the car. She snatched the remote to click off the TV, but not before hearing the anchor rattle off the riot's toll: three confirmed dead, more than twenty injured, eighteen arrests, ten cars torched, two entire buildings destroyed, with five others partially fire damaged.

She took a deep breath as she fingered the cross one last time then bolted out the door.

●　●　●

Trisha's stiletto heels clicked against the concrete pavement of the underground garage. In the distance, the shriek of an ambulance broke the morning silence.

Oh God, where are you?

Millions of Christians were praying. Why have things gotten worse?

If my people will . . . turn from their wicked ways . . . then will I forgive their sin, and heal their land.

As she walked toward her car she thought of Michael Patterson and felt her stomach knot. Michael Patterson, her boss. Her *married* boss. Humbling oneself and praying was only part of it. It was that other part, that part of turning from our wicked ways that was so difficult. But what did she have to feel guilty about? She had crossed no line.

Except in her heart, and didn't God see the heart?

When she reached her parking spot she unlocked the door of her red BMW and hopped in. Within seconds she was cruising down Highway 9 toward Patterson Aviation, a mere twelve miles outside the city limits. Lamp posts and storefronts blurred as she whizzed past, hoping no patrol cars were around. Her meeting was in ten minutes. No time for being stopped by a cop. And she'd be easy to spot on this empty road. It was barely six o'clock.

She searched the radio for more news about the riot while imagining the heartbreak of those who lost loved ones or shops or homes. Even now, the smell of smoke followed her, filling the interior with its caustic odor.

So much violence. Where would it end?

Since Kamal the Blade declared jihad on America and renamed it ISA, the Islamic State of America, fear permeated even the most mundane activities. The threat of carnage was ever present. And who was there to stop it? Not President Thaddeus Baker. He was weak on terror and even weaker on law and order—often siding with the rioters while chiding the police. She was glad his second term was nearly over and prayed that the new president, whoever he was, would do a better job.

When she heard the Singing Donut squeak out its silly jingle, she turned off the radio, then hit the gas. She glanced at the rearview mirror looking for any sign of a patrol car and noticed a white van tailing her. She needed to slow down. It wasn't worth the ticket. At her speed the fine would be hefty. Her boss would have to wait. She eased up on the gas. So did the van; and following too closely—just a few feet from her bumper.

Why didn't it just pass her?

She floored the pedal. Within seconds the needle read twenty miles over the speed limit. The van kept pace. She was getting nervous, now. Kamal had made looking over one's shoulder common practice. And even though Trisha told herself she was overreacting, she continued monitoring her tail.

She got off at her exit and nearly choked when the van followed. But it was no match for her BMW, and after several hair-pin turns, she lost it.

Why had it followed her? It could easily have run her off the deserted road, if the intent was malicious.

Get a grip, Callahan!

Just a teen getting his kicks by trying to frighten her.

But by the time Trisha entered the double doors of Patterson Aviation the matter of the van was still on her mind.

•   •   •

Trisha was about to test her new theory. She was sure it was his eyes that unsettled her. *The trick was not to look at them.*

"Come in, come in!" barked the man behind the desk.

She hovered by the door before entering the lush oak-paneled office that always smelled of Murphy's Oil Soap. "You sent for me?" She settled in one of the two chairs facing the desk; chairs that, Trisha was certain, had been chosen for their discomfort in order to discourage lingering visitors.

Don't look at his eyes. She briefly closed her own.

"Am I keeping you up, Callahan!" barked a deep, masculine voice.

Her lids snapped open and she stared into a smiling face that contradicted the voice. But he was a man of contradictions. She had learned that about him. And other things too; how he moved his mouth to one side in a half smile when something pleased him, or how he chewed the end of a pencil when deep in thought, or the clumsy way his powerful body reacted when forced to handle a fragile object like the toy model of the P1 airplane on his desk.

"Looks like your boys did their usual thorough job of mutilation." He jabbed the copy of her report lying in front of him. Both the voice and finger belonged to Michael Patterson, president of Patterson Aviation. "The active controls performed well, better than expected."

"Yes, I'm pleased." An understatement. The wind tunnel testing on a sample wing of the Patterson II or P2, where it was loaded, twisted and vibrated, had surprised everyone. "The active controls did a fine job of distributing the stress evenly and the wing showed a high lift-to-drag ratio."

"Don't gloat, Callahan. It'll just cut into your bonus." Mike leaned back in his leather chair barely concealing his own pleasure.

The wing design was years ahead of their competition. It was built to move from the conventional position at subsonic speed then fold backward into an arrow shaped configuration at Mach 2 and up without increasing drag. It had been a heavily contested subject between them.

"But vindication *is* sweet." She tried ignoring the feeling that was coming over her again. What was it about him that unsettled her? That made her feel like an iron filing in front of a neodymium magnet?

"Okay, go ahead. Remind me that it was *your* idea and what a tough time you had talking me into it."

Trisha's laughter came out like a string of musical notes. Two years ago she had come to Patterson Aviation or PA as head of their Research and Development Department. She had an impressive resume: a degree in physics and aeronautical engineering, two years of nuclear fusion research at Princeton University, and four years of working at one of the "Big Three." But she had come to this smaller company in hopes of working on her own innovative ideas and Michael Patterson had welcomed her.

"You did put up a whale of a fight. As I remember, you called my idea 'crazy' then contested every inch of my design."

"What you told me was that you were doodling and came up with a sketch you'd like me to see. Doodling? Seriously? Was that supposed to impress me? But I guess I could have been less difficult."

"You mean less mule-headed?"

Mike's eyes flashed with amusement, his large, muscular frame looking out of place behind the desk. It was as though his powerful, athletic body rebelled at confinement, and even now seemed to press defiantly against his blue Armani suit as though in anticipation of being called into some action.

As she watched him undo his tie and toss it onto a nearby chair, she realized her theory about his eyes was quickly proving unsound. In desperation, she studied the gold wedding band on his finger.

"If I concede to being mule-headed, will you admit to your own unbecoming qualities?"

"Such as?"

"A barbed tongue, for one."

"Barbed tongues have their value."

"And that is?"

"They have a way of pricking one out of his complacency."

Mike chuckled as he picked up a pencil and nibbled the eraser. "How's the new composite material?"

Trisha narrowed her eyes. "Incredible. Unbelievably strong and light. Our projections are holding. It will decrease gross weight and increase payload by ten percent. Now . . . what did you *really* get me up an hour early to discuss?"

Mike tossed the pencil on the desk. "The fusion reactor. Your report, regarding the seventy-five simulated flights, indicates an increase in casing deterioration after the first thirty-five."

Trisha nodded. She understood the gravity of this information. The problem was cooling the hot ionized plasma which reached over sixty million degrees during fusion and was contained inside a webbing of magnetic fields, much like Jell-O being held by a net of rubber bands. Success with the P2 and the nuclear power reactors would catapult Patterson Aviation to the prominence of the "Big Three." But failure to solve the cooling problem could jeopardize the entire P2 project and bring down the company.

She watched a look of impatience contort his face. No use in beating around the bush. "We've got a problem with the cooling system, and we can't count on fixing it without ramifications. Nolan, Audra, and I agree we have only two choices. Nolan favors increasing the magnetic field. I'm opposed because the heavier shielding and additional vacuum pumps will increase gross weight thereby decreasing payload. How much? We can't say at this point. But we all agree it would mean portions of the P2 would have to be altered."

Nolan Ramsdale was R&D's nuclear engineer and Trisha relied on him in matters concerning the nuclear power reactor, the NPR910. But this time, she was going against his advice and knew it placed her on shaky, if not dangerous, ground.

When her boss's eyes narrowed, Trisha knew what he was thinking. The greatness of the NPR910 was not in the fact that nuclear fusion was possible, but that it was possible in a reactor the size of a Rolls Royce RB11 engine, the famous engine that had powered Lockheed's TriStar L1011.

"And the second choice?"

"Create a casing made from a new substance."

"Sounds like another one of your crazy ideas." His voice was curt, but his face told her he was interested. "I suppose you have something in mind?"

"Titanium carbide, the composite . . . ."

"Callahan, I already know it's a heat-shield coating and keeps a space craft from burning up during reentry. But it's not new. So why are you talking about it?" It was his habit to shoot questions in rapid fire when something appealed to him.

"Well, a material's ability to withstand corrosion at high temperatures is directly related to the hardness of that thin protective film which stands between a metal surface and a potentially destructive environment. Titanium carbide deposited . . . ."

"Get to the punch line."

"deposited in the range .3 to .5 has less structural imperfections, and the hardness of the films is second in hardness only to diamonds. The processes of surface and bulk diffusion are thermally activated. The major . . . ."

"I don't need a dissertation, Callahan."

"Convince me, you say, then you narrow the tunnel and force me to act as a battering ram to widen it. No wonder I have migraines."

The muscular executive chuckled. "Alright, batter away."

"Where was I? Oh, right . . . the major variable in determining the microstructure of deposited films is . . . ."

"You're referring to T/Tm ratio. Got it."

Trisha iced a smile. It was hard not to be impressed with this man, with his vast knowledge and his love for the things she loved. Instinctively, she touched the large, cross that hung near her throat, a cross fashioned by her mother years ago as a gift.

She was doing that more often in his presence, this grasping for her anchor. And that anchor went deep. Most of her thirty years of life had been fastened to it; years filled with middy blouses and pleated skirts, prayer books and incense-filled churches.

Something *he* mocked her for—a man without a mooring, without restraint or limits.

She cleared her throat. "Yes, T/Tm ratio. And based on this ratio, a sixty to sixty-five million degree temperature would naturally change the .3-.5 deposition. But like I said, it wasn't titanium carbide that I had in mind."

"Then what in blazes have you been talking about?"

"Something *like* titanium carbide."

"Which is?"

"Titanium X."

"Sounds like something out of *The X-files*. Okay, Callahan, what's this about?"

"It's about a substance that will make titanium carbide look like tissue paper."

Mike laughed. He knew titanium X was nonexistent. "And what does Nolan say?"

"Inconclusive data for formulating an accurate hypothesis."

"His very words?"

"His very words."

"You are, I take it, an expert on this titanium X?"

"No, Audra is. She's done a lot of work with titanium carbide and in the process came up with titanium X. I've gone over her notes. More work needs to be done, but I see enough potential to want to pursue it."

Trisha knew this was going to be a hard sell. Airframe manufacturers did not, as a rule, build their own propulsion system. And her boss's inexperience in this area would make him all the more hesitant to embrace something this radical.

"Assuming we go with Nolan's choice, what major change do you foresee in the actual design of the P2?"

"Reduction of passenger space by twenty to thirty seats." Trisha watched her boss's face drop.

The P2 had been on the board for two years. That represented thousands of man hours. Wind tunnel testing on various parts was well advanced, and plans for a full scale mock-up were being developed. A change in the size of the NPR910 would mean scrapping some of what had already been accomplished. Time and money would be lost. And Trisha knew that money, especially, was a critical factor. If, on the other hand, they were to go ahead with their current project in the hope that a new casing material would be found, the loss in dollars would be even greater if the discovery was not realized. The dilemma was awesome.

"And you favor going with a new composite?"

"It's a big risk but the one I'd take."

"If I was afraid of risk-taking would I have hired you? I'm a businessman. No stranger to speculation. But going against Nolan . . . ." His forehead furrowed.

Trisha sat quietly. She wouldn't push. It was a tough choice he had to make. She wondered if he was thinking of her earlier warning that the reactor casing was unstable and not to go ahead with the full-scale mock-up until they resolved the issue?

He picked up the model of the P1 and turned it around in his hands. "How close is Audra?" His tension-free voice told Trisha he had made his decision.

"Very close." She brushed aside her ebony hair that hung like a lion's mane over her shoulders then folded her arms across her slim body trying to appear calm.

"Okay, Callahan . . . do it."

She knew his permission to go ahead with titanium X was based largely on his confidence in her. But it also added to her pressure. If she wasn't successful, the consequences would be dire. "Thank you."

"For what?" he shot back, his eyes sweeping over her hair, the folded arms and slim body. "We've had our differences but that doesn't mean I don't know what a fine job you're doing. But it does present a problem. It's our interim financing. We're overextended so the banks are out. If you want to complete your R&D, I'll have to go through the board."

Trisha nodded. Lack of funds was the familiar shadow that continued to cloud the project.

"It wouldn't have been necessary if the ten C101's, just out of production, hadn't lost their buyer. The freight company filed bankruptcy yesterday, leaving us holding the bag."

"How is that possible? The company's credit history was investigated and given a thumbs-up by Dun & Bradstreet."

"Callahan, don't start acting like you live under a rock. You know the jihad is killing free enterprise. And the constant rioting over perceived injustices by police has compounded the problem."

"I suppose the airlines are out."

It wasn't unusual for airlines to defray some of the development costs of a new plane. It was this very practice that enabled the Anglo-French development of the Concord SST.

"Forget the airlines. The spike in fuel prices is killing them, too, considering that just one Boeing 747 can guzzle over three thousand gallons of fuel per hour. No, it's the board or nothing. So what I want is this: minimal specs, showing barest details."

Trisha nodded in understanding. Although her boss had controlling interest of PA—fifty-one percent—she had heard how his father, in the last years of his life, had mismanaged the company. Since then, it teetered between the black and red world of profit and loss.

"*Minimal* specs," he repeated. "For Gunther's benefit."

Again Trisha nodded. The Middle East situation continued to deteriorate. The black flag of ISIS now hung over most of it, even those once friendly to the west. And one oil refinery after the other had been brought under its umbrella. Oil now moved through the Strait of Hormuz only by their will, creating a global crisis with the price of a barrel of oil reaching two hundred fifty dollars—money used to further finance the jihad.

Unable to afford the fuel or energy they needed to operate, many businesses closed overnight. As common as the stories of terrorism, were the stories of suicide by defunct entrepreneurs and business owners who had lost everything. Unlike the distraught businessmen who, during the stock market crash of 1929, leaped to their deaths from high-rise office buildings, their modern counterparts went home, and without mess or fanfare, overdosed on sleeping pills or other drugs.

Now, PA was coming up with nuclear fusion, something that would constrict the jihad's financial spigot. If safe nuclear fusion was realized, over time ISIS could be bypassed since there was enough deuterium for plasma available in the oceans to meet present rates of power consumption for at least a million years.

It was this argument that won over her boss two years ago—the prospect of America becoming energy independent. And she had clinched it by telling him that one cubic foot of "free" ocean water represented two million BTU's or close to two thousand gallons of number six oil.

But Robert Gunther worked for Tafco Oil, a company rumored to harbor Islamic sympathies and which still had holdings in Syria, holdings that up to now had never been targeted by the jihad.

"Why do you keep Gunther on the board, anyway?"

Mike laughed. "Politics. He has strong ties to D.C. and a horde of influential friends, including those in the Federal Aviation Administration and the National Transportation Safety Board. In addition, Tafco's influence spans the continents in spite of all the negative rumors. Still, nobody believes Tafco or Gunther actually want to see the black flag of ISIS flying over the White House."

Trisha rose. "I'll get working on that report."

"One more thing." Mike's face tightened. "Be careful."

"Why? What happened now?"

"This is not to leave the room. Understood?"

Trisha nodded.

"Two nights ago we had an attempted break-in. It was stopped by a security guard but the intruder got away."

Like most large companies, Patterson Aviation had doubled its security staff because of the jihad. Armed men patrolled PA twenty-four hours a day. After two years of terrorism in the homeland, American businesses could no longer rely solely on the government but employed their own anti-terrorist protection. Armed guards were common place, as well as complexes protected by barbed wire and sophisticated electronic surveillance.

PA's heavy security was well known. And in light of this knowledge, Trisha found an attempted break-in all the more alarming. She wondered if she should tell him about the white van, then decided against it.

"He was trying to get into *your* building, into R&D. And . . . it's the second attempt this month. So observe maximum security measures, and that goes during your off-duty hours. If anyone suspicious starts hanging around your apartment, if you get unusual phone calls or mail, I want to know about it."

Trisha frowned. "Does Homeland Security know?"

Mike nodded. Every company performing a critical function or a function of national defense was listed by Homeland Security as a possible terrorist target and was frequently visited by a DHS agent who assessed its risk, then advised on how to beef up security.

Patterson Aviation, because of its work in nuclear fusion, was on that list. And agent Peter Myers was a frequent visitor to the plant. Evacuation drills for possible bomb threats were repeated over and over. Bulletproof glass was installed in all ground level windows, and extra security guards were hired; all things PA employees had learned to live with.

"So be careful," Mike repeated. "No heroics, Callahan. This is one situation where that cross of yours isn't going to do much good."

Her hand moved to her throat. "If you notice, I'm not the one who's worried."

A broad smile split the rugged face, embedding splinters of wrinkles around the mouth and eyes. "I know how seriously you take that . . . ornament. Though I still don't get it. But just be careful, okay?"

• • •

Mike stared at the door long after Trisha was gone. There was something satisfying about her; something that both relaxed and tensed that huge frame of his. It was a feeling he had never experienced with anyone else.

And there were times, like now, when he felt close to her.

Only, why couldn't she look more like the head of a research department and less like someone who should be sipping a martini and saying "yes," though he had never asked the question.

"Business and pleasure don't mix," he muttered as he stabbed the intercom too roughly. "Have Buck come to my office!" But minutes later, even before there was a rap on the door, Mike knew that someday he would ask.

• • •

Mike watched the tan, leathery face of Buck McNight wrinkle into a smile as he folded his body into a chair, a body that made the chair appear undersized. He was a man in his early sixties and with an easy, unhurried manner. But his hands, whose folds and creases were stained by machine oil, gave away his real occupation. They were hands adept at ministering to the cogs and wheels of complexity. And herein lay the paradox to an otherwise simple life.

Mike rose from his chair and paced as though working out a cramp. Neither spoke, but their silence was the comfortable silence of two people who knew each other well and had nothing to prove.

Buck was "family." As a test pilot and mechanic for Patterson Aviation for over thirty-five years, he had been a friend to the elder Patterson. He was also friend to Mike, a friend who had taken him fishing on lazy summer afternoons when he was a boy. From Buck, Mike had learned how to pitch a tent and ride a horse. It was Buck who had taken Mike up for his first flying lesson. And it was to Buck that Mike went when burdened with problems, first about failing grades, then failing romances, and now failing projects and companies. He was one of the few people Mike trusted completely.

"How much do you know about deuterium?" Mike said, breaking the silence.

Buck expelled a slow, easy chuckle, like sage rolling in the breeze. "Not much. A heavy isotope of hydrogen. You're using it as the plasma in your reactor. Why?" Buck seldom wasted words.

"I'm going to need some. Callahan's having a problem with the reactor casing. It's breaking down. Her solution is typical; wants to develop a new composite material. What all this means is that the seventy-five tests we've done will have to be repeated. I don't want to go to our present supplier. It would raise questions and add to whatever suspicions might already exist. The less people know what's going on here, the better. That's where you come in. How would you like to go into the 'mining' business? How would you like to 'mine' deuterium?"

The large oil-stained hands hung motionless over the arms of the chair. "Seems to me you'd do better with a physicist." His eyes told Mike he had not taken him literally.

"You'll have your physicist. Nolan Ramsdale. Your role will be to purchase land, building materials, equipment, everything Nolan needs. And he'll advise you on this. But I want it done apart from Patterson Aviation. No connections. Not yet, anyway. At the right time my attorney will annex it to the corporation. But until then everything's on a need-to-know basis. When you've set up shop, contact me."

"When do you want me to start?"

"Right away. I'll arrange a meeting between you and Nolan later this afternoon. And Buck, I don't want Nolan to know any more than he has to, either."

"Okay, Mike," he said, as though needing no further explanation. "You can count on me."

"Some things don't have to be said."

• • •

CHAPTER 2

The shock wave knocked Joshua Chapman off his feet as the explosion ripped through the terminal. Cries of pain rose to a crescendo as spears of shrapnel, hurled twenty feet away, injured dozens. Bodies laid everywhere. Joshua watched a small boy collapse against a wall, his blood painting a macabre fresco of red.

"Security, code-four! Security, code-four!" boomed a voice over the airport loud speaker. Within seconds, a squad of guards appeared.

"Everyone stay calm!" one yelled. But his directive had little effect. People continued screaming, and those still on their feet ran in all directions.

"Everything is under control. You must keep calm. The EM team will attend to your wounds. Please. Everyone. Stay calm."

Dazed and with ears ringing, Joshua struggled to sit up and felt pain radiate down his arm where a piece of metal had lodged in his biceps. He left it. No telling how deep it went. Freeing it might cause the type of bleeding he couldn't stop. Besides, he had felt worse pain.

He looked around, mentally assessing the damage. The bomb must have been taped to the underside of a plastic seat and remotely detonated—blasting apart the rows of molded chairs plus the check-in desk by Gate 12—the arrival and departure point for El Al passengers.

No doubt a message from ISA to Israel.

And an inside job.

Who but an employee could smuggle in the explosives? He was sure it wouldn't take ISA long to claim responsibility.

They were the reason he was here. He had to verify Arie Katz's astonishing claim that ISA was being funded by wealthy U.S. businessmen and that they enjoyed the protection of the powerful.

The question was—how high up?

He rose to his feet, ignoring the torn sleeve and blood running down his arm. The medical team, now required in every airport, had arrived and began restoring order. Already, two nurses were assessing the injured. One directed the doctors to those needing the most help, while the other began cleaning and bandaging the less seriously wounded.

But no one seemed to notice the small boy covered in blood and who now lay unconscious, except for the sobbing woman beside him.

Joshua retrieved one of the thin, blue blankets from the pile an airport employee had deposited on the floor and walked towards the boy. But Joshua had seen enough death to know that even before he reached him it was already too late.

He placed the blanket over the child's body leaving his face uncovered, a face unmarred and as peaceful as an angel's. Let the woman remember him that way.

The pressure in his ears lessened and he could hear her screaming, "My baby is dead! My baby is dead!"

"You may not believe this now, lady, but you're lucky," said a middle-age man who had walked over. "He was hurt real bad. I could see that right off." The man gestured to the small, lifeless child cradled in the woman's arms. "Same thing happened to my niece three months ago. Only it was a car bomb. Poor little kid. She never did nothing to nobody. She was just minding her business, walking to school with friends. Wrong place at the wrong time, that's all. She was hurt real bad, too. Trouble is, she didn't die. She's a vegetable now. Poor little kid."

The expression on the mother's tear-stained face told Joshua she had not understood a word he said.

"My baby . . . my baby . . . ."

"Yeah. Poor little kid. I'm sorry. Real sorry," the man said, and walked away.

"Can you do something for her?" Joshua asked the nearby nurse.

She pointed to his arm, "First you," then led him to an area filled with folding chairs and stainless steel trays piled with medical supplies. "Sit. Let's get that nasty piece of work out."

The aging nurse removed the shrapnel, sterilized the area, and after bringing the bleeding under control put a large butterfly bandage over the gash. Then she wrapped sterile gauze around his arm.

"This needs more attention than I can give. Make sure you go to the hospital for follow-up. You'll need stitches. Maybe even a tetanus shot. Swab and bandage, swab and bandage, that's all I can do. But for some of these poor souls it won't be enough." She secured the end of the gauze. "So, who's going to claim responsibility this time?"

Joshua shrugged. He wasn't about to voice his suspicions here. "Could be any one of them. There are so many terrorist groups now."

The nurse grunted. "A person isn't safe anywhere nowadays. So much violence! I tell you son, I see it everyday. It makes you wonder what life is all about."

Joshua watched the paramedics place the lifeless boy on a stretcher then cover his face. "Yes, it makes you wonder."

●　●　●

Joshua tossed his half-empty Styrofoam coffee cup into the nearby trashcan that no one seemed to use, judging by the debris on the sidewalk, then leaned against the wall of the graffiti-covered pawn shop. He pulled out his phone and tried texting Arie Katz, one last time, but got the same signal telling him Arie's phone had been compromised and that his friend was in danger.

It was this very thing that had brought him here four days earlier than planned. After receiving Arie's signal twenty-four hours ago, the Mossad had remotely wiped the phone then pulled Joshua from another assignment and ordered him to the states. So far, Arie still had not coded-in to reinstate the phone, and Joshua needed to find him. He had been scouring the neighborhood for the past two hours, visiting places his friend normally frequented. He didn't dare go to Arie's apartment for fear of blowing his own cover.

The mission was too important to jeopardize it the first day out.

He straightened when he saw a bearded, swarthy-looking man in a hoodie scurrying down the sidewalk then dart into a shop that boasted, according to the sign in the window, as having the largest assortment of video games in America.

Arie!

Thank God.

He crossed the busy street and entered the store, which reeked of weed. Its backroom was a known pot house where marijuana and other illegal drugs were sold. He'd have to be careful. If he caused too big a scene it could garner unwanted attention.

He flipped through a rack of assorted *Mortal Kombat* games then went to another rack containing several versions of *Call of Duty*, all the while watching Arie out of the corner of his eye. And just as Arie turned, Joshua put out his foot and tripped him.

"Hey man! You did that on purpose!"

"Sorry. I didn't mean it."

"Says you! I should give you a busted lip for . . . ." The man's eyes widened when he looked at Joshua for the first time.

"Look, I said I was sorry!"

"Well, I'm gonna make you sorrier!"

A large man with tattooed arms rushed over just as Arie balled his hands into fists. "Take it outside, boys. No fighting in here. It's bad for business."

"You have no quarrel with me," Joshua said, picking up a copy of *Call of Duty*. "I just came to buy some entertainment."

Arie stepped back. "Yeah, well . . . okay. Maybe it was an accident." Then he turned and walked out.

Joshua paid for his purchase and left, knowing Arie would be outside waiting. As soon as the shop door closed behind him, Joshua felt two hands grab his shoulders, felt his body slam hard against the side of the brick building.

"They're on to me," Arie whispered.

Joshua dropped his package and smashed his fist into Arie's chest. Then leaning into him, he mumbled, "Meet me tonight, ten o'clock, under the bridge. I'll get you to a safe house." Another blow sent Arie reeling backward. Joshua hadn't wanted to hit him so hard, but he had to make it look good.

"Put your hands on me again and I'll flatten you!" he shouted. "I told you it was an accident. You punks always have something to prove."

Arie clenched his fist and swung, clipping Joshua's chin. With one punch, Joshua made good his threat and sent Arie sprawling onto the concrete sidewalk. He frowned when he saw blood trickle from his friend's lip.

But better a split lip than Arie's life.

• • •

Audra Shields dabbed lipstick on her mouth like a skilled artisan dabbing her canvas. Behind her the TV droned on about the Everman airport bombing. She was tired of hearing it. It had filled the airwaves all day. Ten people dead, four others critically wounded, a dozen more with assorted injuries.

First a riot then an airport bombing. What next?

She shouldn't be listening to this stuff. It was stressing her, and on her day off when she needed to decompress, especially after Trisha's news yesterday. She was to go all-out with her titanium X experiments. And she knew what that meant. Michael Patterson planned to use it for the reactor casing.

More stress.

She capped her lipstick, tossed it on the vanity, then picked through the crumpled tissues and makeup brushes and jars of cream until she found the remote and clicked off the TV. She ignored the ache between her shoulders that reminded her how tired she was.

But she wasn't about to spend the night alone.

Life was too short. Just ask the families of those who had died at the airport. Everyday there seemed to be another terrorist attack, another riot. Life could be snuffed out in an instant. No guarantee she'd live long enough to collect Social Security. So why sit around moping on her couch? Better to squeeze what she could out of life.

She studied her reflection.

Tom Halleron, her college beau, had said she was beautiful in an Ivy League sort of way. It had pleased her then. But now it seemed so tame, so plastic and Barbie doll-like. Still, there was little she could do about her flawless peach complexion, bouncy blond hair, and well defined lips, though for a while she had considered dying her hair black before deciding against it. For some reason her clean looks attracted dirty men.

And maybe that wasn't so bad.

That meant no proposals of marriage. Not like Tom Halleron's. She had barely dodged that bullet. Cooking, scrubbing, chauffeuring children and pets around in SUVs? Forget it. That wasn't for her. Those were the things that made a woman old before her time. She had seen what it did to her friends—the same friends who were now pressuring her to marry before her thirtieth birthday.

But too late.

Thirty was only weeks away. The thought pricked her, though she didn't know why. Perhaps because it *sounded* so grownup, so mature, as though she should be further along that road of "having it all together" than she actually was.

She picked up her mascara and applied it to already blackened lashes as she thought about the last man she brought home. He had had a disgusting habit of sucking air between his teeth and in the morning had stolen all the money from her wallet.

She was getting careless.

No repeat performances like that, she thought, as she raced out the door. She'd have to be more careful. But not *too* careful. She wasn't going to worry about anything; not her thirtieth birthday or airport bombings or riots or . . . dreary Saturday nights.

●　●　●

Grobens Tavern was already hopping when Audra entered. The familiar five-piece band that played every Saturday night made the walls vibrate, while a stringy-haired singer, wearing a white Stetson and sounding like he had had one Jack Daniels too many, slurred a Blake Shelton song. "You'll be my sugar baby. . . ."

Audra pressed against the bar, her tight designer jeans suddenly feeling too tight. "I'll have the usual."

The dark, burly man behind the bar studied her as he poured out a Black Label. "Here you go, cutie."

Audra winked, then pushed a twenty-dollar bill toward him. She scanned the crowded dance floor where couples gyrated and clung to one another, and saw the usual thirty-something crowd ranging from executives to construction workers.

"Anyone interesting, Ace?"

"Na. You can dress them in thousand dollar Armani suits or put them in jeans, it don't matter. Most of them are jerks. Not the kind a girl like you should bother with." Ace Corbet leaned over the bar. "You need someone with class. And I know just the guy who can deliver."

"Yeah, I bet you do."

"No . . . seriously. I got more class in this here pinkie than these jerks got in their entire bodies. Why don't you wait for me after work and I'll prove it?"

"You used that line last time, Ace. I appreciate the offer, but you're just not my type."

Ace backed away. "From what I've seen, you're not always that particular."

The music stopped and when the stringy-haired singer announced that the band was taking a ten minute break, Audra made her way to the juke box containing a large selection of CDs. Ace Corbet called it an iJuke and had once bragged how it also played WAV and MP3 files.

She took a sip of Scotch as she studied the titles, all the while wondering why Ace's last remark still felt as abrasive as an irritating pebble in her shoe.

Forget him.

He was a bore. Why should she settle when she had no trouble in turning her share of heads? Even though nearly thirty.

She looked for something by Christina Aguilera. Something to dispel the depression and feeling of loneliness creeping over her. Aguilera's *I am beautiful* rolled around in her head. Just the uplift she needed. But before she could find it, a voice broke in.

"Hey, sexy! You gonna move over and let someone else at this juke?"

Audra stared into a handsome, grinning face. "Well . . . I . . . can't find what I want. You go ahead."

"I bet you're a Demi Lovato fan, right?" The lean, muscular man bent over the juke box then paused. "Or maybe you're feeling more in the mood for Adele? Why don't you let me play a few for you?"

"Well, *Someone Like You* is one of my favorites." Audra had never seen him before. There was something disturbing about him. Something that told her to run the other way. Instead, she smiled.

"So . . . what do you say?" He tapped impatiently on the juke.

"Go ahead, stranger." There was flirtation in her voice.

The man laughed a coarse, insolent laugh. "Not stranger for long, I hope. The name is Bubba, Bubba Hanagan." And as he slipped a few coins into the slot, he let his leg brush against her.

● ● ●

The aroma of the bouillabaisse in front of Trisha obscured the scent of the herbal candle sitting in the middle of the table and curling smoke up the sides of its glass enclosure. She watched as her companion, Dr. Daniel Chapman, skillfully opened the huge Maine lobster on his plate then probed one of its claws with a silver pick.

"I see why you're rated the top surgeon in Everman Hospital."

"Don't mention that place! Please. What a day. You wouldn't believe how busy we've been with all the casualties from the airport bombing this morning. I can't tell you how good it is to be here with you. To forget the world outside . . . all the violence." Daniel's serious face gave way to a smile. "Did I say you look gorgeous?"

"Only ten times, but thank you." Trisha's thick, black hair was pulled back into a French braid. Pearls, shaped like teardrops, hung from each lobe, and her green, silk dress shimmered in the candle light. "You're just grateful to see a woman who isn't in scrubs."

Daniel shook his head as he eyed her. "You look like you stepped out of a fashion magazine. I think you're one of the most sensational-looking women I know."

"I thought for sure you knew more than two."

"I know plenty, thank you. And believe me, there's plenty more who'd like to know me. Not that I'm Mr. Wonderful or anything. It's just that 'doctor' still has a magic ring for the ladies. Believe it or not, as liberated as women say they are, they still want their daughters to marry a doctor. I *know*. I've had enough mothers try to set me up with their little beauties. Funny, isn't it?"

"Well, my mother kept telling me to *be* a doctor. She never said anything about marrying one."

Daniel laughed. "Now . . . if they all looked like you."

Even in the dim light Trisha saw the indentation of his dimple. He was more charming than handsome, with a kind, pleasant nature. She watched the dimple deepen as she fished out a clam shell then licked her fingers. "Messy. Definitely an Emily Post no-no."

"You're the only one I know who enjoys food as much as I do. In case you haven't noticed, this body is the lean receptacle of a true epicurean."

"That's because you're thirty-five. Give it a few years, then you'll be sorry!" She dunked a chunk of Italian bread in her bowl.

"See, that's one of the reasons I'm so crazy about you." He looked a bit too earnest as he jutted his chin toward her bread dripping with sauce.

"If I thought you were serious, this would be our last dinner together."

"I know. You're too busy for any real commitment. I get that. But I suspect it also has something to do with you still wanting it to be like it was in Saint Joseph's where a date with a guy didn't mean an automatic trip to the back seat of a car. You like your men eager, hopeful, but not very demanding."

"I thought we were talking about messy food, epicureans, and the like."

"I've decided to change the subject."

"Okay, as long as you have, then let me ask you something." Trisha wiped her fingers on her white linen napkin. "Is that why you never asked me out in high school?"

"I didn't ask because I was too chicken. Then, in college, you seemed uninterested in dating anyone."

"That's because the guys made dating as appealing as mud wrestling." Trisha chased a shrimp around with her fork. "Did you know I was dubbed 'Ice Queen' by the jock fraternities? But I didn't care.

I saw too many girls ruin their lives. I've heard it said that 'men play at love to get sex and women play at sex to get love.' It must be true because I saw it enacted over and over again."

"But aren't you playing, too? Playing it safe by going out with someone like me? Someone you'll only consider as a friend?"

Trisha ignored the ardent look on his face. Lately, things seemed to be taking a turn in their relationship; a turn she didn't welcome. "We *are* friends, Daniel. And I value that friendship. You're like a breath of fresh air. A gentleman with a sense of humor and a brain, and I enjoy your company."

Daniel pushed away his plate then dipped into the nearby finger-bowl of warm water. "Regarding those frat boys—the joke's on them. You have plenty of passion, Trisha. I've seen it on your face, heard it in your voice whenever you talk about airplanes. So when you finally fall for someone, I suspect you're going to have trouble keeping a lid on things. And it makes me wish all the more that it could be me. Still . . . I can't resist pressing the point. We do have fun together. Don't we?"

Trisha nodded.

"And some marriages are built on a lot less, you know."

"Meaning?"

"Well, what would be so terrible if we, you and I, got married?"

"Because we have fun together?"

"Because I *love* you!"

Trisha felt the same emotions as when, in fourth grade, she caught Johnny Lawson stuffing a love letter into her school bag. She would never forget that biting look of humiliation on his face. It was painful to feel what other's felt, to feel their hurts and disappointments. She had tried hating him for his adoration, for transmitting that pain to her like a contagious disease. But she never could. Now, twenty-one years later, she saw that same look of humiliation bite into Daniel's face as he realized the extent of her surprise.

They had never discussed marriage. And being the product of parents who had been happily married, Trisha viewed it as desirable.

She remembered how, after twenty-five years together, her parents still held hands; still, with heads together, whispered their inner-most secrets; still laughed and had fun; and how sometimes they would even steal a kiss on the couch.

It was something she wanted for herself some day. But she couldn't force her feelings, fabricate something that wasn't there. She admired Daniel. They were long-time friends, and he was one of the finest men she had ever known. And she did love him. Just not in *that* way.

"Daniel, you know I love you like a brother."

The dimpled face yielded to the blow of disappointment. "Ouch. I suppose that will have to do for now. But who knows, maybe in time you'll change your mind. I'd like to hold on to that hope. Do you mind?"

Trisha shifted uncomfortably in the chair. "Don't do it, Daniel. I don't see our relationship going any further. And I love you too much to hurt you by being dishonest."

• • •

"So what did he say?" Trisha asked, as Daniel pocketed his cell phone and slipped behind the wheel of his Caddy.

"Don't come."

"He's probably exhausted. He just got in this morning and with the stress of the explosion and all, hardly up for visitors. And it works for me, too. That bouillabaisse had to be laced with tryptophan because my eyelids feel like manhole covers." Trisha tried to sound upbeat, but the awkwardness she felt over Daniel's proposal still lingered, and she was anxious to go home.

"You're not getting off that easy."

"You mean you're still going?"

"Of course. I'm the older brother. I don't have to listen to him. Besides, I want to check his arm. Twenty stitches. That's what it took to close that gash."

Trisha nodded. Daniel had told her all about it over the phone earlier in the day.

"I just wish he'd settle down. All this flying around the world for his software company—I don't like it. When you do that much traveling the odds are that sooner or later you'll find yourself in the middle of something bad. Next time he may not be so lucky."

"He loves his job and he loves Global Icon. He's never going to quit."

"I'll talk to him about it."

"Would you like someone talking to you about quitting your job?"

"Hardly."

"Then be a good big brother and don't talk to Joshua, either."

Daniel squinted through his windshield at the posh apartment complex ahead. "I'm making no promises," he said, as he pulled into the underground garage.

● ● ●

Trisha felt a rush of pleasure when Joshua opened the apartment door. "It's good to see you," she said, smiling and hugging him, careful not to touch his injured arm.

The boyishly handsome man, seven years Daniel's junior, responded with a smile of his own. But his face hardened into a mock frown when he saw his brother standing behind her. "What part of 'don't come' didn't you understand?"

"We won't stay long," Trisha said, entering the spacious apartment leased by Global Icon for their out-of-town employees. "Daniel didn't want to call it a night before checking on you so don't bite too hard."

"Never you, Trisha, but I'd love to take a chunk out of this stubborn brother of mine."

Joshua ushered the pair into the living room that sported a large marble fireplace, a sixty-inch flat screen TV, and mahogany-framed couches and chairs with brown silk upholstery that looked straight out of a Benetti Italia showroom.

"I can only offer you bottled water. Fridge is empty. With all the excitement I haven't had time to stock it."

Trisha sank into the down-cushioned couch. "Nothing for me. I'm stuffed. Daniel wouldn't let me leave the restaurant without having desert, and that tiramisu was enough for four!"

"Let me guess. You went to Bella Luna's?"

"Where else?" Trisha watched Daniel examine Joshua's arm. "Your brother is obsessed with the place."

"Did I tell you that when Joshua came to the hospital his bandage was soaked in blood?"

"I bumped into a wall. No big deal. But you made it as good as new." When Joshua moved his arm up and down to demonstrate, Trisha saw him wince.

"Of course the whole time he stitched me up, Daniel joked about finally getting even with me for losing his favorite Spalding mitt when we were boys. Some brother, huh?"

"When are you moving back to America? Flying is too dangerous now. With your credentials you could get a job here just like that." Daniel snapped his fingers.

"I like living in Israel and being near Global Icon headquarters, so save your breath big brother."

Trisha watched Joshua settle in a nearby chair. There was something off about him. She had thought that for awhile, now. He worked behind a desk all day yet maintained the body and strength of a Spartan. She had mentioned this to Daniel, once, suggesting that his brother might be working for the CIA or Mossad and how his job provided perfect cover. Daniel only laughed.

"I think there's another reason you want to stay in Israel," she said, and was taken back by the startled look on his face. "I think your father has made a zealot out of you. Wasn't he a member of the Haganah?"

Joshua nodded. "And proud of it. After Britain's waning commitment to restoring Israel's homeland, the Haganah began smuggling Jews into Palestine and . . . ."

"Don't get him started. He can go on for hours about this stuff," Daniel said, frowning at his brother.

"and Dad fought under Ben-Gurion and helped surviving European Jews enter the Holy Land."

Trisha noticed the fire in Joshua's eyes. A fire she had never seen in Daniel's when it came to Israel. Joshua's commitment seemed all-consuming and made her, again, feel there was something about him that didn't add up.

"Didn't your dad take part in the attack on a British concentration camp at Athlit?"

Joshua smiled. "He did. And helped liberate over two hundred illegal Jews, then later dispersed them into the kibbutzim. When the Haganah made a truce with Britain in '46, Dad joined the Yishuv and fought with Menachem Begin. Even after Israel was declared a state in '48, Dad remained in the Yishuv. He knew the declaration would enrage the Muslim world and that their armies would immediately cross the Palestine borders in an effort to forcibly nullify the partition resolution."

"Yes, but then Dad came to *America*," Daniel added, taking a seat beside Trisha. "And he became an *American*. And that's what you are, Joshua . . . *American*. And *this* is where you should live."

"I have dual citizenship, like Dad did, remember? I belong in Israel, too. And even when Dad came here, he continued fighting for Israel by forming Supporters of Israel to lobby congress regarding matters concerning the Jewish state.

"Israel needs all its men now. Who knows what will happen with Russia's Marine Brigade 810 fighting alongside Hezbollah Special Forces in Syria? It's just a matter of time before they go after our oil fields in the Golan. They've already begun drone surveillance. They claim it's confined to Syria, but who knows? And they've established a base in the coastal city of Latakia, installing batteries of S-300 anti-aircraft missiles. And why? ISIS doesn't have an air force. And what about the arrival of four Russian Sukhoi 30SM tactical jets already in Latakia and the half-dozen MiG-31 interceptors on a runway in Damascus?"

"What's your new assignment?" Trisha asked, seeing Daniel flush with anger, and regretting she had brought up the subject.

Joshua raked his hair. "Global Icon has been hired by Senator Philip Merrill's campaign. Seems their computers were hacked and they want additional security."

Trisha's eyes narrowed. "Why now? The election is in six months, and unless someone discovers that Senator Merrill is an ax murderer or an international drug dealer, he'll be our next president. He has a double-digit lead in all the polls. So, why spend all that money? Global Icon isn't exactly cheap."

Joshua looked at his watch. "No skin off my nose how they spend their money. And if they want to use it to keep me employed, that's fine with me." He yawned then glanced at his watch again. "Nine thirty, guys. I'm bushed. It's been a long day."

When they said their "good-byes" Trisha leaned closer to Joshua. "Be careful," she whispered, not understanding why she said it.

"What? Be careful of loose women? Be careful of exploding computers?"

"Just be careful."

● ● ●

Joshua made his way to the bridge, the one connecting lower and upper Everman. Below it ran the Wachupa River, a narrow silty body of water that, surprisingly, still contained catfish. He maneuvered down the bank toward the huge, concrete abutment anchoring this side of the beam bridge to lower Everman. His shoes squished in the mud as he walked. He hoped Arie would already be here. He wanted to tell him that the safe house had been prepared and that two Mossad agents were, even now, on their way from Tel Aviv to help get him out of the country.

In the meantime, Joshua's mission still held: confirm Arie's last encrypted message to headquarters stating that U.S. President Thaddeus Baker had connections with ISA, and that Baker had, in fact, given them a directive—disrupt the streets of every major city in America by targeting police and fomenting riots.

And Joshua was to do it all without the help of the CIA or FBI or DHS, and before Israeli Prime Minister Yossi Behrman entered talks next month with the U.S. concerning Israel's oil discovery in the Golan Heights. Prime Minister Behrman needed President Baker's support in the already brewing dispute over who owned the oil rights. Syria, backed by Russia, claimed it was theirs, stolen from them by Israel in the Six-Day War. Without U.S. help, the issue was sure to find its way to the UN, a notoriously anti-Semitic organization; one that had issued sixty-one resolutions condemning Israel for human rights violations while Egypt, Saudi Arabia, Yemen, Jordan, Lebanon, Qatar and the UAE had never received even one.

Arie's accusation seemed fantastic. But he was one of Mossad's best. Never careless, never sent information he hadn't corroborated. Still, Joshua needed confirmation.

The closer Joshua got to the abutment, the deeper he sank into the mud. The sucking noise of his shoes hardly made it stealthy. But even in the dark, he saw no one was here.

Now, there was nothing for him to do but wait.

When his legs began to ache and his feet became numb from cold, wet mud seeping into his shoes, he checked his watch. A half-hour gone. Arie was never late . . . unless. Joshua couldn't afford any more time. His friend must be in trouble. He'd have to chance it and go to the apartment.

His cover be hanged.

• • •

Joshua pulled the hood over his black wig then pushed his night glasses tighter against his nose; glasses that resembled a pair of Carrera readers and enabled him to see in the dark, though everything had a green and silver hue.

He walked down the street that smelled of smoke and garbage, ignoring the rats scurrying among the debris. The further he walked the more graffiti-covered the buildings became.

A group of men loitering on one of the corners eyed him as he approached. The biggest, with tattoos covering both arms and a red bandana around his forehead, stepped in front of him.

"Hey, what's up man? Whatcha doing here?"

Joshua slipped his hand into the pocket of his sweatshirt and gripped the handle of his 9 mm Beretta, the outline of which could be seen when he twisted it inside his pocket and pointed the barrel at his adversary.

The stranger forced a laugh. "Hey, no problem, man. I don't want no trouble. But if you don't want trouble, either, then don't go too far with *that*." He gestured with his chin toward Joshua's bulging pocket. "The pigs are out. Just a block away. About ten squad cars."

Joshua eased his finger off the trigger. "What happened?"

"Someone lost his head." With that the man stepped aside.

Behind him the others snickered. "Yeah, someone lost his head," one of them said.

Joshua shrugged. "Too bad." But his heart pounded as he walked away. Arie lived up ahead. He couldn't move too fast. Couldn't look too anxious. He sauntered down the street, past the remains of the two buildings burnt down the night before, then spotted flashing lights and a sea of blue uniforms.

Curious tenants streamed from their apartments and clogged the sidewalk. The closer Joshua got, the thicker the crowd. Young men cursed and waved their fists in threatening gestures toward the police who were busy cordoning the area with yellow tape.

The tension was palpable.

It wouldn't take much to start another riot.

Joshua pushed through the crowd, stopping a few feet from the tape. He eyed the massive oak door of Arie's apartment building where his friend lived under the assumed name of Abdul Kabani. Chiseled into the door were the words, "*Allahu Akbar*" and a crude carving of a crescent.

"What happened?" he asked a young boy standing next to him, his tone emotionless.

The boy casually took a drag from his cigarette. "A beheading."

"Who was it?"

When the boy shrugged, Joshua pushed his way to the front just in time to see the medical examiner and his attendants wheeling a covered body toward a waiting van.

"A John Doe?" one of the officers asked the ME.

"No, his ID says he's Abdul Kabani, and they found a bunch of jihadi literature all around the place. Pipe bombs, too. They're bagging some of it now."

"Makes no sense. Have the jihadists started killing their own?"

The ME frowned. "Could be a sunni-shia turf war. They're crazy, these people. Beheading the guy wasn't enough. Someone went and carved a crescent into his forehead."

Joshua faded back into the crowd barely under control. He knew of only one person who would carve a forehead. It was Kamal's calling card; a man who knew how to inflict maximum pain before killing his victims.

Had Kamal broken Arie?

If so, what information had Arie given him? Was Joshua compromised? And why had Arie gone back to his apartment when he should have stayed in a public venue where it was safer?

Arie was a pro. There had to be a reason. Had he gone to retrieve something or leave something . . . something he wanted Joshua to find? He needed to get inside the apartment no matter the risk. He couldn't let it go, not now. Kamal had raised the stakes.

He had made it personal.

Again.

• • •

Joshua wore the same hooded sweatshirt and black wig he had worn earlier. He even smudged dirt on his face. It would make him harder to remember should a confrontation arise, though it seemed unnecessary in this darkness.

The quarter moon was obscured by clouds, and most of the street lights had been vandalized by thugs hoping to hide their activities from patrol cars that roved less and less frequently since the riot.

He had parked his rental car four blocks away making the last and most dangerous part of the journey on foot. The baseball bat he carried and the gun bulging in his pocket had deterred most aggression so far. He had to pull out his gun only once, and that ended quickly with the assailant fleeing into a nearby alley.

At Arie's apartment building dim lights shone through grease-smudged windows and cast an eerie glow around the entrance telling Joshua the stoop was deserted. He covered the four steps in two strides, then opened the heavy wooden door. It was three in the morning and still he heard a TV blasting.

He made his way to the second floor, to the door marked twenty-eight. Ignoring the yellow police tape, he pulled a lock pick from his pocket and within seconds was inside.

Placing his bat by the door, he maneuvered to the only two windows in the apartment and pulled the shades. Next, he felt his way to the bathroom, brought out a towel and stuffed it along the bottom of the apartment door. Only then did he turn on the lights. Even so, he was taking a chance that someone would notice a glow from the windows. But how else could he examine the place?

The room was a shambles with blood everywhere, most of it in the middle where the body had rested, though no chalk markings or tape outlined it.

The police hadn't finished processing the crime scene because near the large blood spot was Arie's phone. No point retrieving it. It was one of Mossad's new phones that employed fingerprint technology and automatically sent a signal to headquarters, and other agent phones in the group, if an unauthorized person tried using it without first punching in a special code. And if they did, it was remotely wiped.

He stepped through the littered field. Everything had been picked over by the intruders. Even the couch cushions were slashed. Kamal must have thought Arie was hiding something, too.

He decided to explore the less disturbed areas and entered the bathroom where he checked the medicine cabinet for hollowed-out shaving cans and false toothpaste tubes. Finding nothing he went to Arie's closet and checked shoe soles and jacket pockets.

Next, he inspected the wood furniture and stopped when he saw an "AK" carved into Arie's nightstand.

AK for Abdul Kabani *and* Arie Katz?

With all the nicks and scratches he had almost overlooked it. He ran his fingers along the sides searching for a crevice where a note could be stashed. Finding none, he turned his attention to the scarred headboard and took his time going over every inch until he saw an "R" scratched on one of the square legs; something Arie knew Joshua would notice since it was the letter Joshua spent the better part of a year scrawling across his files and gym equipment.

R for Rachel.

His fingers probed all four sides until, at the back, he felt a piece of loose wood. He pushed the bed away from the wall, then, with his lock-pick, pried away the wood exposing a small carved-out niche containing a piece of white, folded paper. He pulled it out. Instead of words there was a crude drawing of a crane . . . or ladder—it was hard to tell—some barbed wire and the letters TO.

Obviously, Arie left this message in coded form for fear Kamal or his bunch would find it. But what did it mean? What was Arie trying to tell him? Did TO mean he was to go to a specific place?

And if so, where?

He'd run it through his own decoding software as well as send it off to headquarters in Dimona. But now he had to get out of here. He sprang to his feet, flipped off the lights, grabbed his bat, and within seconds exited the building.

• • •

CHAPTER 3

Trisha glanced at the rearview mirror and watched the white van inch closer to her bumper. It looked like the same van from the other day, but she couldn't be sure. To her, all white vans looked alike. She pressed the accelerator and when she did, the van kept pace. This time she wasn't going to keep it to herself. With one hand, she fished for the phone in her purse and made a mental note to get a smaller bag.

She was about to dial Buck, to apprise him of her situation, when the van suddenly changed lanes and sped past her, then exited the highway. She felt foolish as she slipped her phone back into the purse. Her imagination had gotten the better of her.

She took a deep breath trying to regain her composure. The sun warming her arm through the open car window felt good. So did the swirling breeze playfully rearranging her hair as she sped down the road that felt like a ribbon of glass.

The highway was open, deserted and well-paved, and led to a small, tight-knit community of Cherokee, one of the Five Civilized Tribes which, her mother said, included the Chickasaw, Creek, Choctaw and Seminole.

She forgot the van as she sang along with the CD blasting out a favorite tune. "'Jesus, Jesus. He's as close as the mention of His name.'"

God was *so* good even in the midst of a dangerous and chaotic world. She couldn't imagine life without Him. Her mother had taught her about Jesus when she was young. And Trisha couldn't remember a time when she didn't love Him. He was the center of her life, the very reason for her existence. How could she be anything but joyful?

And she was.

But . . . .

Her joy would be complete if only she could get her *boss* out of her mind.

She pulled down a street lined with tidy brick dwellings and manicured lawns, then parked by a house with Kelly green shutters and a thick crop of azaleas clustered along its front.

When she got out of the car she headed straight to the back of the house. On a day like this Mom was sure to be working in her vegetable garden. She waved when she saw a tall, trim woman in denim carrying a bag of mulch. At once her mother dropped the bag and extended her arms.

"How was the ride?" the elder Callahan said as she embraced Trisha.

"Long."

Her mother laughed and brushed aside shiny strands of black hair that had escaped her ponytail. Her complexion was darker than Trisha's and her features squarer, bolder. But by everyone's account, she was a fine looking woman.

"You look great, Mom. As usual."

"And you look tired. You're working too hard." Mrs. Callahan led her daughter to the back door and into the kitchen, then retrieved a pitcher of iced tea from the refrigerator and poured two glasses.

"How are you doing, Mom? Really? Still missing Dad?" Trisha pulled out a chair and sat down.

"One doesn't spend a lifetime with a person then get over losing him in six months. Yes, I miss Paddy, that wild Irishman, *very* much."

"You could move to the city. Closer to me. That way I could see you more often."

"I would never leave my people, Patricia. You know that. And I'm happy here."

Trisha nodded. She knew how much her mother loved tribal customs and history. How often had she told Trisha the story of the Trail of Tears, when the Cherokee were forced off their land by the government because the white man found gold on it? Or about the Cherokee's love for learning and books? Or how many notable people had come from their tribe: artists, musicians, politicians, writers, lawyers?

Trisha also knew her mother had a deep spiritual connection and often spoke about a spiritual nation inside the political one. "We are of the lost tribe of Israel. A very spiritual people," her mother often said. And when she did, Trisha would just nod, knowing that only three writers in the seventeen and eighteen hundreds believed the Cherokee were descendants of Jews.

"Come, let's sit on the porch."

Trisha rose and followed her mother out the front door.

As the elder Callahan rocked, Trisha sat beside her, enjoying the cool breeze sweeping down from the nearby hills. She tilted her head back to catch the wind before reaching over and taking her mother's hand. "How many hours have we sat on this porch together, do you think?"

"Too many to count."

"I remember every one of them and all our conversations, too. And I don't think I've ever said, 'thank you.'"

"For what?"

"For providing a happy, peaceful home in which to grow up. I know there were times you went without in order to put braces on my teeth or give me a new school wardrobe or for a class trip or some other thing that kids are always needing or wanting."

"What brought this on?"

Trisha shrugged. "I don't know. Everything is so topsy-turvy now with all the rioting and violence. I don't think we can afford to leave things unsaid anymore. Who knows what tomorrow will bring? Plus, I'm getting older—at least old enough to appreciate you, to appreciate all you did for me."

"I'm a mother, Trisha. I did no more than other mothers down the ages have done for their children."

Trisha squeezed her hand. "We both know that's not true. You put up with a lot."

"Are you talking about your junior high years?"

"Yes. And I'm sorry. Sorry I was . . . ashamed of you, ashamed you were half Indian, ashamed I was a quarter."

"I know how much that word 'half-breed' can sting. You didn't want to be different. You didn't want to stand out. It was a hard time for you . . . when learning and growing, tears and joy, all seemed to fold together in awkward adolescence like a jelly roll. Do you remember what I told you?"

"Never allow anyone to make you ashamed of who you are. That God made me and I must not insult Him by my shame. You were so wonderful and wise. And then you told me not to be afraid. That I was to soar like an eagle."

"But you are afraid now."

Trisha turned to her mother and frowned. "How could you know that?" When her mother didn't answer, Trisha nodded. "Yes, I'm afraid. But only of myself, of my own weakness."

"I have sensed that for some time, Patricia. And I've been praying. The world is a difficult place and you are alone and vulnerable. You need a proper husband. Hasn't Daniel proposed yet?"

"We're friends, Mom. Only friends."

"I don't think Daniel would agree. And perhaps you would give him a chance if you . . . didn't love another?"

"Mom! Why would you say that?"

"Because it's true. And it's someone you are ashamed of loving."

Trisha tensed. "I don't want to talk about it. It's something I need to work out myself. Let's talk about something else. Tell me what's new with the council."

Mrs. Callahan withdrew her hand from Trisha's. "Some of the members have had visions of a coming danger. They say when it comes, the Cherokee must go to their safe place in the hills. They saw armored trucks and soldiers and a camp."

"They're always having visions. You can't put too much store in them. You can't guide your life by them, Mom."

"Scoff if you want, but I've had dreams, too. Dreams involving you and . . . . "

"And what?"

"Danger. You and some danger."

Trisha laughed, but even to her ears it sounded hollow. "Mom, how many times have I told you not to eat chili before going to bed?"

"The thing is, I can't get you to safety. Though I try . . . I try. You must be careful, Patricia. You must be very careful."

"What are you trying to tell me?"

Her mother compressed her lips.

"Well, please say it. Do I die or something?" When her mother didn't answer, Trisha pulled on her arm. "Mom?"

Mrs. Callahan leaned her head back in the rocker and scanned the sky. "It looks like a storm is coming. You better head back."

Reluctantly, Trisha rose, all the while wondering if her mother was speaking of the darkening clouds overhead or something else.

●　●　●

Audra couldn't believe it was Sunday night and *he* was still here. She glanced at the large body sprawled across her bed, clad only in briefs. The handsome, square face was studying its new object of lust, a sizable Granny apple. After a few bites he tossed it on the floor.

"Too sour!"

His attention then turned to his massive biceps. They quivered in brief, isometric jerks. *He* was into body building and possessed the powerful physique of an avid weight lifter. He had told her that aside from women, lifting weights was his only passion.

Audra had scoffed at what she considered an ignoble pursuit, and had asked what he saw in it. "Power," had been the reply, which he followed with a demonstration by twisting her arm.

Now, Audra looked at the discarded apple and thought of what her mother would think.

Like mother like daughter?

No. Her mother had been married, at least for a few years, then divorced when Audra was two. According to her mother, marriage was a dying institution; a farce that had outlived its usefulness. And hadn't she told Audra that the only good thing she got out of that marriage was her daughter?

Audra wondered if her father had been like Bubba. She knew little about him. Her mother seldom spoke of him but when she did the adjectives were always the same: weak, lazy, selfish. And Audra, who had no reason to doubt her, grew up applying these same adjectives to most men.

But she wished she could remember her dad. He had been a shadowy figure, visiting her every weekend until she was five. Then one dreary Saturday her mother told her he wasn't coming anymore, that he had died in a car crash.

Audra walked over to the apple. "You're such a slob!" she yelled, nudging the apple with her foot. "I don't know what pigsty you came from but here we don't throw food on the floor!"

The blond, blue-eyed man rippled his quadriceps and chuckled. "Sorry Audra, just one of my bad bachelor habits." But he made no move to pick it up. "What's on TV?" he asked, sounding bored.

"Look for yourself!" Audra didn't even try to conceal her irritation as she tossed the TV Guide onto the bed, just a bit out of reach so Bubba had to pull himself over in order to get it.

"You broads are all alike."

Audra looked down at the discarded apple, debated whether to pick it up or make a scene, then finally bent over. "And you men are all alike!"

But even as she walked into the kitchen, carrying both the apple and her anger, she knew she wouldn't ask him to leave tonight, just as she hadn't asked him to leave the night before. In fact, she might not ask him to leave for sometime.

He was crude, brutish, possibly even dangerous, and these things she didn't like. But he was a companion to fill the lonely space that seemed to gnaw at her more and more the closer she got to her thirtieth birthday.

But wasn't this the life she had chosen? Instead of the tedium of marriage and raising kids, hadn't she decided to pursue a career? She had worked hard to get where she was, and diapers and dirty dishes weren't part of the picture. Men were simply to enjoy. That's where her mother had gone wrong, by trying to fold a husband and family into her career. And Audra had learned from her mother's mistake.

She glanced back at Bubba.

He wasn't exactly the type of man she had envisioned for herself; even for a one-night stand. She would have preferred a more educated, cultured man. Sometimes reality lowered standards. But the one good thing about someone like Bubba was that things would never get too serious. There would be no talk of marriage, no temptation to walk down the aisle and drive SUVs in suburbia. No husband who would go and die on his five-year old daughter.

"Hey, Audra! Get me a brew while you're up, will you?"

Audra opened the refrigerator and reached for a Bud Light, regretting, for the first time, that too many Bubba Hanagans of the world seemed to populate her life.

●　●　●

Joshua sat in the living room of his posh apartment and stared at the two agents who had been sent to retrieve Arie. The younger one, Nathan Yehuda, was clean shaven and bright eyed. The other, Iliab Nahshon, with deep facial scars and dark brooding eyes, intimidated him, though Joshua would be hard pressed to admit it.

Iliab was a member of the elite Kidon, the assassination wing of the Mossad. Many in the agency had heard of him, but few actually knew him, and fewer still had ever seen his face. And like most Kidon agents, Iliab had been recruited from IDF Special Forces. Compared to him, Joshua, who often worked out of two separate Mossad departments—Collections, their espionage wing, and Technology, their development wing—was a rookie.

Iliab sipped from his bottle of water while his partner, who had yet to speak a word, sat beside him. "Headquarters has instructed me to tell you we have confirmed Arie's last communiqué as valid. Someone in deep cover was able to get us a message. President Baker *is* behind the rioting or at least has authorized some American Muslim leaders as well as members of the Muslim Brotherhood to instigate it."

"Why would a U.S. president want to destroy his own cities and foment unrest?"

Iliab replaced the cap on his bottle. "That is for us to find out."

"Then you'll be staying? Even though Arie is . . . ?"

Iliab's eyes narrowed. "Our source tells us that the Brotherhood assured the president they 'knew just how to do it,' just how to make the riots appear spontaneous and tied to some killing or another. And that Kamal may be spearheading the operation."

Joshua nodded, finally understanding why someone like Iliab was assigned to Arie's collection detail—a routine mission—and why he had been ordered to remain. "Then I assume I am to contact you with any new information?"

"Me or Nathan, here, and of course headquarters directly."

Nathan smiled as Joshua retrieved his phone, then punched in the numbers rattled off by Iliab.

"Any word on the information I found in Arie's apartment? I've had no luck deciphering it." Joshua said, after the contact numbers were entered.

"No." Iliab rose to his feet, his action prompting his companion to rise with him. "But headquarters will figure it out. It always does."

• • •

CHAPTER 4

The first thing Joshua noticed when he entered Merrill Campaign Headquarters was the noise. A dozen people, all young and eager-looking, with phones glued to their ears, sat behind desks requesting contributions or extolling their candidate's virtues. In the background KFOM spewed out the latest poll numbers on a small wall-mounted TV. Another half dozen volunteers pounded computer keys or pulled stacks of bumper stickers from cardboard boxes.

Joshua stopped and smiled when he saw glossy handbills scattered across one of the desks, proclaiming, in bold lettering, that Phillip Merrill was a man they could trust. Beneath the letters was a color photo of a lean, serious but pleasant-looking man with short, salt-and-pepper hair.

"You Joshua Chapman?" asked a young woman appearing from nowhere. She looked like someone you'd find at a rock concert with her black nail polish and short purple-tipped hair. But her violet eyes—eyes Joshua found remarkable for their size and color—were serious, thoughtful. "Joshua Chapman?" she repeated.

When Joshua nodded, she jerked her head sideways. "Follow me. Senator Merrill is waiting in his office. We're going to have to cram a lot into twenty minutes. He's on a tight schedule and has to leave for a fundraiser in New York."

"We?" Joshua said, struggling to keep up. The woman was moving so fast she could be on motorized skates.

"Yes, I'm database manager, Cassy Merrill," she said without bothering to turn around.

"Merrill? As in Senator Merrill? A daughter?"

"A niece."

Joshua had finally caught up. "Any more relatives I should know about?" When she didn't answer he added, "I hope you don't expect any special treatment. I'm here to do a job, not babysit family members or conduct special tutorials to bring them up to speed." He had heard how political campaigns were often populated with irksome family members.

Cassy stopped in front of a closed door. "Let's be clear, Mr. Chapman. My Uncle is paying your company an exorbitant amount for your new security software. They say Global Icon is the best in the business, but frankly, I don't think you're worth it. And I'll be watching to make sure we're getting all we're paying for."

She placed her hand on the knob. "And save your tutorials. As part of a project for Homeland Security, a team of ten software engineers were commissioned to see if sKyWIper could be blocked by a firewall. Six months. That's all it took us. And I was project manager."

While Cassy rapped on the door then twisted the knob, Joshua swallowed his surprise. sKyWIper was a program developed jointly by Israel and the U.S., and among other things was capable of intercepting keyboard strokes and wiping data. It was called a "veritable tool kit of cyber-spying programs" and its code considered "unprecedented in complexity."

With effort, he pulled his gaze from the woman in front of him and directed it to the open door where a dignified man sat behind a desk, smiling.

"Come in, Mr. Chapman. We have a lot to talk about."

● ● ●

Trisha bent over a long, metal table cluttered with paper, made several notations, then stopped and smiled. She loved the P2, her sleek lines, her promise. Once more she scanned the specs, not with her usual critical eye, but with the eye of love that filters imperfections.

"Mind if I sit down?"

Trisha felt something touch her fingers then saw a large, powerful hand next to hers. "How can I?" She looked up and smiled. "You're the boss."

Mike eased himself onto the bench beside her. "I love this room."

She had heard him say that before and knew why. It was nothing to look at; a giant cafeteria-style area with large, metal tables and benches set up here and there. Against the far wall, partitions separated the space into cubicles containing small, metal desks. Each cubicle belonged to a different employee of R&D; a place where their books and notes were kept, a place to go for quiet thought when not in one of the busier rooms containing the reactor or the wind tunnel or the computers that displayed a different spec on a screen at the touch of a finger.

But in this drab place, vision turned into reality.

"How are you doing on that report?"

Trisha thumbed through some papers. After finding the right ones, she slid the pile closer to him.

"Not bad," he said, scanning it. "But you'll have to complete the rest without Nolan. He's on special assignment."

"No problem." Though her curiosity was aroused, she didn't question him. His passion for secrecy was legendary. If he wanted her to know about the "special assignment" he'd tell her.

"I guess that's about it, except . . . thanks for not asking about Nolan."

"You're welcome, J. Edgar."

"J. Edgar? As in J. Edgar Hoover? The former FBI Director?"

"Exactly."

Mike chuckled. "Are you suggesting there's a similarity?"

"You could be twins."

"From what I hear, he was pretty tough on his boys."

"He was."

"Well, keep that in mind, Callahan."

"What?"

"That you're just one of the boys."

• • •

Audra's perky, blond hair bounced around her head as she walked beside Trisha.

"Here's your new space." Trisha's arm swept the premises as though she was showing off the Taj Mahal instead of a drab, unimpressive room where Audra would conduct her experiments. Next door was the nuclear reactor.

Her stomach knotted. All eyes would be on her now. The eight-member team of R&D would follow her progress closely. Two years of hard work made them emotionally invested. Now, it was up to Audra to see it didn't fail.

She eyed her boss, a boss she never liked.

On the personal side, Trisha was far too ordered for her taste; far too rooted in conventional morality.

But professionally, Audra grudgingly respected her. A few minutes on Google revealed that Trisha had worked at Princeton with the tokamack or Princeton Large Torus, a doughnut shaped nuclear fusion test machine that used deuterium in four neutral beam heating devices to achieve near fusion threshold.

Audra knew that fusion had never been achieved because of insufficient plasma densities and confinement time. But under Trisha's direction at PA, these and other problems had been solved, problems such as eliminating impurities from the hot plasma held at the core of the magnetic doughnut—the very impurities that cooled the plasma and retarded fusion.

Audra frowned. Yes, Trisha Callahan's successes were impressive, while *hers* remained to be seen.

"You do have a back-up plan, right? I mean, while I'm doing this, Nolan will be working on the shielding and vacuum pumps, won't he? Just in case?"

"Afraid not. Mike wants to put all the eggs in your basket."

"Risky, isn't it? I have faith in titanium X, but suppose . . . ."

Trisha threaded her arm through Audra's as she led her down the hall. "It's a lot of pressure, I know. Just remember, you're not responsible for what the executive office decides. You can only do your best. And that's all I ask. Everyone is here for you." Trisha stopped in front of a door and opened it.

When Audra saw that the door was unlocked, her anxiety increased. Patterson Aviation's eight-building complex sprawled, like a sleeping lizard, in the desert twelve miles south of Everman. R&D's Building Six formed the tail. Its front and back entrances were always locked. But Audra had heard the rumors of a recent break-in. So why weren't the individual rooms of the research department locked? It seemed careless.

"I've instructed everyone to give your needs top priority," Trisha said, entering the room. "Just remember, you're not alone. Don't try to assume all the pressure and burden. When you're stressed or have problems, come to me."

Audra scanned the familiar concrete bunker-like room. A large, glass window gave a clear view into the connecting room and at what looked like a jet engine in a type of sling device. The special glass, the concrete walls, all unnecessary precautions as essentially no radioactive waste was produced by deuterium. In front of the glass, an array of buttons and switches dotted a panel like miniature cookies on a platter. The engine was controlled from outside.

Audra eyed Trisha who was pressed against the glass like a mother viewing her newborn through a nursery window. No, she didn't care for her boss. The holy-roller prayed before eating lunch and even went to church a few times a week. She couldn't imagine Trisha bellied up to a bar and ordering a Black Label on the rocks; or using four letter words; or bringing strange men home to enjoy for the night. But she had to admit Trisha knew her job, knew every nut and bolt that went into this project.

Now, Audra only hoped she knew hers well enough to solve perhaps one of the most difficult problems of all.

"I have confidence in you," Trisha said, taking her eyes off the NPR910.

"I appreciate that," Audra muttered, feeling like she was about to heave her breakfast.

● ● ●

The pile of papers hit the desk top with a thud. "Here you go, boss," Trisha said. "One briefing as ordered."

"The name is Mike or Mr. Patterson, take your pick."

"I like, 'boss.'" She smiled. "On top of the pile you'll find a short outline encapsulating the entire report. And I've made six copies, one for each board member."

Mike flipped the edges of the pile like a deck of cards. "Did you go to secretarial school, too?"

"No praise, please. I accept cash or credit cards only."

Mike leaned back in his chair. "I suppose you do deserve a raise. You're a constant surprise, Callahan."

"The name's Trisha, Patricia, or Miss Callahan."

"Thanks, *Callahan*," he said, with warmth in his voice as he picked up the top pages. For a moment Trisha felt his dark, searing eyes bore into her own; felt their heat. If she let him, he'd burn right through her defenses and expose her vulnerability.

She turned away.

For a while Mike remained silent, nibbling a pencil. "By the way, we're having a party Friday night," he finally said. "And before you say 'no,' let me add, you can't refuse. It's for my wife's political friends, but I'm combining it with business. Much to her distaste." He paused to chuckle as though picturing his wife's anger and finding it amusing. "Three rich, influential cattlemen have just purchased an EX4 apiece, and our sales director is hoping to sell them part of that C101 order we got stuck with."

Trisha visualized the corpulent sales director with his pleasant, red face.

"He's going to pitch the idea of transporting livestock by air. If successful, some of the other cattlemen may follow suit. It could mean big money for PA."

"But I know nothing about the cattle industry. What exactly am I supposed to talk about?"

"Talk? Who said I wanted you to talk? I need you as window dressing. Wear something sexy."

"There are dirty words for women like that."

"I . . . suppose."

"I thought I was just one of the boys?"

"Well . . . ."

"Of course I'll expect a raise."

"I know, cash or credit cards only."

"See, you are temperate. I don't know why anyone would call you unreasonable."

"Someone called *me* unreasonable?"

"It doesn't matter."

"Who said it?"

"You shouldn't take these things personally."

"Who, Callahan?"

"Well . . . I have called you that once or twice."

Deep, throaty laughter filled the room. "Alright, Callahan, would you mind coming and giving our sales director a hand?"

"I'd be happy to. I assume your invitation includes my date?"

"Your *date*? Well . . . I guess . . . . But it's going to be all shoptalk, boring . . . but yes, fine, bring a date."

The black, flowing hair hung like an ebony cloud around Trisha's shoulders. She brushed it from her cheek as she thought of Daniel. Perhaps she shouldn't ask him. She still hadn't forgotten that look of humiliation on his face after his proposal. Maybe she should leave it alone. She didn't want him taking it the wrong way. It would be cruel to give him false hopes. But Daniel would provide a buffer between her and Michael Patterson.

And she really needed a buffer right now.

"Then we'll both be there," she said as she moved towards the door. "And regarding the board meeting—just remember what Lincoln said. 'You may fool all of the people some of the time . . . but you can't fool all of the people all of the time.'"

The athletic body rose from its chair like a mountain rising out of the sea. "It's obvious Lincoln didn't benefit from Despreauz's wisdom." In only a few strides he was beside her, his hand on the door next to hers. "'Greatest fools are oft most satisfied.' Now beat it, Callahan, before I qualify you for unemployment."

• • •

Mike returned to his desk and sat down. The massive hands folded over each other into a beige knot. They were hairless, smooth hands with large, square, well-manicured nails. But they were also strong, sinewy, with knuckles like walnuts. They were hands not only at home on the top of a desk, but on the throttle of a four hundred ton machine. Mike had wanted to put them on her. Instead, he had fabricated a story so flimsy a child could see through it, all to draw her closer.

He had done this twice before. "Compulsory business parties," he had called them. But this desire to bring her close always stopped short of any real intimacy. And it had nothing to do with mixing business with pleasure. It had to do with fear. If one touched, then one could be touched. It was the kind of risk Mike had avoided all his life.

He could sense the threat like a hunter senses the lion in the bush. Even a tame circus lion was unpredictable, dangerous. But this time *he* had come too close. He had felt an inexplicable jealousy because of her desire to bring a date. Even now it gnawed at him.

A strange feeling, jealousy. An alien emotion. Uncomfortable and overwhelming. In ten years of his open marriage, he had never once been jealous—not even when one of Renee's lovers turned out to be Mike's friend. So how was it possible to feel jealousy over a woman he had never even touched above the wrist?

His hands moved across the desk to pick up the outline. There was comfort in the crisp, white paper, in the bold, black lettering, in its . . . inertia; to be moved only at his pleasure, at his will.

It could be controlled.

Presently he began reading. "Page One. Patterson II. Aerodynamic Control Surfaces . . . . "

●　●　●

"Page Four. Patterson II. Subassemblies. Please note that in spite of the wide body and considerable passenger capacity, weight without payload or fuel is only two hundred thousand pounds. Now, if you flip to the last page you'll find the estimated cost for total development of our SST. Two hundred and fifty million, the bottom line, gentlemen. Only ten million above our last projection. A mere pittance when you consider the development of the Concord cost over nine hundred million."

The pinstriped suits clustered together like a gray lotus. Pages turned with a crackling noise as heads bent together. Mike paused to allow the five men sitting around the large, rectangular conference table time to digest all he had said.

One did not chew bitter herbs readily.

"You're aware that we have been unable to replenish our R&D fund since it was depleted during the creation of the EX4, even though that aircraft has been leading the industry in the executive craft category for over a year. We've gone over the reasons before and I see no need to rehash them now. The problem I want to focus on is how to get the additional ten million needed to complete the P2. In the past we obtained several grants from the government, but even that source has dried up.

"Once before, when we were first developing the fusion reactor and before garnering government interest, I asked you to procure loans for its development, using your influence and prestige to attract investors. I now make that same request. Naturally, stock warrants will be issued, same as last time."

Mike studied their faces. As expected, all were favorable except one. The dissenter, Robert Gunther—a thin, sickly looking man—was one of three board members affiliated with an oil company. And of the three, the most powerful. Mike needed his support.

"Your reaction, Bob?"

The pasty lids blinked over dull eyes. It was as if he had not heard the question. But Mike knew better than to underestimate Gunther. What he lacked in stature and strength, he possessed in knowledge and cunning.

"Well Mike, I'm not impressed." He thumped the papers in front of him, his blue veins visible beneath the thin, tissue-like skin of his hand. "Where are the progress reports on the NPR910? Where are the test results? We have already stuck our collective necks out far enough. I think before you ask us to stick them out any further we need the performance data. Just *what* have you done so far?"

"You're talking about highly sensitive material. Only a handful has access to it. DHS insists we keep it that way. I need not remind you that in our business industrial spies are not uncommon. As for why you should stick your necks out again, here's a reason: to guarantee the return of the money your investors have already made in the NPR910."

"And if the P2 fails," Gunther said, "not only will we lose our investors' capital but our credibility."

"A valid consideration, but if you don't back me now the project cannot progress further and we'll have no chance of recouping the R&D funds already invested. That could mean bankruptcy. And what, gentlemen, would that do to your credibility?"

Four of the executives went into an immediate huddle.

"Alright," Gunther said, breaking up the conclave. "I believe you've made your point. No one here wants to see Patterson Aviation or the project fail. However, at present PA is overextended. Perhaps if you suspended your R&D, brought this matter up in six months or a year, then backed it with some performance data . . . ."

"Six months! A year! In less than six months I could produce a full scale mock-up. In a year the P2 could be rolling off the assembly line!"

"The reactors . . . you're that close?" Gunther appeared stunned.

"We're that close."

"And the mock-up? Six months or less?"

"That's right." Mike looked at the other four and knew he had them. Then he searched out the dull eyes of Robert Gunther and smiled.

Men of cunning always understood each other.

• • •

Joshua wished Cassy Merrill wasn't stuck to him like gum on a shoe. She had not left his side for longer than ten minutes at a time, and he needed more than that to clone the senator's hard drive. He had promised headquarters they would have it soon. Maybe now he'd catch a break. Just moments ago, she told him she had a phone call to make, then disappeared.

He unzipped his attaché case and was about to pull out the cloning software when Cassy's head popped through the doorway. Her hair was green-tipped today, her nail polish—purple, and in addition to the customary jeans, she wore a gray MIT sweatshirt.

"What is it *now*?" he said, shoving the disc back into the bag. The girl, the woman—he didn't know what to call her because sometimes she seemed both—was getting on his nerves.

"A little testy, aren't we?"

"We? No, *I'm* testy. I'm trying to get work done here which, as you have so gracelessly reminded me, is costing your uncle a bundle, and you keep interrupting."

Cassy smiled and sauntered into the office, then took the seat next to him. "Since it's my uncle's money, I can interrupt as much as I like."

Joshua frowned. "And what's with the MIT sweatshirt? Is that your way of telling me you went to a great school for your software engineering degree? Or was it a present from someone who did?"

"You don't like my wardrobe?"

"It doesn't bother me. Just makes me wonder what you're trying to say about yourself. Your tipped hair, your dark nails, your crazy anarchist T-shirts, your . . . ?"

"I just got a message from my uncle. Garby's campaign is filing a complaint against him, charging him with a federal campaign-law violation by failing to display a disclaimer on his official website. Seems there's no mention of who's paying for it, which is required. The campaign's paying for it! Who else! And this was clearly indicated on the site twenty-four hours ago which means someone hacked in and removed it. Seems like there's nothing that crowd won't do to stop us. Guess we'll be working overtime. Dinner's on me tonight. A burger."

"Is that all you eat? Hamburgers? I'm tired of smelling them in the office everyday."

"Boy, you *are* testy!"

Joshua shot her an angry look. "My contract doesn't require me to be nice."

When he saw her smug facade crack for an instant and reveal a vulnerable core that could be hurt, he sighed. "Look, I'm sorry, okay? I don't mean to be a jerk. I just want to do my job which your uncle really *is* paying a lot for and I'd like to see that he gets his money's worth. And it would be helpful if I didn't have you looking over my shoulder every minute. I don't need babysitting. You can trust me to do my job. I won't disappoint you, I promise."

Cassy pinched her lips then made a funny sound as she blew out air. "I'm not trying to be a pain and I'm not sitting next to you because I don't trust you. Truth is, I'm impressed. I've never seen anyone expose vulnerabilities in software as fast as you did ours. And your suggestions for security hardening are brilliant. You *do* know your business and I thought . . . well, I thought here's someone I could learn a thing or two from."

Joshua hadn't expected that. He studied her face. He had done enough interrogations to know when someone was lying. "Okay, truce?" he finally said.

Cassy brightened. "Then you'll let me observe?"

"Yes," he said, knowing it was going to make his job harder. How was he going to poke around the senator's files with her leaning over his shoulder?

"Thanks," she said in a near whisper.

"Okay, but that doesn't include meals together. I don't want to be around when you're eating one of those awful frozen hamburgers you nuke everyday."

• • •

CHAPTER 5

Mike stood before the full length mirror adjusting his tie. A lady "friend" once told him he was handsome enough to be a male model. He took it as an insult. His physique was powerful, his face, rugged, not "pretty" like those on the fashion pages.

"Admiring yourself?"

Mike watched Renee's approach in the mirror and noted, with amusement, that her black, floor-length dress was tight and had a neckline plunging to her waist. "I never admire myself when I can admire you."

"That's because you already know how handsome you are. But I suspect if you were less so it would preoccupy more of your thoughts. People are generally preoccupied with what they don't have."

"Looks mean nothing to me, Renee. I learned long ago that a man doesn't need them to make money, a deal, or a woman. But I admire good looks in the female species. And you *do* look incredible. Out to impress someone? You've certainly baited the hook. Anyone I know?"

"Don't be vulgar."

"You'll be hard to resist. I've always said you had the finest figure of any woman I've ever known."

"It got you, didn't it?"

"Yes, sex can sell anything."

"Our ten years together haven't been so bad, have they? I've made a good partner—with my looks, money and social status. I've been your 'gracious hostess' and used my influence for the benefit of your company. You got everything you wanted."

"Not everything."

"You're not going to bring that up again? I can't help that I'm unable to have children. I don't see why you resent me for it."

"I don't resent you for it. I resent that you're *glad* you can't have any. It's your easy-out of unwanted responsibility."

Renee laughed. "Look who's calling the kettle black! You don't want that kind of responsibility, either. Only, you won't admit it. You can't push a child away as easily as you can a wife."

"Don't make it sound so one-sided. You got what you wanted, too."

"You were Daddy's choice, not mine, remember?"

"Save it, Renee. I've heard it a hundred times. But you never mention that it didn't take much for 'Daddy' to persuade your straw-haired veterinarian to leave town. I understand it cost him less than fifty-grand to send him packing. And if you were so in love, why didn't you follow him?"

Renee's face reddened. "Well . . . Daddy convinced me that love was overrated, that wealth and power were more important, so I settled for you."

Mike thought of Trisha and wondered what it would be like to be married to someone like her. "I guess we both settled. But don't kid yourself, if you had married that vet of yours, you'd be taking a solo trip to Reno within a year. No, Renee, you got what you wanted, what mattered to you—total freedom and a chance to get that small town chip off your shoulder. I was everything your tyrant father was not."

"He wasn't a tyrant! He was generous and gave me everything I wanted."

"Yes, and kept you under his thumb. Corralled you like one of his heifers."

"He . . . had a reputation to maintain."

"For heaven sakes, Renee, he never allowed you to go more than fifty miles from the ranch! Maybe he thought this cloistered life would keep you innocent." Mike laughed. "Guess that didn't work out too well."

"Just how would you describe me, Michael?"

"Petty, cruel . . . selfish."

"I see. And how would you describe yourself?"

"Ambitious and selfish."

"So . . . it seems we are well suited."

"But are you *satisfied*? Don't you want more? Something better? A child could bring love into our lives. Maybe bring us together, like a real family. It could be our last chance. Don't you want that?"

Something flickered across Renee's eyes, a softness he rarely saw, and for an instant Mike knew she was considering it.

"You're not the only one with dreams, Michael. I have them, too. And they don't resemble scripts from *Leave it to Beaver*. Besides, I've never asked for your love, never expected it. You can't go changing the rules now. You want too much from me, from yourself. Maybe if we had started out better . . . maybe . . . ." She shrugged.

"And don't kid yourself, you're more like Daddy than you realize. Why do you think he picked you? In your own way you want to corral me like a heifer, too; fit me into some mold you think will make *you* happy. But what about me? What about the things I want?" She threw her hands in the air. "I'm done. I don't want to talk about it anymore!"

"You never do." He turned away. How could he explain his growing need for some warmth, warmth that would touch his life, make it glow like a well-heated coal in his later years? He was pushing forty and had begun thinking about those years. Renee had teased him, told him he was going through a premature aging crisis. He had tried to stave off that crisis by speaking of adopting a child. A son would stoke those fires, rekindle that dying coal. A son would be someone to whom he could leave his company, his legacy. "I guess one child in the house is enough," he added dryly.

"I assume you're referring to me, darling. Well, I do like getting my way and love being pampered. And I'm over-indulgent with money. And . . . yes, I can be cruel. But you already knew all this before marrying me. And you've always dealt so beautifully with it by never dealing with it. So don't change now."

When Renee brushed against him, he reached for her. "We don't have to live like this," he whispered, his arms encircling her. "If both of us tried harder maybe . . . ."

She pushed him away. "I thought I made my feelings clear. I'm satisfied with things as they are. Besides, haven't we got everything?" She slipped her arm through his and led him to the top of their grand staircase. As they descended, she leaned closer. "You've been prickly lately. What you need is a vacation . . . or a good fling."

Mike remained silent until reaching the bottom step when he barked at a passing servant to open the French patio doors. Had he been thorny of late? Yes. But how could he explain to Renee it was due to ten years of him not caring enough; ten years of her not caring enough; ten years of unstoked fires, of chilblain, of cold.

Ten years of drafty emptiness?

Suddenly, music came blasting from the patio. "You've hired a band!"

Renee smiled demurely. Her green, cat-eyes watched him. "Darling, snap out of it. I want you at your best. There are people coming I want to impress, and I'll not have you rude and irritable."

"You know how I hate dancing with all those plump, gray-haired wives," Mike returned, bombarding her with his frustration as if the last ten years had been all her fault. "Especially tonight. I've business to discuss."

Renee leaned over and kissed him on the cheek. "You'll survive, darling. I want my party to be a success and women love to dance. They expect to when they bother getting all dressed up."

"Then *you* dance with them!" he snapped, and walked off.

● ● ●

In spite of her husband's ill humor, Renee was certain this would be a great party. All the right people were coming. And she had spent the better part of two weeks preparing. The woodwork had been repainted, the rugs shampooed. She even had some "Spanish" touches added. The *artesonado* ceiling with elaborate boxed out squares of wood, one foot by one foot, and centers filled with grille work were new. So was the parabolic archway at the room's main entrance.

It was sure to impress Senator Garby who had spent several years as ambassador to Brazil before becoming a U.S. senator, and now, her party's presidential candidate.

She had aligned herself with the government crowd. In Everman, that consisted mainly of petty bureaucrats. Now, she had a chance to broaden her scope, to step into a grander, more important life, and the Garbys were the doorway.

Since meeting them at a fundraiser eight weeks ago, Renee had seized every opportunity to be in their company. Her hope was to assist in his campaign, to help raise funds so he could beat his opponent, Senator Phillip Merrill, even though she found Garby's poll numbers a bit off-putting.

She normally backed winners.

And though she hated to admit it, Garby was so far down in the polls that it would take a miracle for him to become the next president of the United States.

Still, he was a useful stepping stone with his influence in Washington. And for Renee, Washington had become the Mecca of proper living, of all that was desirable. The important people of the world traveled through its gates, and for some reason she had begun envisioning herself as one of them.

When she saw her husband standing in a group, her stomach knotted. Cattlemen! How she hated them! She had spent too many years around these rough, course types. Even her father, a rich cattle baron himself, had often embarrassed her with his poor manners and poor grammar.

She had been furious when she learned her husband had invited some tonight, and had shouted a warning how they better not bring in any cow dung on their boots!

But her irritation was forgotten when the doorman announced the new arrivals. As she rushed to greet them, her sling-back heels made a hollow, tapping sound all across the large, mosaic vestibule.

"Senator and Mrs. Garby! How wonderful to see you again!"

The tall, spindly senator made a slight bow while the fragile-looking woman beside him offered an anemic smile. "Mrs. Patterson . . . ."

"Renee."

"Renee," continued Senator Garby, "allow me to introduce you to a good friend of mine, Mr. Alexander Harner, president of Tafco Oil."

"Alex to my friends," the gray-haired executive said. Until now, Renee had not noticed him nor had she noticed the delighted expression on his face as he viewed her wide, plunging V.

"I hope you don't mind, but I insisted that Alex accompany us here."

Renee eyed Harner. She viewed oil men with the same disdain as cattlemen, though there were many here tonight. But didn't politics often necessitate doing the unpleasant? What oil men lacked in breeding, they had in money. And a trip to Mecca was expensive. "Don't be silly, Senator. Your friends are my friends. Mr. Harner . . . Alex is welcome."

The tune of the *Mexican Hat Dance* came blaring from the patio. "Don't you just love Spanish music?" Renee said, failing to see the sneer that passed between the senator and his wife.

She led them to a long, rectangular table covered with food. To one side were platters of lobster tails, chateaubriand, crystal bowls of caviar, oysters Rockefeller, shrimp, and dozens of salads and vegetables. To the other: tureens of *gazpacho* on top of a bed of ice, platters of *tostadas* and *enrollados,* steaming mounds of *albondigas* and *empanadas,* a large tongue in almond sauce, *paella, pollo escabeche,* and *garbanzo salad.*

At Renee's parties, food was served all night.

"Just tell them what you want and they'll take care of you." Renee gestured toward the staff that stood in starched, white uniforms like plaster statues.

The couple smiled but showed no interest in the food.

"Perhaps a drink then," Renee said, sullenly, then signaled to the man she had hired for the evening to attend the rolling bar. "Dewers and water, Bubba."

Bubba Hanagan made the drink and handed it to Renee, then looked at the others. "The usual Hanagan," Alex Harner said. "And how's it going?"

"Fine, Mr. Harner." Bubba mixed a Scotch and soda.

"Still lifting weights?"

"Of course, sir."

"You know each other?" Renee asked. When Hanagan ignored her, she shot a glance at Alexander Harner.

"Bubba used to be my body guard."

"Small world as they say," Renee replied, already losing interest. And while her attention was on the senator and his wife she failed to notice the bartender slipping a piece of paper into Alexander Harner's suit pocket.

• • •

"Nice party," Trisha said, smiling at Patterson Aviation's corpulent sales director as she smoothed the side of her silk, oriental looking dress that nearly touched the floor. Slits on both sides of the skirt reached to her knees, revealing long, shapely legs. Around her throat arched a stiff collar, and passing between her breasts, a long row of tiny silk-covered buttons. In contrast to the severity of her gown was the casual manner in which her hair was piled on her head, leaving soft, black wisps to frame the sides of her face like a picture.

The sales director smiled broadly. "Trisha, you look wonderful!"

He took her hands and pressed them between the chubby palms of his own. "I swear, if I weren't a happily married man you'd be in constant danger of my advances."

She gave him an affectionate kiss on the cheek before he introduced her to the three cattlemen beside him.

"My friends were just telling me how this jihad madness has affected their business. Many of their trucks have been bombed or hijacked. Between that and the energy crisis, the cost of getting their beef to market is skyrocketing. I was telling them that a good alternative would be transporting their cattle in a fleet of cargo carriers. It's quicker. No stops on the way. Less chance of having something go wrong. All plusses to offset the added fuel cost of air transportation. In the long run, they'd save money considering their current loss of both cattle and trucks."

The director paused and chuckled. "Actually, Trisha, I was about to seduce them into buying our C101's. That is, until you came and otherwise seduced us."

Trisha smiled at the salesman who blushed with pleasure. "I'm afraid real seduction is your department."

● ● ●

Someone's plump, gray-haired wife managed to drag Mike from his sales director and the three cattlemen he had invited. But he continued observing the four men while politely bobbing his head for the benefit of the matronly woman stepping on his toes. After Trisha joined the group, Mike ceased bobbing and excused himself.

"May I have this dance, Miss Callahan?" he said, his voice low, husky. Before Trisha could respond, he pulled her out to the patio where he began leading her in what resembled a slow two-step.

"You look good. Although I've seen sexier dresses on ten year olds. Still . . . you look good." He hoped she couldn't detect the joy he felt at seeing her.

Trisha smiled. "How was the board meeting?"

"Gunther wasn't happy. He wanted more data on the NPR."

"So what happened?"

"He gave in because the others went my way."

"They usually follow him. How did you manage it?"

"By promising them the P2 mock-up within six months."

"No! How could you? What if Audra can't come up with the new casing and we have to enlarge the shielding?"

"I want you to join Nolan. And I want it done secretly. I've already purchased two hangars a hundred miles from here. It's an isolated spot, the remnants of a private airstrip that belonged to an eccentric old geezer who always wanted to take off over the sea except that the strip wasn't long enough. You could say the project never got off the ground."

"Very clever," Trisha said sarcastically. "Okay, you have two old hangars by the ocean, is that supposed to mean something?"

"Deuterium," he said, as if that explained it all. And to Trisha, he knew it did.

"So, *that's* what you've had Nolan doing. You *are* clever. But are you clever enough to convince the board to finance the P2 if the casing fails?"

"In a few weeks I'll give the orders to tool-up."

"Why do you keep ignoring my questions?"

"In the meantime you'll start building the engineering mock-up."

"You can't build an airplane like this. It's backwards. Besides, how can you expect only a handful to accomplish such a mammoth task?"

"I expect you to get it rolling and when the time is right, I'll assign others. No one said it would be easy, Callahan."

"I don't expect easy. But how about sensible?"

"Was it sensible when you came to me two years ago *begging* me for a chance to build the first fusion powered aircraft?"

"I didn't beg."

"Oh . . . then what do you call groveling on all fours?"

"Exaggeration," Trisha returned, and the pair laughed.

"By the way, what happened to your date?" The sudden realization that Trisha was alone pleased him.

"Something came up. At the last minute Daniel called from the hospital telling me there was an emergency and he couldn't get away. He's a doctor. Things like this happen."

"You were stood up."

"No I wasn't."

Mike grinned. "Don't worry, Callahan, you won't end up an old maid. You still have a few good years left."

"You're ridiculous."

"I want you at Gibs Town in three days. Your room is booked at a local hotel; although we'll be working such long hours you won't get much chance to use it."

"You made no mention that you'd be there."

"Didn't I?"

"No. Is . . . this . . . wise? I mean . . . you shouldn't start anything until after we've developed the casting. This could jeopardize your company."

He noticed the faint flush on her face. He had unbalanced her, hit a nerve. He'd have to think about what that meant. Maybe it was a good thing. For him. "Look, I know a lot is riding on this. So, what I need is for you to tell me you're with me."

Trisha narrowed her eyes. "You already know that. But you're not going to turn me into a yes-man. This approach is crazy and you know it. But I'll work the skin right off my fingers trying to make it succeed."

His hands traveled down the hollow of her back as the music stopped. "Maybe you can try being a yes-man just once?"

Trisha pulled away. "I think that's what the big bad wolf said to one of the little pigs before he ate him."

The broad chest shook with laughter, and even after Trisha left him amid the Mariachi band and lamp posts strung with red and orange streamers, she could still hear it.

● ● ●

"Trisha! Trisha, how divine you look."

The engineer turned toward the silky voice.

"Thank you, Renee."

"Marvelous dress, dear. So cute with all those little buttons down the front."

Everyone's eyes went to Trisha's high buttoned collar and then to Renee's plunging V. Senator and Mrs. Garby appeared embarrassed, while Alexander Harner seemed delighted.

"Isn't it terrible about those two British school teachers?" Senator Garby said hurriedly, as though trying to change the subject. "You know . . . the two British teachers on vacation in Cyprus who were brutally murdered this morning? Kamal's crowd, or rather one wing of his group, took responsibility. Ever since he declared war on western educators for teaching 'lies' about Muslims and Islam in their schools, his followers have been killing any they can get their hands on."

"Violence and terrorism . . . that's all you ever hear about anymore. I can't bear all this cruelty," Mrs. Garby said, looking wide-eyed and troubled. "When will it stop?"

"As long as it's big business, never," returned the barrel-chested Harner.

"Big business? What do you mean?" Renee said, sipping her Dewers.

Harner smiled. "It's well known that Arab oil countries have been financing terrorist groups for years. Sunni countries like Saudi Arabia have funded al-Qaeda, Hamas, the Muslim Brotherhood and even ISIS, while predominately shia countries like Iran and Iraq funded groups like Hezbollah. But now the lines are blurring—'the enemy of my enemy is my friend' thing.

"In addition, armed men extract money by force from their own people, like the Palestinians, for example, and even those in refugee camps. Didn't Libya's ex-president, Gaddafi, take six percent from the pay of Palestinian exiles working in that land to help subsidize jihad?"

Senator Garby nodded. "True. It's estimated that last year's combined income of Fatah and Hamas surpassed that of the nation of Jordan. Terrorist revenues are in the billions. They're so rich they even act like multinational companies and make legal investments via the world stock exchanges. And now that oil is over two hundred fifty dollars a barrel, they're getting even richer."

Alex Harner chuckled. "To be sure. Fatah has invested over ninety-five million in London alone."

"How can they be so wealthy? The PLO went bankrupt after Arafat backed Saddam Hussein during the Gulf War," Trisha said.

"Old news," returned Harner. "Money is now pouring into both Fatah and Hamas from Iran. Clearly, Iran is getting ready for war. You've heard of the 'Iran War Dial'?" When no one answered, Harner continued. "It's the clock that compiles various expert predictions on how close we are to an Israeli/Iranian conflict. The clock is almost at midnight. Many in Iran are desperate to bring about world chaos in order to usher in their Mahdi, their Messiah."

"Gentlemen, please." Renee pursed her lips. "No one wants to hear about wars or Messiahs. And you make terrorists sound like . . . well, like . . . entrepreneurs."

"Exactly," Harner returned. "And their commodity is terror which they sell. They even have their own bureaucracy with office staffs of forty-thousand-dollars-a-month men, complete with secretaries and company cars. And it's the faction that does the most damage that gets the most money. So all the groups, including Kamal's, have to outdo each other in order to get the big bucks. It's like an incentive program."

"Come now, we're here to enjoy ourselves," Renee said, picking at her diamond bracelet. "This conversation is depressing all the ladies. Let's hear no more of it."

Trisha glanced at Alexander Harner and Senator Garby. "You both seem well informed."

Harner smiled and leaned closer to Trisha as though about to reveal a secret. "Neither the senator nor I uphold violence and terrorism for any reason. We are, however, not unsympathetic toward the Arabs. We believe they have been maligned and misrepresented to a certain extent. I own and operate one of the largest oil companies in the west and . . . ."

"I know who you are, Mr. Harner," Trisha said.

"Alex, call me Alex, please." When Trisha remained silent, Harner shrugged and continued. "With the energy crisis being what it is, and with Middle East hostility being what it is . . . well, I have to keep informed."

Trisha frowned. "This sympathy of yours isn't due to the fact that your company has never experienced any major terrorist attack? Rather startling good fortune when you consider that no other oil company can say the same."

Alexander Harner shook with laughter. "Money, Trisha, money! I pay protection. Simple as that. Are you shocked? Of course, I see by your face that you are. But you needn't be. Businesses do it everyday. Oh . . . maybe not in outright payments, but in the form of 'gifts' shall we say. 'Gifts' given to the right people can buy a remarkable amount of friendship."

"You mean you're paying off the terrorists? That you are giving money to our enemies?"

"Oh no, no. You misunderstand. I'm paying a protection force to guard my oil fields in hostile lands. Perfectly legal. Nothing untoward."

Trisha studied him. There was something about the man that made her uneasy. "Well, Mr. Harner, politics seem vastly more complex than airplanes."

• • •

Mike pulled off his suit and flung it across a chair.

"You know, I forgot to congratulate Trisha on her achievement," Renee said, as she lingered nearby.

"What achievement?" Mike hoped he didn't sound too interested.

"Getting you to dance so long. It must be a new record. You know how you abhor it. How in the world did she manage?" After a brief pause, her lips curled into a smile. "Or is she your newest playmate? That isn't like you, Michael, mixing business with pleasure, although I've always thought that rule of yours rather silly. Well, is she . . . are you two having an affair?"

Mike pulled an undershirt over his head. "No."

"Really? Then why do I sense something between you?"

"That's your own dirty little mind working overtime. And why the interest? You've never questioned me about anyone before."

"Well, it's just . . . . ."

"Trisha is not the type who would have a cheap, little affair with the first guy who asked."

"Cheap? Not a word you normally use when discussing our 'arrangement.' I don't understand . . . unless . . . unless you *did* ask and she refused. Michael, did she refuse you?" Renee released what sounded like croaking laughter. But when her husband didn't respond she positioned her body into what was supposed to be a seductive pose, except too much alcohol had made her clumsy and almost comical looking.

"Save it, Renee," Mike said frowning. "I'm not up for it, not when you approach sex like a vampire. I don't feel like being drained just so you can feel replenished."

"It's always turned you on before. Besides, I like knowing that while I mean little to you, no one else means more."

Her honesty startled Mike. He supposed it was the liquor talking, making her so unscripted. She was sure to forget about it in the morning. He watched her sink onto the bed.

"Michael, the Garbys have invited me to DC to help host a big fundraiser and I've accepted."

"Well, isn't that what you've been angling for all this time? I'm happy for you. Maybe now you'll see how unsuitable they are to lead our country."

"I've heard the talk, too. But since when do you pay attention to rumors?"

"I know about the crowd he hangs with, and they're bad apples, Renee."

"You mean Alexander Harner? I don't think much of him either. He's an *oil* man. But the Garbys . . . well . . . they're the kind that shapes history."

"But what *kind* of history?" Mike asked in a mocking tone.

"Don't act so superior. Just tell me what you heard about Senator Garby that makes you so cynical?"

"For starters, while in South America he formed some unsavory friendships . . . some *dangerous* friendships."

"Like?"

"Like with known terrorists."

"*Terrorists?*"

"It's no secret that Garby is sympathetic to the Palestinian cause, and during his senatorial campaign it was rumored that some finances came from these sources, in a round about way, of course. The money was well laundered, and nothing was ever proven. It's also no secret that he works closely with pro-Islamic lobbyists in Washington."

Renee jutted her chin. "That doesn't prove anything. Lots of senators and congressmen are backed by special interest groups. Personally, I refuse to listen to such gossip. I don't care what anyone says. I like the Garbys. They fascinate me. And . . . they are powerful."

Renee was right. In spite of the controversy and Garby's plummeting poll numbers, money kept pouring, like Monsoon rains, into his presidential campaign. The news outlets, including all the major TV anchors, were pushing hard to make the senator a household name. It was as though an edict had been issued to "puff" Garby. But careful evaluation revealed a poor performance record. His attendance in the senate was spotty; his voting record exposed inconsistent views and conflicting loyalties. In reality, he was a lackluster candidate with no record to extol.

"You don't realize how powerful Senator Garby is," Renee pressed.

"Is that why you've been following after him like a hound?"

"Oh Michael, really, you're impossible. Why am I trying to explain? You just don't understand. Your problem is you associate with too many cattlemen."

"No, that's your problem. Deep down, Renee, you're terrified you'll never get rid of the smell of cow dung. And you're right; you'll never be anything but a small town girl."

• • •

Audra lay naked beneath soft pastel sheets. Next to her was Ace Corbet. "That tickles," she said as he traced her face with his finger.

"You *are* cute, cutie." Ace grinned as he stared at her from his propped position.

"And you do have class," Audra returned in a mocking tone which Ace failed to discern.

"I told you you wouldn't be disappointed."

"And you were right," she lied, as she sank deeper into her pillow and thought about the past hour with Ace. She had been feeling especially lonely. Bubba Hanagan had more or less moved in, and against Audra's better judgment, she had given him a key to the apartment. He had reciprocated by giving her, his. But she had seen that mocking look on his face because he knew she'd never use it. What woman in her right mind would ever go to his apartment? But after all was said and done, the arrangement worked. Both went their separate ways, no explanations necessary.

But Bubba had not been to the apartment for three days, and it was Saturday night. That gnawing ache inside had taken her to Grobens. Five Black Labels on the rocks had made Ace Corbet's usual advances, enticing.

Now, she was filled with mild disgust, coupled with boredom, and she wished Ace would leave. It was three in the morning and she wanted to get some sleep. But he didn't seem to be in any hurry. She was thinking of how to get rid of him when she heard a voice.

"Hey, Audra! Looks like you're having quite a party. Don't mind me. I just came for my boots."

The couple sat up. Ace clenched his fists in anticipation of having to fight an irate lover and looked dumbfounded when he saw the muscular Hanagan leaning calmly against the door frame—arms folded like a cigar-store Indian, a big, toothy grin plastered across his face.

Audra was white with rage. "You could have knocked or something! You could have shown some common decency!" Her anger was fanned by the knowledge that Ace wouldn't have to use those clenched fists.

Bubba just laughed. "I won't take long. You two keep doing whatever it was you were doing." With that, he entered the room, rummaged through the closet until he found a pair of tan work boots, tied the laces together, and slung them over his shoulder. "Catch you later." He flashed a smile again then disappeared.

In one swift motion, Audra jumped out of bed, and not even bothering to put anything on, ran to where Ace's clothes lay piled on a chair. "Get out! Get out!" she shrieked, as she threw his clothes at him. "Just get out of here!"

● ● ●

CHAPTER 6

"God, where are You?"

Trisha knelt in the front row pew of her little church in upper Everman. Her heart was broken. Only this morning a bus of Everman elementary children was blown up by a terrorist bomb. Forty children died. Only four survived and all with life-threatening injuries. And last night, after police tried arresting a known drug dealer in lower Everman, a riot—the second one in a month—broke out, killing two policemen, injuring a dozen more, with thirty rioters arrested.

Trisha was already an hour late for work but still she remained kneeling. Her mooring was slipping. That had never happened before. No matter the circumstances, she had always felt God's presence, had know that all would be well.

But now . . . everything seemed fluid.

The world was going mad. Innocent people were being murdered on a scale never seen before. And her personal life was rocky, too. Tomorrow, she'd be going to the seaside hangars where the very future of PA hung in the balance; where the success of their P2 could have profound effects on the war on terror.

So much pressure.

And *he* would be there, too, adding to the stress—a man she had no business loving. She kept her head bowed for what seemed like hours until at last she felt that familiar stirring in her heart, heard that still small voice.

"I am your refuge and strength. A very help in times of trouble. Whom shall you fear? You can do all things through Christ who strengthens you."

● ● ●

Joshua installed his cloning software on Senator Merrill's computer. He didn't know how much time he had, an hour maybe. That's how long he figured the meeting for the campaign staff would last. He had to maximize the opportunity. Headquarters was waiting for the cloned data. It would prove if Merrill was the friend to Israel he claimed to be.

More than ever, Israeli Prime Minister Behrman needed to know just how much he could count on Merrill after he became the new U.S. president. Important information Behrman would need at the UN since Israel had so few allies left.

Pressure was mounting for another land-for-peace deal that included Israel surrendering its lucrative oil rights in the Golan— where barrels of oil were said to be in the billions. Their offshore Mediterranean natural gas rights were also in question. Then there was Russia. Their troops and weaponry were all over Syria, a country that bordered Israel.

Headquarters already knew Senator Garby's position to be staunchly anti-Jewish, and with clandestine ties to ISA, the Islamic State of America.

Joshua watched the screen tick off the cloning progress. He had already removed the malware that had corrupted the system and necessitated calling in Global Icon. The malware was sophisticated. Hardly what you'd expect to be used against a political campaign.

That raised the question of who sent it and why—all questions headquarters would have to answer through their secretly owned company, Global Icon, the very tool that enabled the Mossad to gain access to numerous Fortune 500 companies looking to secure their systems. GI obliged by giving them state-of-the-art security software, but software containing a "back door" for the Mossad to enter and scoop up a plethora of information such as which companies or executives supported ISA.

Joshua drummed his fingers against the polished cherry wood desk. The task was taking longer than expected. And with Cassy, nothing was certain. It would be just like her to leave the meeting and pop in to see what he was doing. He let out a sigh of relief when he saw the screen flash "completed."

No sooner did Joshua slip the cloned hard drive into his briefcase then Cassy came bouncing into the room. Her brown hair was tipped orange today.

"How's it going?" Cassy slid a chair close to his and leaned her elbows on the desk.

"Did you know your uncle's computer contained malicious code that could send information back to the attacker?"

"Yes, I just didn't know how to get rid of it."

"Well, it's gone now, and you won't have to worry about it again. I've installed several security layers. I defy even the NSA or Echelon to hack you now. The question is why would anyone want to infect *this* computer with such a sophisticated virus?"

Cassy rose, her face taut. "Opposition research. Every campaign is always looking for dirt on the other guy, to use wherever they can. That, and to learn their opponent's strategy. Things like budget, names of big donors, where they're going to put their marketing dollars, etcetera." She tapped the leather bound notebook in her hand. "That's why I keep that kind of information in here."

"You won't need to after I've completed my installations."

"We'll, see," Cassy said, not sounding impressed. "I have to go. I'll check back with you in a few hours. Oh . . . by the way, do you own anything beside casual business wear? Like a decent suit?"

"Of course . . . why?"

"You'll need it. Remember there's a cocktail party here tonight for our important local contributors."

"Nothing to do with me. Count me out."

"No can do. Read your contract. It says right there in black and white that Global Icon agrees to assist in auxiliary matters for the appropriate fee."

"You've got to be kidding! How does a cocktail party qualify?"

"You're an internationally known company. I want our donors to know that their private information is being protected. So, see you at eight." Then she bounded out the door leaving Joshua puzzled.

Up to this point, Cassy had barely left his side. Now she seemed to want to distance herself. His Mossad training had taught him to observe changes in behavior and he clearly saw that Cassy's behavior had just changed.

But why the invite to the party?

It didn't make sense. And something else, too. She seemed to know more about the malware and why it was installed than she let on.

Okay, he'd play her game.

It would give him more time to dig around Senator Merrill's computer. So far, his preliminary investigation showed nothing of interest. But between his continued scrutiny here and headquarters doing its analysis in Dimona, maybe that would change, too.

● ● ●

"So you came."

Joshua ignored the smug look on Cassy's face as he adjusted his tie. Truth was, he was curious about why he was invited. That, and he wanted to see her in a social setting. He was curious about that, too, though he'd probably let his tongue be cut out before saying so. It implied he was interested, the last thing he wanted to admit to himself or anyone else. Still, a woman with violet eyes the size of plums had to be someone worth getting to know.

"I can't believe you're actually here," Cassy added.

"You'll get my bill in the morning."

"I was hoping this was pro bono."

Joshua ignored her as he scanned the campaign headquarters. It was filled to capacity with elegantly dressed women laden with expensive jewelry, and men, some wearing two-thousand dollar Armani suits, a few others wearing twenty-two thousand dollar Zegnas—the donors Cassy talked about, and big ones.

"Nice turnout." He was about to reach for one of the crystal Champagne glasses carried by a black-tux-clad waiter when Cassy caught his hand.

"Not so fast, mister. You're on duty." With that she pulled him through the large room that had been emptied of desks and chairs, and began introducing him to everyone along the way. And for more than an hour, they made the rounds.

"I think that's about it. I think we've covered everyone," Cassy said, steering him to a quiet corner.

"You missed the wait staff. Maybe we should go back and do it all over again."

"Very funny. But the point was made. People know that Global Icon is on the job."

Joshua pulled out his cell and began video taping the room. Sweeping it slowly from right to left.

"What are you doing?"

"Capturing the moment. Some day I might want to show my kids that I once hobnobbed with the rich and famous, with senators and mayors and the beautiful people, all while the world was blowing itself up." He sent the video to headquarters then powered off his phone.

"You're a strange one. I still can't figure you out. You don't want to be here, yet when I introduced you, you studied each person as though you were a computer filing away information. I bet you can name every person in this room, recall every word they said. Who *are* you?"

"I'm an Israeli Jew. We've learned the importance of knowing who we're with, of sizing them up in a moment to know if they can be trusted. It's a skill acquired after years of living with terrorism. We've been at this a lot longer than you Americans have."

"Your resume says you have dual citizenship, that you're also an American."

"True," Joshua said, noting Cassy had removed the orange coloring from her hair and that she looked rather fetching in her black strapless cocktail dress. "But I identify more with Israel. Americans are asleep. They don't take anything seriously." He gestured with his hand at the crowd drinking Champagne and nibbling hors d'oeuvres. "This is what you live for. To be rich and famous. To live the 'good life.'"

"That's unfair. I know many people who . . . ."

"And while you call yourself a Christian nation, you don't even care that thousands of Christians are martyred by ISIS every year."

"Wow, what brought this on?"

"Let's just say I've had too many friends die at the hands of terrorists. But this is not the time or place for that. We're at a party, which reminds me, you look nice."

"Really? You mean you finally approve of my outfit?"

"I never disapproved of your clothes."

"No, but you implied . . . okay, what does my wardrobe say to you?"

He had wondered how long it would take her to ask. Most women were conscious of how their clothes affected others. Obviously, Cassy was too. "All this punk-gothic stuff it not the real you."

"Well, mister-know-it-all, who is it then?"

"Someone trying to tell the world she was not establishment, not her uncle."

"But it says something different to you?"

"Yes . . . 'I'm lost, please help me.'"

Cassy waved to a passing waitress to bring her a drink. "Well, there's where you're wrong. I'm not lost. I'm just shattered."

• • •

Audra sat slumped over the small, white Formica desk in her bedroom. The pressure of her new assignment was getting to her. It was the third night this week she had taken work home. And there was no end in sight. She was exhausted and yawned as she tossed her pen onto the desktop. Time to call it a night, she thought, when a voice startled her.

"You're really working late! All work and no play, you know, makes little Audra a dull girl."

Audra glanced behind her and saw the muscular frame of Bubba Hanagan. Then she looked at the small digital clock on her nightstand. Three A.M.. She had no idea it was so late.

"Where have you been!" she snapped.

The words were barely out when she realized that was not what she wanted to say. She cared little where he had been. His comings and goings had never mattered before. They mattered even less now. Ever since Bubba had walked in on her and Ace Corbet, Audra had become increasingly irritated with him. After weeks of living together Audra knew their relationship was drawing to a close. It had never been a good one, anyway. He was still a stranger, and what Audra had meant to say to this stranger but didn't was, "How dare you walk into my apartment at this hour!"

Bubba ignored her and sauntered over to the desk. He peered down at the papers cluttering the top. "What are you doing?"

"None of your business!" She scooped her notes into a pile, shoved them into the bottom drawer of her desk and slammed it shut. Then with a stiff, angry motion, she locked it.

"Okay, okay. Don't bite." He sounded unruffled but his face hardened. "What's the matter? Got the rag on?"

"I hate that expression! Only you stupid men would use it!" She stood up.

"Just who are you calling stupid?" Bubba asked between clenched teeth.

"There are only two of us here," Audra answered, all the hatred and frustration of her life pouring from her. "And I'm not the one who resembles a gorilla."

"Why you . . . I don't take that from any broad." He grabbed the lamp from the nightstand and ripped its cord from the socket, then raised it, like a weapon, over her head. For one sickening second Audra thought he was going to smash her skull. But slowly the angry lines on Bubba's face dissolved and he threw the lamp on the bed.

"You broads are all alike. You want to play in the big leagues but you don't have the stomach for it."

"And you men are all alike," she spat. "You have more brawn than brains. I want my key back, and I never want to see you again!"

Bubba's lips curled into a sneer as he dug into his pants pocket and pulled out a key. With a gesture that was both arrogant and threatening, he flung it onto the floor by her feet. "And good riddance."

Long after the apartment door slammed shut, Audra hugged her knees and sat shaking in the middle of the bed. "Oh, god!" she cried as the image of her smashed skull filled her imagination. She had to get a grip. Her life was spinning out of control. This was not what she had envisioned for herself. "Oh, god!" But even as she whispered it again, she knew her supplication was useless. "'No deity will save us, we must save ourselves,'" she mumbled, quoting her mother's favorite line from the *Humanist Manifesto*. But the question her mother had failed to answer was *how*?

How did one save herself?

• • •

The blustery wind filled Trisha's sweatshirt and blew it out like a sail. Now and then she tried flattening it over her jeans as she and Buck walked along the deserted airstrip, but it was pointless. "It's beautiful here. It helps you forget all the violence back home."

"Yeah." Buck grinned beside her. "Look over there, how the strip leads to the very edge of the cliff. If a plane isn't airborne by then it's all over."

Trisha's eyes followed the direction of Buck's finger where the strip continued for another quarter of a mile, then ended abruptly as the land ended abruptly. She couldn't see the jagged rocks forming the sharp drop into the ocean. But she could hear the muffled sound of the pounding surf.

"Seems like there's plenty of strip for a safe CTOL," she said, scanning the length of the runway before the two turned and headed toward the hangar.

"The P2 won't have any trouble taking off here, not with the power she's got. But for conventional aircraft it would be risky. The winds are strong, unpredictable. And there's no way to enlarge the runway, except by leveling that mountain on the opposite side."

Trisha looked at the mountain that rose high in the air like a huge monolith. Nestled beside it was a hangar, which in comparison to the size of the mountain looked like a metal doll house. "I see you joined the two hangars," she said, scanning the shiny corrugated metal of the midsection.

Buck nodded. "You've got four hundred thirty-five thousand square feet of work space. Enough room to build one heck of an airplane."

"Do you really think we can do it?"

"Kelly Johnson and his Skunk Works crew at Lockheed designed, wind tunnel tested, and completely built a ready-to-fly XP-80 in just one hundred and eighty days. We've been working on the P2 for two years."

"I know, but we need to solve the casing problem first."

"Relax, Trisha. I know it's going to be a bumpy road, but everything will work out. You'll see."

Although his voice was optimistic, Trisha doubted Buck really believed that Kelly Johnson himself would ever build an airplane in this manner.

"And good news," he continued. "I spoke to Mike this morning and he's decided to send another small, hand-picked crew of mechanics and shop workers tomorrow."

She was about to say that was a step in the right direction when they were greeted by shouts and waves as they stepped through the hangar door. After responding with her own greetings, she leaned closer to Buck. "Is this part of the bumpy road you mentioned?" Her chin jutted to the chaos around her and to a group of men opening large crates of equipment and machinery.

"Yep. It's going to take a lot of work to make it happen."

"It is exciting though when you realize that we have a chance to make history right here."

"I suppose so. I don't think about it much. My interests are narrower, more selfish."

"You love him, don't you?"

"Mike? Yeah. We go way back. In some ways I raised him as much as his father did."

"I know, I've heard."

"I guess that means I have to take credit for the bad as well as the good."

"Meaning?"

"Meaning that I love Michael Patterson like a son, but I know he has faults."

"What are you saying?"

The leathery man chuckled. "I like you, Trisha. I liked you right off, when you first came to PA. You looked to me like a scrawny, wide-eyed kid then, but when you opened your mouth and started talking about airplanes, you didn't seem like such a kid anymore."

Trisha squeezed his arm. "I like you too, Buck."

"Then you won't mind me talking to you like a father?"

"I'd be honored."

"Okay, what I want to say is that Mike's not the kind of man I'd want my daughter to get involved with, if I had a daughter that is.

His favorite toy was always the one he couldn't have. You understand what I'm saying?"

"If you're saying what I think you are, then you have no worries. He's married."

"Exactly. And you're what my generation called a 'nice girl.' And nice girls and married men aren't combinations that add up to a happy ending." Buck draped his arm around her shoulders. "But we can't always help how we feel, can we? We can only help what we do with those feelings."

"I wasn't planning on doing anything with mine."

"I didn't expect you would. But you see, I also know Mike, and he's . . . well, he's attracted to you. Don't ask me how I know, it's little things that wouldn't mean anything to you. And *he* may act on his feelings."

Trisha's face darkened. "You're very blunt."

"I'm sorry if I've overstepped, it's just that I like you, and I know Mike, and I think he's working himself up to making a good old-fashioned pass. I've seen him work himself up before."

"I thought 'guys' were supposed to stick together? You don't seem to be looking out for his interests."

"Oh, but I am. Aside from liking you, Trisha, I don't want to see Mike get involved for his own sake."

"And why is that?"

"Because you're the type he'd fall in love with. You're the kind who could break his heart."

"Is this the kind of sleazy gossip going around the PA lunchroom?"

"I doubt if anyone in the world knows how you feel, including Mike. I'm not much of a talker, Trisha. I do more watching and listening. And I saw it coming over Mike, just as I saw it come over you, like a slow growing cancer."

"Cancer? I guess that's a good word for it."

"You're tough, Trisha. You can get over this. Not all cancers are incurable. But Mike, he's the one I'm worried about. He's never been in love before."

"You make him sound like some innocent school boy, when you know the opposite is true."

"He's far from innocent, but he's vulnerable, more vulnerable than even he knows."

"I suppose I should thank you for wanting to be my conscience."

"I don't need to be that. You've already got one. I was thinking more along the line of 'friend.'"

"I'd like that. I think I'm going to need one out here."

"In return, can I count on you for something?" Buck gestured toward an organized section in back, full of bottles and holding tanks. A man in a white shirt and khaki pants stood, by what appeared to be a large pump, writing something on a pad.

"What's Nolan up to?" Trisha said, following his gaze.

"Well, that's the thing I'm counting on you for. I was hoping you could tell me. I can never understand what he's saying."

She gave Buck's hand a squeeze. "He's brilliant, you know. I'll go see what he's doing. And I'm *very* glad we're going to be working together," she said before walking away.

"Nolan, hello! I heard about your special project. How's it coming?" Trisha approached the tall, thin man.

Nolan had a serious but comely, almost girlish face. He rarely smiled and was, in fact, generally pessimistic. Now, his face knotted into little bows of consternation as he put down his pad.

"Considering the circumstances under which I am forced to labor," he paused, allowing Trisha to observe his makeshift lab, "I suppose I'm doing well."

"Seems like we're all going to be working under adverse conditions." She thought of her conversation with Buck.

"Yes, I was advised of operations moving here." He looked utterly wretched as he scanned the disorder around him. "I think this entire adventure is ludicrous. What type of mentality would conceive of building an airplane mock-up without first perfecting its propulsion system?"

"I'm afraid, Nolan, that necessity is often the enemy of rational thought."

The physicist grunted. "Of all people, I thought that you, at least, would try to prevent this."

"I did." Trisha looked at his note pad. "What's this? 0.0042869?"

"I was just going over some notes. That's the mass change of the deuterium nuclei. Using the relativity relation $E=MC^2$, this gives 4.5×10^{13} calories per gram atom of deuterium. Thus, about 0.1% of the mass is converted to heat energy. Naturally, the greater the heat energy the greater the destruction of the casing by the plasma. We know there was no evidence of breakdown in the first thirty-five tests. I propose to find the exact point at which our metal began breaking down. Based on what I've done so far, I think if we use one more water cooled vacuum switch tube with its capacity to control another twenty-five million watts, plus additional shielding in each . . . ."

"The tubes alone are three hundred and twenty pounds apiece; times that by four reactors on one P2 that's 1,280 additional pounds, just for starters, without even getting into the metal shields or additional vacuum chambers."

"True, but the alteration of the P2 may not be as drastic as first anticipated. If we pursue this course, maybe in six months we can begin the mock-up."

"In six months we must complete it."

Nolan's girlish face warped in panic revealing his ignorance of Michael Patterson's new plan. "I . . . I am a scientist; a logical being who deals in facts and then proceeds in careful, precise action. You are also a scientist, Trisha. I have always held you in the highest esteem. How can you submit to such chaos? How can you submit your staff to this chaos?"

Trisha understood Nolan's frustration. A person didn't expend his energy, his very life into building something revolutionary, then casually accept the possibility of it being tossed into a scrap heap.

"Nolan, there are things involved here that neither you nor I have any control over. What happens here, though, will control the future of PA. This makes our work more vital than ever. We have to pull together regardless of our personal feelings. I need you. And I need to know I can count on you one hundred percent."

With a sigh he picked up his pad, "Trisha, you know the answer to that."

● ● ●

"Looks like you need a break, Callahan," said a voice that seemed to fill the hangar with a gusty breeze of its own.

Trisha brushed the dust off her jeans, then the dirt smudges from her face, as she turned toward the voice. For the past several hours she had been helping to rig one of the large mobile platforms.

The tall, muscular man smiled broadly, thinking how pretty the face was and feeling unusually pleased at seeing it. He took her arm then guided her through the maze of crates and boxes until they reached the rear of the hangar where a dented metal pot sat on an old, paint-chipped table. "Come on, I'll buy you a cup of coffee."

"I could use one."

"Looks like you're moving along fine."

"Well, boss, we've gone from total chaos to semi-chaos so, as they say, progress is being made."

Mike poured two coffees and handed Trisha one, then they both sat down on metal folding chairs. He remained silent as he stared into the steaming liquid. When he looked up his forehead was furrowed. "Why is it that we never call each other by our first names?"

"Does it matter?"

"Yes. After two years of working together I think we should be friends. And friends are on a first name basis."

"I have no objections," she said, her smile looking forced. "After all, I am one of the boys."

"Seriously, Trisha, you're the first woman I've ever been able to speak to as if you were a man."

"Nice of you to say so, boss . . . ah . . . Mike." She shrugged. "Guess it will take a bit of getting used to."

Mike sipped his coffee, his eyes never leaving her. He liked the way her thick, black hair was gathered at the neck by a scrunchie. It exposed the faint blush creeping over her ears. Had he hit a nerve, again? Whatever it meant, it fueled his courage. He reached for her hand, his fingers lightly touching hers. "Trisha . . . I wish . . . we had all the money in the world so we could build this airplane properly." With that, he rose and disappeared among the maze of boxes, feeling like a coward for not saying what was really on his mind.

● ● ●

For the next several hours Trisha helped assemble the huge mobile platforms and ladders which resembled scaffolding in a shipyard. By the time they were completed, she was so exhausted that when Mike said, "Okay everyone, let's knock off," she was one of the first to leave, and quickly slipped out the side in order to avoid her boss.

All afternoon she had managed to keep her distance. But this was an impossible situation. How had this happened? How did she wake up one morning in love with a married man?

Buck called it a cancer. The question was how to get rid of it? The most obvious answer was to quit. Walk off the job. But could she do that? Could she leave the project in a lurch?

Still . . . the way he had looked at her! He said he wanted to be friends, but did he know, like Buck did? Had he seen something on her face, heard something in her voice that told him how she felt? There was only one way out. As soon as the project was finished, she'd hand in her resignation.

Mike's reputation with women was legendary. As Trisha walked to her car she imagined his face contorting with laughter; envisioned her name scrawled over some dirty urinal in some dirty men's room; heard it bantered about in a locker room heavy with male perspiration; visualized his friends slapping him on the back in congratulations over his latest conquest.

The half moon made usual shadowy objects appear more luminous. But some things were best left in shadows she thought when spotting the helicopter bearing the name of Patterson Aviation and the initials M.P. in gold and white lettering. He was a man used to flying in and out of people's lives, oblivious to all the turmoil he created, as if it could be easily tidied-up. How many hearts had he broken? How many lives had he damaged?

Suddenly, she felt angry—at herself, at her weakness. And when she pulled into the Sea Breeze parking lot she was still angry even though she had tried to dispel it by driving around for nearly an hour.

She parked her BMW in front of a marble horse-head post with a large brass ring through its nose. The Sea Breeze was a converted mansion, and several touches of the former splendor still remained. It was here that Michael Patterson had rented one entire wing for the Gibs Town staff.

When she neared room twelve, she stopped. "Mike . . . what are you doing here?"

"My room's beside yours," he answered casually, but his face was anything but casual.

She stood looking at him, her silence prevailing like a great shield of armor between them. Then the strong, powerful executive took the key from her hand and unlocked the door.

"Look, I'm tired." She tried slipping past him but she wasn't fast enough for suddenly he had hold of her.

"There was something I wanted to tell you, over our coffee earlier."

"What's that?"

By way of answer he kissed her and when he did, she felt pulled by some invisible tide, felt herself being swept away. Then, just as suddenly she felt herself leaning against the frame of the door looking into the face that a moment ago had been so intimately a part of her own.

"Trisha, I can't explain what I'm feeling now. I don't understand it myself. I know that I want you. But it's more than that, too. I also know you're not the type to look twice at a married man. But my feelings are so strong I can't be silent."

"You have no right to say that to me. As you pointed out, you're married. You're talking about *adultery*."

"That's an ugly word. And I've never viewed it that way. I like to think of it as two consenting adults." He shrugged. "I had to try. You of all people know how impetuous and impatient I am."

Buck had known this was coming. He had warned her. But in her heart, Trisha didn't believe her boss would actually make a pass. Now that it had happened it seemed so silly, like something out of a romance novel, and yet so . . . frightening, too.

Mike gently grazed her cheek with his thumb, his face inches from hers. "Don't look so worried, Trisha. You're not going to have to spend all your time at Gibs Town fighting me off. But just so you know, the door between us locks both ways. My side will remain open. Good night." With that the powerful frame disappeared into room eleven.

Trisha entered her own room, closed the door, and without turning on the light made her way to the bed.

Lord you are my refuge and strength. A very help in times of trouble. Whom shall I fear? I can do all things through Christ who strengthens me.

And as she sat in the dark, she heard that still small voice.

"I will never leave you or forsake you. I love you with an everlasting love."

● ● ●

CHAPTER 7

Joshua leaned back in Senator Merrill's tufted executive's chair and stared at Cassy in disbelief. "Why have you waited so long to tell me this? You realize that every change you make will cost you? I've already started encrypting the second server."

"I decided the volunteers don't need the extra security. They'll have nothing but call numbers for pitching to small donors or voters. A few will have Photoshop and other tools for creating brochures, etcetera. Nothing to worry about."

"Your uncle contracted for two encrypted servers. Why the sudden change?"

"I'm thinking of the cost."

"That's not the place to save money. Especially since you've already been hacked."

"Actually, I want to put that money toward the first server. In addition to it being encrypted and with fingerprint recognition, I want the self-wiping feature so if the system is breached, all information will be erased. We already back-up our servers so no problem there."

Joshua tented his fingers. "You've paid for one of our best security systems but it doesn't come with a self-destroyer. Sorry."

"I've done my homework and I know of companies that have Global Icon's new app. I believe you actually call it, *The Destroyer*."

Cassy smiled and tossed her head, making her spiked hair, which was dyed all blonde today, swish pleasantly around her face. "I think it's an equitable tradeoff. Only one encrypted server *and The Destroyer.*"

Joshua eyed her, thinking how the new hair color made Cassy look like a young Meg Ryan. He liked this brainy non-conformist, though at times, like now, he found her annoying. "You're making changes late in the game and you know I've already started upgrading both servers."

"How much do you want for the changes?"

"You still owe for that cocktail party. But tell you what. I'll make a few modifications to your general office server, leaving off our pricier features. It will still give your office more protection than it has now. And you, your uncle and the campaign manager's computer will get the works."

"No, not the campaign manager's. He'll be fine with your basic package. But my uncle's and mine—I want them as secure as Fort Knox."

Joshua pulled himself closer to the desk and tapped on Senator Merrill's computer. "What's on this thing that you need such tight security?" He hadn't found anything interesting so far and neither had the Mossad. "And don't tell me it's none of my business. It would help to know what I'm trying to safeguard. And forget about telling me it's to protect Senator Merrill's campaign strategy."

Cassy picked at the black leather bracelet on her wrist. "How much extra?"

"Look, Cassy, if I knew what was so important I could better tailor the package to your needs. You're leaving me in the dark here."

"My uncle has enemies. Okay?"

"All presidential candidates throughout history had enemies. Tell me something I don't know."

"He's had death threats."

"You mean like drop out of the campaign or else?"

Cassy shook her head. "No, much more serious."

"Has he gone to the police? Or FBI?"

Again Cassy shook her head.

"If he reports this, the Secret Service will assign him additional bodyguards."

Cassy's eyes brimmed with fear. "His enemies are powerful and well connected."

"Are you talking about Senator Garby?"

Cassy flipped her hand in the air. "No, he's nothing more than a puppet for the current administration. But Tafco Oil for one . . . and others."

"You want to tell me about it?"

"How do I know I can trust you? I don't know who to turn to anymore. Who to trust. And Uncle Phillip won't bring in the authorities. He says it's because there's no one we *can* trust. But I need to trust somebody. I can't sleep nights and I . . . ."

"Okay, take it slow, what's going on?"

Cassy stared at her leather bracelet as she twisted it around and around.

"Cassy?"

"My uncle has information some powerful people would like to get their hands on. Information he has been getting via email. Not long after they started showing up in his in-box, his computer got hacked and the death threats started coming."

Joshua straightened. Tafco Oil. He knew that name. Tafco Oil—TO? Was that who Arie meant when he scribbled those initials on the paper? He thought of the ladder-crane-like drawing. An oil derrick? It didn't make sense. The Mossad already knew of Tafco's ties to terrorists.

Joshua stared at the woman in front of him. All his instincts told him she was frightened about something. But was it really the big deal she made it out to be?

"Your uncle has erased all the emails on his computer. Does he still have a record of them somewhere?"

"Yes, hidden in a safe place. But the emailer said there was more to come. And when they do, his computer needs to be fully secure so no one can hack in and see what information has been sent. If they don't know what he has, maybe that will protect him, and maybe that will cause his adversaries to think twice for fear that Uncle Phillip has made provisions for releasing this information should anything happen to him." Cassy rose to her feet. "The emailer has put my uncle's life in danger. I've told you enough that you should understand how important your security system is to us."

"Maybe I can help. Not just with your software."

"I don't think so." Cassy walked to the door. "Though I wish you could."

"Meet me for dinner and we'll talk." When she shook her head, he added, "I know a great hamburger place."

● ● ●

Mike toweled his wet body before throwing open the bathroom door. When he did, he was surprised to see Renee moving about.

"You're up early. It's not even ten." He wrapped the towel around his waist suddenly feeling awkward. He was not used to being home. He had spent few nights here during the past month.

"I have a lot to do." She rummaged through a huge mahogany dresser. "I'm going shopping. The Garbys have seen my entire wardrobe, everything decent anyway."

Mike chuckled. "Since when did you need an excuse to spend money? But I guess that means you plan on doing more fundraisers?"

"The senator has roped me into three more. And he keeps insisting I wear the same black gown with the V neckline."

"I can't imagine why," Mike said sarcastically.

"Truth is, I'm getting bored with it."

"Bored? With all that attention from, what did you call them— people who shape history?"

"I don't like being treated like a glorified event planner. Don't get me wrong, DC was exhilarating and I won't have missed it for the world. And, yes, I still believe Senator Garby would make a great president though the closer we get to the election the less likely it will happen. But I resent being taken for granted. The Garbys expect me to drop everything and be their 'little hostess' whenever they call."

"So when are you leaving?" Mike asked, smearing shaving cream over his face, his mind already on Gibs Town. He hated leaving it. Hated leaving *her*. He was sure he was in love with Trisha. Problem was, he didn't know what to do about it. "So, when are you leaving," he repeated, trying to sound interested.

"In a few days. And Michael, the Garbys would like you to come, too. To be their guest at their big gala dinner next week."

"Impossible."

"Why? We haven't gone away together in some time. A little vacation would do us both good."

"There's too much happening at the plant. I can't go anywhere, not for a long time."

"You're just saying that because it's the Garbys."

"Renee, right now the Pope himself couldn't induce me to leave my company."

Renee laughed. "Poor illustration, darling. You're a Methodist and in name only. No, you've let the rumors prejudice your opinion of them."

"We've been through all that. I'm not going to defend my position. And you're right. I'm not interested in spending time with the Garbys. I'm particular about the company I keep. I'm at a point in my life where when I do have free time, I want to spend it with people I like. Can you understand that?"

"Of course, Michael. What it boils down to is that we like different people. But it's a shame. Senator Garby has taken an interest in you. And if you made half an effort you could be friends. He can do a lot for you, for both of us, even for Patterson Aviation. And for someone as ambitious as you, that should mean something. At any rate, he asks about you all the time."

"Really?"

"Yes, mainly about your company, the kind of planes you build, that sort of thing. I told him you're so secretive I don't even know what goes on."

Mike's face knotted. "What else?"

"Nothing. Well . . . he did ask why you were so secretive. Why are you?"

"Ever hear of corporate espionage?"

Renee made a face. "He also mentioned how he'd like to visit your plant, and then Alex, Alex Harner said . . . ."

"He was there?"

Renee nodded. "And Alex told Senator Garby it would be good publicity for his campaign, you know, senator visits factory, mingles with the common worker and all. Then Alex suggested the senator enlist you in his campaign."

"And *that's* what this invitation is all about? You're supposed to reel me in, is that it?"

"I wouldn't put it like that."

"And what were you supposed to get out of this? An invitation to the 'inner circle'?"

"Well, I . . . I . . . ."

"Just how far would you go to get a little attention from your precious senator? Maybe it's a good thing you *don't* know anything about my company."

"You're being a bore."

"And you're being naive. Grow up, Renee. These boys don't give anything away, not even their time or attention, unless there's something in it for them."

Renee threw up her hands. "Believe me the senator doesn't give a hoot about your company. The thing he didn't understand was that I don't either!" She slammed one of the drawers shut. "And don't look at me like that. You know I've never been interested in your company. And ever since you started running off to that secret workshop of yours, you haven't been the same. Michael, honestly, you can't get so worked up over an airplane!"

"Drop it, Renee."

"For heaven sake, what's wrong with you? You have an opportunity here to make something of yourself and . . . ."

"*Make something of myself?* I thought I already had."

"I didn't mean it like that. It's just that Senator Garby is powerful and I don't think it's wise to deliberately offend him. Surely you can't refuse . . . ."

"I can and do."

Renee's face reddened. "Well, what am I going to tell him?"

A sudden rap on the bedroom door ended the conversation. Mike quickly put on his robe and answered it.

"I . . . I'm sorry to disturb you, sir," said one of the maids. "A phone call for you, a Mr. Buck McNight. He said it was urgent."

Without another word, Mike rushed to the adjacent sitting room and nearest phone. "Yes, Buck, what is it?"

The voice on the other end sounded strained. "There's been an explosion. The autoclave. Mike, the whole wall is gone! Five workers injured and on the way to the hospital. Thank God there weren't more."

"I'll be right over," Mike said, and hung up.

• • •

Mike paced his office floor as he listened to Buck retelling the events of the morning. "It's a miracle it wasn't worse," he said when Buck finished.

Adhesives, which Lockheed helped develop, had replaced riveting in large fuselage panels. The adhesives were also used to apply titanium straps. Those parts of the aircraft on which adhesives were used had to be put into the autoclave—which functioned like a giant pressure cooker—and bonded the adhesives under tremendous heat and inert gas pressure.

"How could this happen? There were safety devices, strict guidelines. Any indication of a malfunction?"

Buck clicked a boot heel against the leg of his chair and shook his head.

"Then we have to consider sabotage or terrorism. That means Homeland Security will be crawling all over us. Let's just hope it won't scare away any of our employees. In the meantime, I want constant updates on our injured linesmen. And see what can be done for their families while you're at it."

Mike stopped pacing and sat down at his desk. "We're backlogged with the EX4 and C101 deals . . . ." His voice trailed off. PA's sales director had sold all ten C101s, plus five more. These five, plus the EX4s he sold earlier, put production schedules on an overtime basis. They couldn't afford to be without the autoclave. It meant loss of productive man hours and that meant loss of revenue.

"We've survived worse," Buck said.

"We'll double the overtime. Thank God for the C101 money. It'll help defray costs here and over at Gibs Town."

"There's something else. The rumors are flying."

"What rumors?"

"That you're building some kind of 'super plane.'"

"It was just a matter of time." Mike had been trying to keep the P2 under wraps for the last two years. Only R&D knew the real nature of the project. And now, aside from them and the Gibs Town crew, no one knew about the seaside hangar and the nature of the work being done there. But everyone knew something was afoot. It was difficult not to notice when key co-workers failed to show up for work.

"Can we keep the lid on?"

"Not for long. The plant's buzzing." Buck had flown with Mike in the helicopter from Gibs Town. They had been in Everman less than twenty-four hours.

"The trouble keeps mounting, doesn't it? I just hope PA survives. You're the only one I'd ever admit this to, Buck, but I'm a bit unnerved by the prospect of losing my company."

"You're not your father, Mike. You're strong and not afraid to take risks. You have guts. You know I liked your dad but . . . I love you like my own. Stay focused. We still have a chance to pull it off. By the time anyone knows what's going on at Gibs Town, it'll be too late."

● ● ●

Joshua handed a bulky, laminated menu to Cassy. "I already know what I want."

After a brief glance, Cassy tossed the menu onto the oilcloth-covered table. "I'll have what you're having."

"Then be prepared to eat the Hoppies Special, a half-pound Black Angus burger topped with lettuce, tomato, onions, mushrooms and avocados."

"I can handle it."

Joshua gave the order to a young pimple-faced waiter then turned his attention to the woman sitting across from him. They had come straight from work and in separate cars. Joshua guessed the separate cars, which was Cassy's idea, was for the purpose of a quick get-away if the conversation proved not to her liking.

Now, he sat across from her thinking how nice she looked with her blonde hair framing her face that way. And there was something about the softness of her violet eyes that drew him. It's strange what can turn a man's head. Whoever thought that for him it would be a pair of violet eyes?

"So . . . what's life really like in a campaign? All I've seen of it is a bustling office."

"It's hectic. Nerve-racking. Stressful. Emotionally draining."

"Wow, all that? I never knew a database manager had it so bad. But it looks like Senator Merrill's a shoe-in. I don't see how Garby can pull it out, now. Not with his poll numbers. Your uncle is still ahead by double digits. You must be proud of him, proud to be part of it."

"My uncle is working his tail off. He has for over a year, now. Campaigning isn't for the faint of heart."

"What's his schedule like tomorrow?"

"A town hall meeting in the morning, a rally in the afternoon, a fundraiser at night. But his handlers are working just as hard."

"His handlers?"

"Yeah, the campaign manager works like a plow horse and carries the biggest load, but there's also the speech writers, the scheduler, finance director, communications director, policy advisers, volunteer coordinator . . . ."

"Whoa. I get the picture. How about we bag the shop talk and move on to a more interesting topic? *You.*"

"Why?"

"Maybe you're someone I'd like to get to know better."

"Then what? Go back to Israel? No thanks, I tried that once. I don't do long-distance relationships."

Joshua smiled. "I wasn't thinking that aggressively. I was thinking more here-and-now. Really, Cassy, I'm just trying to break the ice. This past month you've been constantly looking over my shoulder. I know you said it was because you wanted to learn, but it felt more like you were an adversary, questioning all my decisions.

"Then today you talked about someone wanting to kill your uncle, and that concerns me. I'm a security specialist. I know people who might be able to help. But I need to determine who I'm dealing with. Am I dealing with Cassy, the flapdoodle with purple-green-orange-blonde hair, or Cassy the genius who blocked sKyWIper?"

"My hair bothers you?"

"No. I'm speaking metaphorically here. But as long as we're on the subject, you do look better with all one color. You're attractive when you fix yourself up. I already told you how good you looked at the cocktail party last week."

"If this is a pass, save it. I'm not . . . ."

"No pass. I have someone . . . had someone . . . never mind. Look Cassy, just tell me if this is for real. Tell me that it's not your imagination. That your uncle really is in danger. I can see that you're scared. But I need to know how credible the threat is."

Cassy opened her mouth then closed it when the waiter brought their burgers and placed them on the table. When he disappeared, Cassy pushed her plate away. "Who are these people you say can help? Are they part of the government?"

"They don't have to be. I know those in and those out. Global Icon has powerful friends everywhere."

"If I tell you, it can't go any further unless I say. Swear it?"

"You have my word."

Cassy picked up her fork and speared a French fry. "My uncle has proof that Tafco Oil is building internment camps right here in the United States."

Joshua frowned. "For what purpose?"

"He doesn't know. But he thinks it has something to do with . . . ." Cassy shook her head. "This is crazy. I shouldn't be telling you this."

"You've gone this far, don't stop now. You need a friend, someone who can help. And I promise I'll try my best to be that friend, *if* you level with me."

Cassy let the fork drop to her plate. "I don't know if I'm doing you any favors by involving you in this. It could put you in danger, too. But you asked for it. Uncle Phillip thinks it has something to do with *President Baker*."

•   •   •

Mike watched Trisha's face knot as he talked about the autoclave incident. She had not gone with him to Everman, and until now, no one at Gibs Town knew of the explosion.

"Praise God that all those injured are going to be alright." She lowered her voice as though not wanting to be overheard. "You think it was a malfunction?"

"Doubtful."

"What does Meyers say?"

"What would you expect any Homeland Security agent to say? He parses his words like a politician. But his boys will go over the autoclave with a magnifying glass and then he'll give us his official ruling."

Trisha walked over to the dented coffee pot and poured out two cups. She handed one to Mike then sat down in the folding chair beside him. "It doesn't make sense. Why blow up an autoclave? Why not the entire plant?"

"Terrorists aren't logical. Who knows why they do what they do? You're not dealing with the rational mind."

"Then, Patterson Aviation may be the latest target of ISA."

"Possibly." Mike watched her face drop.

"You're not going to get all wobbly legged on me, are you? I've never known you to back away from a fight."

"I'm not afraid. Only . . . ."

"Only what?"

"Never mind, you wouldn't understand." Trisha sipped her coffee.

"Try me," he said, hoping to draw her closer, ever closer, and yet never quite managing it. She was always warm, friendly. And always out of reach. "Try me," he repeated.

"The whole world is like an open wound, Mike, and all the time there is *Jesus*. Loving us and wanting to heal our lives, wanting us to love Him, but so many won't."

Mike rose to his feet. "But you love Him."

"Yes."

"You'd be better off looking for a man to love. He bent over her, nearly touching her head with his lips. "I missed you." The words worked through her hair like a ribbon. "I'm falling in love with you, Trisha. I'm sorry, but I am."

"I know," she said softly.

"How do you feel about it?"

"Mike, you're married. That's the beginning, the middle and the end of story. And I can't add anything to it."

"Can't or won't?"

"Does it matter? I know you're sincere, that you believe what you say. But your kind of love is different from mine. I think you're more in love with the idea of me. In love with the challenge. Not really me at all."

"You couldn't be more wrong," he said straightening. "I only wish we had met ten years ago."

● ● ●

Audra walked down the hall of Patterson Aviation's R&D Department clutching her purse. Her stomach churned. She had eaten little breakfast. Ever since the autoclave explosion her nerves were as tight as bow strings. Peter Meyers and his group had swarmed through the plant like a regiment of locusts, inspecting every inch and asking question after question.

The entire company had been in an uproar for days. Everyone knew Meyers was Homeland Security. And he meant trouble. Words bounced from one department to another like ping pong balls.

Sabotage.

Jihad.

ISA.

Suddenly, everyone began seeing bogeymen. Bushes blown by the wind covered hidden assassins. A tailgating car became a pursuing vehicle of terrorists. The latest gory newspaper stories were traded like baseball cards. Fear can be as contagious as the flu, and PA experienced an epidemic.

Audra had also seen her share of bogeymen. She had thought, but wasn't sure, that someone was outside her front door. She had thought, but wasn't sure, she had heard breathing and then the knob turning.

If only she could find a nice man who shared her values, who was interested in living an unconventional life, one she could respect and who respected her. She needed to reevaluate her dating habits, but in the meantime she felt sorry she had thrown Bubba out. He was a brute, but he was a big, strong brute. And a big, strong man, be he brute or no, was a comfort in times like these.

But he was no longer there, so she had to buy her comfort elsewhere. It came in the form of a licensed .25 caliber handgun; a small silver and black pistol, perfect for a woman's purse. She took it everywhere.

Audra moved stiff legged down the hall, not releasing the grip on her bag until she stepped into the room that was outfitted for her titanium X experiments.

Madness, it was all madness. The world was going mad.

She just hoped she wasn't going to go mad with it.

●　●　●

CHAPTER 8

Joshua was momentarily distracted by Cassy's perfume as he looked over her shoulder and watched her pull up her uncle's newest email. It was the first time he had noticed a woman's perfume since Rachel.

"There it is," Cassy said, scrolling down and stopping at an email entitled, "secrets from the dark side."

She opened it and began reading. "There are now three internment camps completed. Locations unknown. Best guess, look west of Everman, 500 miles."

The email was from someone calling himself "concerned."

Cassy rose and offered Joshua her chair. "Can you track the source?"

Joshua settled behind the computer, then began pounding keys. Fifteen minutes later he shook his head. "No good. It's the same as last time. He's rolling his IP address. He's packaged up the email like an onion with layers and layers of destinations that go through known remail servers having no tracking."

He couldn't tell her that the Mossad had been trying to trace the last two messages announcing each of the other camp completions. She only knew he had "friends" in the security field working on it.

"The campaign is at a good place. I'm not needed right now. And you're nearly done. What say you we take a few days and drive around?"

"Better yet, how about we hire some mercenaries I know at Blackwater? Former decorated rangers, I might add. Let them take a look-see—no questions asked."

Cassy shook her head. Her hair was longer now, and Joshua couldn't help thinking that she was getting prettier every day.

"You've been great these past few weeks. You even convinced my uncle to hire Blackwater bodyguards for extra protection. But I know that secretly you've questioned my story. How real was it? Was it as bad as I made it out to be? And now I have a chance to prove it to you . . . to myself. I guess I need to be assured that we've not been duped by some nut. And if we find that camp maybe I can convince my uncle to come out in the open with his file."

"Your uncle is paying me to do a job. How would it look if I walked out on it now? Before it's finished?"

"You're into final testing and that can wait a few days."

Joshua frowned. What would headquarters say? He already knew they believed the threats on Senator Merrill's life to be credible. They had messaged Joshua their concern after restoring Merrill's deleted files, including emails. They had also told him that Merrill was the real deal. That he was pro-Israel and was certain to back them at the UN and elsewhere.

Nothing must happen to him.

The election was only months away and they had sent two of their best undercover men, posing as Blackwater guards, to keep an eye on him.

But to bring a civilian into the operation? That was crossing the line.

"Look Cassy, I understand your point. I get it. But I work for Global Icon and they'd take a dim view of me putting one of their clients in danger. Let the professionals handle this."

Cassy logged off her computer then picked up her bulbous black purse which, Joshua suspected, could carry all her computer equipment plus her entire wardrobe. And that wardrobe, judging by what she wore everyday, and not counting that one black silk dress she wore at the cocktail party, consisted of a few pairs of jeans and assorted tank tops.

"I'll see you in a few days," she said, slipping her laptop into the bag.

"Just where are you going?"

"About five-hundred miles west of Everman."

Joshua grabbed her arm. "What you're planning is crazy."

When Cassy's look only became more determined, he heaved a sigh. "Alright. Come on. We'll stop at my apartment first, then gas up the car."

Cassy grinned. "What? You need fresh clothes, pretty boy?"

"No, my gun."

●   ●   ●

"Say that again, Audra!" Trisha shouted into the receiver. She had been praying for this news but now that it was here she was having trouble believing it.

Trisha knew Audra had been working long hours, spending nights on her office cot. Some of Audra's colleagues had become concerned and told Trisha they thought the metallurgist was ready for burnout. Others had confided in Trisha that they believed Audra stayed at the plant, locked in her research lab, because she had become paranoid over the rioting in Everman and the recent explosion at PA, and couldn't bring herself to go home. They also told Trisha about the .25 caliber Audra kept under her pillow at night. And about another gun Audra claimed she kept at home.

Trisha hoped Audra wasn't on the verge of a breakdown.

"I think I've found it," Audra repeated. "I think I've found a way to stabilize titanium X."

Trisha sent up silent praises to God. "How did you do it?"

"I've been concentrating on the films."

Trisha already knew it would be Audra's initial focus. It was the thin protective film that stood between a metal surface and a potentially destructive environment. "I gathered that," she said, impatient to hear more.

"In the past I concentrated on promoting the formation of a non-crystalline surface through laser glazing."

Again, no surprise. A noncrystalline film produced a more effective barrier to corrosion than a crystalline one. "Okay, so what's the end result?" Trisha said, thinking she was starting to sound like her impatient boss.

"The laser melted the outermost layer of titanium X and when the beam was removed, the rapid cooling produced a glassy metal coating. But even after this the film wasn't hard enough and couldn't stand up to the corrosive microworld of fusion. That's when I thought of ion implantation."

Trisha's excitement grew.

"I was able to alter the surface of my metal, disorder its atomic structure, and render it glassier. I bombarded the titanium surface with an ion beam in a vacuum chamber, which then drove thousands of atoms into its surface layers. It took me awhile to convert all the variables into a successful formula, but I think I've got it now."

"Audra, I'm so happy I hardly know what to say!"

There was a brief silence on the other end. "Don't get too excited. I've had some success, but more testing is needed. Maybe in three months . . . ."

"We don't have three months."

"Well . . . maybe I could cut it shorter. I don't know. I'm working eighteen hours a day as it is . . . ."

"Forget all that. We're going to test it on the reactor itself by making a titanium X casing. We're fighting the clock. That means taking short cuts."

"Trisha, this is so irregular. I must register an objection. It's not like you to be unscientific and imprudent. But . . . if that's what you want to do . . . you're the boss."

"It's not what I want to do, it's what I have to do. I'll send Nolan tomorrow. Let him go over what you've got. He'll help you from here on in. That should take some of the pressure off you. And Audra . . . ."

"Yes?"

"You did a spectacular job."

• • •

When Joshua floored the gas he was surprised to see Cassy remain calmly flipping radio channels. Most women would be yelling for him to slow down. He had an appetite for speed and drove much too fast. That's why he had decided to take his rental.

He wanted to drive.

He had sent headquarters an encrypted message telling them he was out looking for the new internment camp and that he had taken Cassy. He decided it was best to let them know. In return, he received two curse words in Hebrew.

That was fine.

At least they hadn't ordered him to cease and desist. And at least they knew he was with a civilian, but it still made Joshua uncomfortable.

Now, he and Cassy were speeding to lower Everman instead of heading west and the open highway. By the time they had gathered their things and readied the car, breaking news of a riot filled the airwaves.

"You sure you want to do this?" Cassy removed her hand from the radio as a broadcaster talked about the carnage. "You heard the news. Things are getting out of control. People are carrying signs saying 'Roast the Pigs.'" She jerked her chin toward the radio. "Listen."

"Two buildings are now ablaze. One, the Apartment Arms, the other, a large pawn shop. Looters are out in force. And rioters are refusing to let in the fire trucks. If the fire spreads it could be a very incendiary evening, in more ways than one. Already a policeman is down and two rioters have been killed. This is . . . ."

Cassy lowered the volume. "Joshua, does it seem like there's a movement going on here in Everman and elsewhere to emasculate the police? You won't believe it, but the other day I saw a kid reading a comic book where a superhero was punching a policeman, as though *he* was the villain. And I see it elsewhere, too. Newscasters constantly denigrate the police; disrespecting them and showing them in the worst light possible. I don't get it. Why do that?"

"It makes sense if you want to deliberately create anarchy."

"But who would want that?"

"Those who want to initiate a power grab. Chaos and violence are two ingredients capable of making people willing to be controlled. Remember Rahm Emanuel's famous quote, 'You never want a serious crisis to go to waste.'? Meaning, it's an opportunity to do things you couldn't otherwise do." Joshua shrugged. "But what do I know? I'm just a computer specialist." It wouldn't do to arouse Cassy's suspicions by sounding like he really had some inside information.

But Arie's intel about the riots being deliberately instigated and staged was playing out in real time.

"Riots are dangerous, you know. Unpredictable." Cassy fidgeted in her seat.

"I know."

"And you still want to go?"

"Yes."

"Why?"

"Because I want to take some pictures."

"What is it with you and your picture taking? Are you some kind of undercover cop? Sometimes you act like it."

"If I was, would you mind?"

"You bet I would! I've sworn off cops. I was going to marry one once . . . until he went and got himself killed."

"I'm sorry, Cassy." He wondered if that was what she meant when she told him at the cocktail party that she was shattered. They never had a chance to discuss it that night. Shortly after her statement, he had been surrounded by people with a barrage of security questions.

"I know how hard it is to lose someone, especially to violence, but I'm not a cop. And don't worry. I'll leave you and the car a safe distance from the action."

"That's what you think! I'm going with you!"

$$\bullet \quad \bullet \quad \bullet$$

Joshua wanted to kick himself for letting Cassy come. His plan was to take a few pictures, send them to headquarters, and be gone. Now, he had to worry about her safety.

"Stay close," he said, weaving through the crowd, his cell in hand.

If only he could get to higher ground and video the area. He wouldn't get much here amid the sea of bodies except the backs of some heads.

Suddenly, he heard cursing and glass splintering as bottles crashed into a convenience store window—Molotov cocktails by the look of the flash and fireball. More glass shattered as Joshua took pictures whenever he could get a clear shot.

Up ahead, a dozen police in riot gear tried to seal off the street, while a helicopter buzzed overhead, attempting to disperse the crowd. Looters, with grotesque masks or bandanas over their faces, broke down a liquor store door and ransacked the place. A nauseating smell of burning rubber filled the air, and out of the corner of his eye, Joshua saw a car blazing. Nearby, men rocked another car, overturned it, then doused it with kerosene before setting it on fire.

In response, police fired tear gas and rubber bullets into the crowd.

Joshua grabbed Cassy's hand. "Come on, let's go."

"What about your pictures?" Cassy coughed and covered her nose to keep from breathing the smoke. Thick, blanket-like smog hovered overhead—fumes from the burning building and torched cars and tear gas. "I can handle this. Do what you came to do."

She was wheezing now.

"No point. I won't get any decent photos in this muck." He pulled her through the crowd, then stopped. Not more than fifteen feet away was a dark, sinewy man lobbing flash grenades at a police line.

Kamal!

So, he *was* still here. Joshua fingered the Beretta in his pocket. It would be easy to squeeze off a shot in this crowd and be gone before anyone was the wiser. He had already heard several bursts of gunfire coming from the crowd. He was about to move closer when he glanced at Cassy. She was having trouble breathing.

"Are you okay?"

"Just my asthma acting up. I'll be fine."

He studied her. It was obvious she couldn't take much more. How could he leave her in this condition to go after Kamal? He cursed himself for not making her stay in the car. He had waited two years for an opportunity like this.

He removed his hand from the gun and pulled out his phone. The only thing he could do now was let Iliab Nahshon and headquarters know about Kamal. Ignoring the anger knotting his stomach, he grabbed Cassy's arm, snapped a quick picture, then pushed through the crowd and headed for his car.

• • •

"I'm taking you to the hospital." Joshua helped Cassy into the front seat of his rental.

She wheezed as she shook her head and fumbled in her purse. "I've . . . got this."

She held up an inhaler, then inserted it into her mouth, closed her lips around the mouthpiece and pressed on the canister as she breathed in. She repeated this once more before tossing the inhaler back into her purse.

Only after Joshua saw Cassy rest her head against the seatback and begin breathing normally, did he close the car door and slip behind the wheel.

"You're starting to look better, but maybe you should get checked just in case."

"Wow! That hasn't happened in a while. I almost forgot how terrible it feels to be unable to breath. And no, I don't need a doctor. I'm fine. And I only have trouble when I'm around smoke or if it's very cold outside, which is one of the reasons I moved to Everman."

Joshua pulled out of his parking space and sped down the road trying to put distance between them and the smoking neighborhood. "You still want to do this? Drive five-hundred miles for parts unknown?"

Cassy nodded. "So what upset you back there?"

"What do you mean?"

"Something got to you. You should have seen your face. If looks could kill . . . someone would be dead now."

"What are you talking about? We were in the middle of a riot with guns firing, buildings burning, and you practically turning blue! I think what you saw was a little healthy fear."

"Stop acting like just because I spike my hair, I'm brainless. I know what I saw. And for your information, I've seen that look before . . . on Chad, my fiancé the cop. Sometimes he'd look like that when talking about a case. And by the way, for a supposed computer nerd you handle yourself well."

"*Supposed* computer nerd?"

"You weren't rattled a bit. You surveyed the area, the buildings, the street, the people, assessing it like a cop would. You sure you're not a cop?"

"I think you took one too many puffs of that inhaler. I'm a security specialist, remember, and work for Global Icon."

"As if cops never go undercover. And just so you know, I could never fall for another cop again. It's too painful."

When Joshua entered the highway he floored the gas. "I've already said it, but I'm really sorry about your fiancé, Cassy. I know how hard it is when you lose someone you love."

Cassy sighed. "Even so, you seem pretty together. I'm still . . . a mess. How long did it take you to get over losing the woman you loved?"

Joshua's hands tightened around the wheel. "Who said I was talking about a woman?"

"Weren't you?"

"No . . . I was talking about my two best friends, David Rosen and Benjamin Cohen. We went to college together. David never graduated. Before he could, he ran across five skin-heads who wanted to teach him the finer points of anti-Semitism. They beat him so badly he was unrecognizable. In addition to internal injuries requiring surgery, he lost the sight in both eyes. A week later he died in the hospital. I think he just gave up; decided he didn't want to live in a world so full of hate.

"Then my friend, Benjamin, died two years after joining the IDF, the Israel Defense Forces. His parents wanted him to be a lawyer. He would have made a good one, too, with his analytical mind. And he had come from a long line of professionals. His family had immigrated from Russia. Just three generations of Cohens in America produced two medical doctors, one psychiatrist, two lawyers, one judge, and two college professors.

"He was killed by trying to stop a terrorist from detonating his vest. They say his action gave dozens of people the chance to get clear of the blast, and saved their lives.

"Is that the reason you identify more with Israel than America?"

"Only one. When push comes to shove a Jew can only count on another Jew. America, Britain, the rest of Europe, they've all let us down; betrayed us at one time or another. And they could do it again.

"Look at the British and their White Paper. In 1917 the British issued the Balfour Declaration, which favored establishment of a Jewish homeland in Palestine. It was even entered into the canon of international law, and aside from the Arabs, was recognized by the entire world.

"But then in 1920, when oil was discovered in the Persian Gulf, Britain's already waning commitment to a Jewish Palestine waned even further. Finally, with the pressures of a world war to contend with, Britain issued their White Paper in 1939 which completely renounced their obligation outlined in the Balfour Declaration.

"The White Paper called for a phasing out of all Jewish immigration to Palestine and an end to land sales. It froze the size of the existing Jewish population, having in mind an independent Palestine in the future, with an Arab majority.

"It was politics at its worst. Britain foresaw their involvement in a world war. Jewish opposition to the Nazi regime was certain. But Arab good-will had to be purchased. The White Paper was the price of that good will."

"Well . . . thanks for the history lesson."

"Sorry. Sometimes I get carried away. It just galls me how much Jewish history has been marked by betrayal."

"But things are different, now. Muslim terrorists are attacking the whole world; they are against all nonbelievers, not just Jews."

"Yes. At least on the surface. But underneath, it's often a different matter. Remember it was Russia who fanned the fires of Islamic zeal and hatred for years. Before the collapse of Communism, they used the terrorist activities of the PLO and other groups for their own purposes.

"After the collapse, and Russia became a federal republic, they realized that five of the fifteen republics were predominantly Muslim. That could mean trouble. Fearing an Iranian backed Muslim insurrection in these republics, Boris Yeltsin made a covenant with Iran. Iran would keep hands off. In return, Russia would back Iran in any future military operations.

"Additionally, Yeltsin installed nuclear plants in Iran and helped train Iranians in nuclear technology. All this did was embolden Iran and produce an increase in global terrorism.

"Now, we see Iran on the threshold of becoming a nuclear power and Russia supporting Syria as well as Iran, and trying to get their hands on our oil fields."

Cassy's fingers brushed against Joshua's arm. "You're not alone. You have friends who are sympathetic."

When he didn't respond, she turned her gaze to the passing scenery. "So . . . what was her name?"

"Who?"

"The woman you loved. The one you avoid mentioning by talking about everything else."

"Rachel," Joshua said, as though the name came out on its own power. It was the first time he had said her name aloud in months. "Her name was Rachel. She was beautiful and funny and smart."

"How did she die?"

"She was killed by Kamal, the head of ISA, the man I saw at the riot today, the man I've been tracking for two years."

Cassy turned from the window. "I think you're more shattered than I am."

"What do you mean?"

"I lost someone I loved, but I don't want to kill anyone."

•　•　•

When Trisha told Mike about Audra's news, his first words were, "No overtime today. Tonight we celebrate!" And in spite of all her cautious, almost nervous reminders that Audra's achievement, while a major breakthrough, was still not a "sure thing," he whistled and hummed through the rest of the afternoon.

And that evening, after he sent Trisha to the hotel, he disappeared on a mysterious errand and returned forty-five minutes later carrying a large, brown bag. He knocked on door number twelve and before Trisha could answer, let himself in.

"Dinner's on me tonight." He placed the package on the coffee table, opened the bag, then deposited an assortment of white paper containers on the round table.

"For the lovely Miss: Wonton delicacies, shrimp toast, and Szechuan scallops. For the handsome gentleman: egg drop soup, spare ribs and lobster Cantonese."

Trisha clapped her hands in delight. "Chinese food! Where in the world did you ever find Chinese food?"

"I cannot divulge my source, madam. But allow me to present my next surprise. An after dinner treat."

"Yes?" She was smiling now.

"An old Laurel and Hardy movie on channel three. I thought it would be a nice way to spend a quiet evening together."

He watched the smile fade. "I've invited Buck. He'll be along soon. Hope you don't mind."

Trisha's smile returned, and Mike hoped she was learning there was more to him than she thought.

● ● ●

"Look how much we've done." Trisha gestured to what resembled a giant whale's skeleton. Beside the huge rib-like section was the jig, over which would be assembled the fuselage panels. Nearby, men were joining the upper and lower assembly of the flight station, and to the left, several others were completing the radome.

Mike gestured toward the large, overhead crane and halter used for moving the nose section into position for mating with the mid-fuselage. "We should be using that by now!"

"The forward fuselage will be completed by the end of the week. Things aren't all that bad."

"Oh, yes they are!" returned a deep, masculine voice. The pair turned and watched Buck head toward them, his leathery face twisted by some unknown trouble. "Let's go over here," he said, leading the couple to the partitioned coffee area that was somewhat removed from the bustle around it.

"It's Nolan," Buck said, as they settled in their chairs. "He crashed about twenty miles from here. The helicopter is destroyed. The inside badly burned. Nolan was thrown ten feet away. They had to go by the company markings to know who to call. Police contacted PA in Everman and were given my cell number. They're taking Nolan to the morgue and need someone to ID the body."

Mike had agreed with Trisha's decision and sent Nolan in the helicopter to PA. But before going ahead and building the titanium casing, he had wanted the physicist's reaction. Nolan was to return this evening with his report. They had been working late, awaiting his arrival.

"Do you want me to do the ID?" Buck asked.

"No, go to the crash site. And fast. Not much you can do tonight. But stay over to see nothing is touched until you've had a chance to inspect everything, piece by piece."

"What are you thinking? More than an accident?"

Mike's face darkened. "We can't afford to overlook any possibility."

The recent autoclave explosion proved to be deliberate. As a result, PA security was tighter than ever. New computerized ID badges were issued to all employees. Sophisticated burglar alarms replaced the old ones. Iron grille-work covered all first floor windows while two armed guards were now stationed at every entrance.

PA was beginning to look like an armed fortress.

"Well, one thing I already know," Buck said. "This accident shouldn't have happened, either. Your helicopter is serviced regularly, and Nolan was a good pilot."

Mike remained silent as he pictured the area where Nolan had worked for the past several months. Nolan had been proud of his work; had gone to great lengths to explain to Mike how his large, silver pump forced sea water into a round, metal drum and then from there through small, rubber tubing from which tiny quantities of water were released at regular intervals and subjected to an infrared laser which dissociated the deuterium molecules and deposited them into six-inch-long glass vials.

It was Nolan's own procedure which he had modified and which he had initially borrowed from Sidney Benson's carbon dioxide infrared laser that irradiated dichlorethane where about one in two-thousand molecules of the substance contained an atom of deuterium.

But Nolan had every right to be proud. His procedure was faster and cheaper, and solidly demonstrated the ease at which deuterium, as a virtually inexhaustible source of energy, could be obtained.

The great pump was silent now; the lab equipment positioned neatly, the way Nolan had left it; his clipboard hanging on a bent nail.

When Mike glanced at Trisha, he saw tears well in her eyes. She would feel Nolan's loss the most. He watched her reach over and take Buck's hand. He had seen their friendship deepen these past months but he couldn't help wishing it was his hand she had reached for.

"I've never seen you cry before," he said awkwardly. "What does a person say at a time like this?"

"Nothing," Trisha answered. "There is nothing to say except perhaps, why?"

• • •

While Buck went to the crash site and Mike went to ID Nolan's body, Trisha remained in her room listening to the news of last night's riots.

Parts of lower Everman were still smoldering. She and Mike and Buck never did get to see their Laurel and Hardy movie. Instead they watched live coverage of the Everman carnage.

When she couldn't listen any longer she flipped off the TV and tried sleeping. That ended by her thrashing around until the covers were in knots. Finally, she dressed and left.

She walked the mile to the hangar, then walked the length of the old, cracked runway. Leaning over the edge, she stared down at the rocks and waves. Moonlight made the water glisten as it pounded the shore. She watched the violent action and thought of Nolan and the twisted helicopter. Wave after wave rolled over the sand and rocks, first like sprays of madness, hissing and tearing, then calming to resemble the foam of soda in a glass.

"Where are you, God?"

She walked the long strip back to the hangar and picked a flat grassy patch where she could rest. She didn't know how long she sat. Minutes, hours—they all blended together as she gazed at the stars.

No point in returning to her room. She wouldn't be able to sleep. She'd stay and watch the sunrise. It was tranquil here; a tranquility that oozed into her shattered emotions and made her feel closer to God, feel His enormity and power. And gradually she entered His peace.

He was a big God. An all-encompassing God.

Perhaps she'd never know why Nolan died, why some evil hand had reached out and robbed him of his life. Or what evil was now causing the citizens of lower Everman to tear their community apart. But she was sure of this. No matter what evil existed in the world, God was still in charge.

● ● ●

News of Nolan's death traveled through PA like brush fire. And when Peter Meyers and his boys showed up again, the plant sizzled with speculation. Was this just a tragic accident or another terrorist attack?

Ever since Homeland Security confirmed that the autoclave had been sabotaged, a heightened uneasiness hovered over the plant. And in spite of all the additional security, it wouldn't go away.

Like other PA employees, Audra had trouble coping and developed her own cure: two glasses of wine at bedtime. It was the only way she could sleep. Even when she spent the nights at PA, she needed the wine.

She plunged herself deeper into her work.

The complexity of her research, the intense interest it held for her, enabled her to escape from her fears for a time, but always they returned.

It was worse when she went to her empty apartment. There, thoughts of what could happen . . . all those real or imagined dangers that lurked behind every minute . . . crowded her mind.

Audra took three large gulps of her Dewers as she pressed against the bar.

Tonight was not a "two-glasses-of-wine" night. Nor was it a night she could stay alone. Like others from PA, she had left work earlier than usual, taking the news of Nolan's death with her.

At home, she had bolted the door and just when she thought she was safe, she had noticed the drawers of the dining room hutch were open. And a living room chair was slightly ajar as though someone in a hurry had knocked into it.

She had pulled her gun from her purse before entering the bedroom. There, she saw that the locks on the desk drawers were forced, the drawers wide open and empty; all her duplicate research notes gone.

How was she ever going to tell them at PA?

She had sat on the edge of the bed fighting dry-heaves and thinking of Bubba Hanagan. This was his handiwork.

The pig!

He must have used a duplicate key because the apartment had not been broken into. And he knew just what he wanted and where to look because the apartment had not been ransacked, either.

He had emptied her hutch. Taken all her silver. Expensive pieces. Heirlooms from her grandmother: two candle holders, part of a silver service, a candy dish. They would fetch a good penny from a pawnbroker.

By why her notes? To sell them to a competitor? It was the only explanation. What else would a muscle-bound ignoramus want with such technical material?

She'd have to look into changing her lock. But not tonight. Without even shedding her work clothes for the customary designer jeans and fresh silk blouse, she had slipped her pistol back into her purse and left.

Now, with a shaky hand she swallowed another mouthful of Dewers.

"Whoa cutie!" chuckled Ace Corbet as he fixed her another drink. "Too much too soon ain't good. It's like other things, if you know what I mean."

He winked, and for a moment she felt sick again.

"Now let Ace here take care of you. I'll set your pace. That way you'll be able to get up tomorrow for work." He winked again and leaned his elbow on the bar.

Audra glanced around the tavern. It was Thursday night. A few silhouettes moved in the semidarkness to the twang of a country western song.

Meager pickings. Where was that respectable, modern man she was looking for?

She visualized the empty drawers and took another gulp of scotch. What was she going to do? She couldn't go back to an empty apartment. Not unless someone went with her, even if that someone was Ace Corbet.

"Well, what do you say?" Ace said, grinning like a hyena.

One more sip then Audra smiled. "That's very generous of you. I think I'll just put myself in your hands. And if there's the teeniest possibility of my not getting up tomorrow, why, you could be there and see to it that I do."

• • •

"Sabotage!" Mike boomed. "Are you sure?"

"Yes," Buck answered, as he eased himself onto one of the chairs in Trisha's room. The three had met here at Buck's request. He had told them he wanted to share this information in private. "Someone tampered with the helicopter."

"What about autorotation?"

Autorotation insured that if the power failed and the rotor was disengaged from the engine, it would still continue to turn freely.

"Useless if a jamming device was used."

"Do you have proof?"

There was a clinking sound as Buck handed Mike several small pieces of twisted metal.

Mike studied them in silence. It was like a jigsaw puzzle where nothing seemed to fit. Who? How? Why? He jiggled the metal together then tossed them onto the coffee table. "Who would have had time or opportunity to do this?"

"It wouldn't take long for someone who knew choppers. There were traces of acid on the engine wires. By the time the engine failed, the rotor was jammed. Pretty clever. From what I can see it's a miracle Nolan was able to get as far as he did. The helicopter was exposed at PA's landing field for almost twelve hours. Even with the increased security it would have been possible for someone with phony ID in a mechanic's uniform to get to it without being stopped."

"That means a professional job," Mike returned.

"No doubt."

"Then we have to assume it's ISA."

"That'd be my first guess. But if so, we may have an even more dangerous situation on our hands."

"Meaning?"

Buck frowned. "We have to consider that you were the target."

Trisha, who had been listening nearby, moved to the edge of her seat. "He may be right, Mike. After all, it was your private helicopter. The saboteur could have staked out the runway, knowing that every few days you flew to PA, spotted your helicopter and not knowing it was Nolan who flew in, sabotaged it, expecting you to fly it back here."

Buck nodded. "It's possible, Mike. We'd be foolish not to consider it."

"Okay. It's possible. I'll give you that." Mike noticed the concerned look on Trisha's face. "But don't worry, I'm not easy to get rid of. You should know that by now."

She met his gaze. "I guess it's time to start praying for your protection."

• • •

CHAPTER 9

"There's nothing out here but desert," Joshua said, speeding down the vacant highway, grateful for his car's air conditioner. It was fall but the glaring sun beating down on the car and asphalt road still made heat stroke possible. "I think we've seen enough. I'm turning back."

Cassy pulled off her sunglasses and squinted into the distance. "You can't quit so soon!"

"So soon? We've been at it for three days. We need to get back." Joshua couldn't tell her that the photos of the riots he had taken and emailed to headquarters proved invaluable. In addition to having Mossad's face-recognition program confirm that the man Joshua saw was indeed Kamal, the Mossad had identified one of Kamal's top lieutenants and some of his flunkies. And though Kamal had disappeared by the time Iliab Nahshon arrived, Iliab was able to locate the lieutenant and take him out.

Headquarters had given Joshua only seventy-two hours to find the alleged internment camp or return to Everman. Along with his job at campaign headquarters he was to photograph all future local riots.

But two questions nagged him: what part had Kamal played in the recent riot? And where was he now?

"It's time we turn around," Joshua repeated.

"Just another ten miles. *Please.*"

"You said that twenty miles ago."

"Yes, but this time I mean it."

Joshua turned to Cassy and frowned. "You're as stubborn as . . . . If I do go on, promise me you won't complain when it's time to head back."

When Cassy didn't answer, Joshua slowed the car to make a U-turn.

"Okay! Okay, you have my word. No more complaining and no more arguing."

Joshua straightened the car, punched the accelerator, and continued heading west. "The election is less than two months away. I'd think you'd want to get back to the office and see how things are going."

"No need. All polls indicate that Uncle Phillip is going to be our next president. Truthfully, I'd be happy to see anyone in that office as long as it isn't Senator Garby. He'd only extend President Baker's agenda. And we see how that's worked for us."

Joshua nodded and thought of Arie's intel about President Thaddeus Baker being behind the riots. The new information, that Kamal was somehow involved, confirmed Baker had ties to ISA as well. But just how deep had to be determined.

"I'd vote for your uncle. Though I see strengths in Garby, too."

"You've got to be kidding!"

Joshua grinned. "Yes."

"Whew! You had me worried. I thought you were a bright boy. I hate being wrong. So . . . when you said I was stubborn, did you mean as stubborn as . . . Rachel?"

"Why do you assume I was referring to a woman?"

"Elementary my dear Watson. Men don't talk about other men in those terms. If a man is stubborn, his friend would call him tenacious or determined or having grit."

"I guess you're right. And yes . . . Rachel was stubborn, but never annoying like you."

Cassy sighed. "I know I can be annoying. And I'm sorry. Sorry for saying that you were worse off than me because you wanted to kill someone. That was unkind. I guess a lot of people want to kill Kamal. He's caused a ton of grief."

The muscles in Joshua's face tightened. "If you weren't with me, I would have killed him during the riot." He felt Cassy's eyes study him.

"Yes, I believe you would. And he'd deserve it. It's hard to understand a butcher like Kamal. I was surprised to learn he had gone to Lumumba University in Moscow. I guess there's your Russian connection again."

"Yes. And did you know that at one time Lumumba was the collection area for Third World students where they received, in addition to their university curriculum, heavy doses of Communist indoctrination? The brightest and most loyal continued training as members of the KGB. The cream of the crop was then trained by Department V, the KGB's Assassination and Sabotage Squad."

"That was cold war days. You're not suggesting it's still going on?"

"I'm not suggesting anything. I'm saying things are rarely what they seem."

"Even so, Kamal's educated. How could an educated man be such a beast?"

"Because a lot of his education was based on hate—*surahs* or chapters in the Quran encouraging violence toward all nonbelievers, especially Jews. Kamal himself admits *surah* sixteen was his inspiration. It told him how Jews corrupted themselves when they turned from Islam and how Muslims are justified in punishing them, i.e. *killing* them."

"But God made his covenants with Abraham and the Jewish people over twenty-five hundred years before Muhammad was even born and founded Islam."

"I didn't know you were interested in Torah . . . the Bible."

"It's an interest acquired since the cocktail party."

Joshua glanced at her and smiled. "Starting to fall for me, are you?"

"Don't be ridiculous."

Joshua's smile deepened. "Did you know that both Kamal's father and grandfather were with Hamas? And that by the time Kamal was ten he had slit the throat of his first 'corrupt' Jew? Most of their arms, as well as directives, came from Moscow. Most of their funding came from PLO Headquarters in Tunis.

"When the Soviet Union ceased to exist and PLO funds dried up after Arafat and Rabin reached their historic agreement, Kamal's family wasted no time in making alliances with elements in Iran, Syria, and Libya.

"It didn't take long for Kamal to rise in the ranks. The entire world became his target, all nonbelievers the enemy. He really bought into what Islam teaches its children, even now, 'today Friday, tomorrow Saturday, then Sunday.'"

"What does that mean?"

"It means Friday is the day of worship for Muslims, Saturday for Jews and Sunday for Christians. Kamal is sunni so that means first the shia Muslims and those Muslims not following the Quran faithfully enough must be subjugated or killed, then the Jews, and finally the Christians, until all the world is Muslim—at least the right kind of Muslim."

"I'm sorry you didn't kill Kamal," Cassy said, closing her eyes and resting her head on the seatback. "And I know it's my fault."

• • •

Mike looked down at the pile of folders scattered across his desk. The sun streamed through the closed window and cast a long beam of light across the oak floor. Even so, it couldn't penetrate the gloom shadowing the office.

Peter and Buck sat frowning nearby.

"I've gone through all the personnel files of employees hired by PA within the past four months and nothing jumps out." Mike's deep voice obscured the drone of the air conditioner. When he saw the look of disappointment on Pete's face, he added, "I know you hoped the person responsible for both the autoclave explosion and the helicopter crash would be among them. And yes, it's possible the terrorists have planted an inside man. But I can't tell from these files."

Pete straightened in his chair. Boyishly handsome and somewhat out of character in his dark blue suit, he had that youthful, all-American look, but closer observation revealed him to be a man in his mid forties. Over the past two years, he had come often to scrutinize the progress of the P2 on behalf of Homeland Security.

PA wasn't the only company researching nuclear fusion. There were several, and all more well-known than PA. But what happened at these companies could have far reaching effects in defense, and DHS was protective of them. And something like the death of Nolan Ramsdale caused concern. As a precaution, DHS ordered the deployment of armed DHS guards around the company grounds.

Pete twisted a paperclip back and forth. "My people are already investigating these employees, but I had hoped you could add to it."

Mike pushed the files away. "You know I'm rarely here anymore, Pete. Most of the time I'm at Gibs Town. I can't even match a face with these names."

"There is one I've noticed," Buck said. "Nothing concrete, just a gut feeling. That, and he seems out of place. I'm told he isn't very motivated by his assembly line work; that he's careless and often distracted. His supervisor is thinking of firing him."

"Who?" asked both Pete and Mike in unison.

"Najjar Haddad."

Peter shrugged. "He was vetted. No red flags. But I'll have my boys give him an extra once-over."

Mike glanced at Buck. He had come to trust his friend's instincts and was usually sorry when he didn't follow them. He tapped the pile of folders "You have a lot here. Mind if Buck does a little snooping? Let him take Haddad."

The tall, blond laughed. "I'd welcome the help. We're at war here, and stretched thin." Then leaning across the desk he added, "But don't get your hopes up, Mike. Most terrorists are trained and fanatical. They either hit, run and disappear, or sacrifice themselves, kamikaze style. They rarely plant an inside man. If that's what happened here, we'll have a shot at him." He picked up the files. "If not, we may never find out who did this."

After Pete left, Mike slid Haddad's file across the desk toward Buck. "Good luck."

"Anything else?"

"Yes. Watch out for Trisha."

"You're asking for trouble. Leave it alone, Mike. Don't go where only fools tread."

Mike watched Buck's leathery face fold in sympathy. In all the years he had known him it never occurred to Mike that Buck had ever been in love. Now, Buck's blazing eyes said there had been someone once, someone special. "Are you speaking from experience?"

Buck frowned. "Trisha reminds me a little of her. Maybe that's why I feel so protective. And my woman, like you, wasn't free, either. So I know what I'm talking about. There's no happiness in this, Mike. I foresee only heartbreak for you. And Trisha, too."

"I'm just asking you to look out for her. Nothing more."

"In that case, I'll look out for both of you."

● ● ●

At that moment Trisha would have welcomed a guardian angel in any form. Nolan's death had left the P2 project in jeopardy. She had relied heavily on his judgment and knowledge. Now, it would all be on her shoulders.

She rubbed her neck, already tightened by the new strain, as she finished reading Audra's notes. She couldn't hand Mike another disaster. What would Nolan have advised? His notes concerning his meeting with Audra had been burned in the crash.

Trisha looked at the file in her hand. Audra's latest experiments were promising. But Audra had been right. They weren't conclusive enough to commit it to use in the reactor casing.

Trisha tossed the papers onto her desk. There was little she could do but stick to her original decision: complete testing of a titanium X casing on the reactor in actual simulated flights. It was a short cut, a gamble.

But so was everything related to this project.

• • •

Joshua floored the gas making the car groan under the steep climb it was ordered to make. This was do or die. Either they saw something from the top of the ridge that overlooked the flatland below or they were heading back to Everman. When he reached a level patch of ground he pulled to the side and stopped the car. Then he and Cassy got out.

"See anything?" Cassy said, as Joshua pressed binoculars to his face.

"No." He did a one-eighty and stopped. "Wait . . . what's this?"

"Let me see!" Cassy pulled the field glasses from Joshua's hand and peered through them. "Good grief! Is that what I think it is?"

Joshua didn't answer. He was busy retrieving his phone from his cargo pants. He pressed zoom and took a video of the area. Then he pressed 'send'. Based on his GPS the Mossad would take satellite photos for their analysts to study.

"Come on. Let's drive closer," Cassy said, handing the binoculars back to Joshua. "Now we can get some real evidence! Maybe this will make Uncle Phillip sit up and listen!"

"We're not going there," Joshua said, heading back to the car. "If it's what we think, the camp will be patrolled by armed guards. There are just two of us and only one gun. I've already sent it off to someone I know. They'll take aerial shots and get us the proof we need."

Joshua thought for sure Cassy was going to argue, but she just pursed her lips and slid onto the front seat. They drove several minutes before she turned and said in a near whisper, "That's how Chad died; going into a situation outmanned and outgunned."

• • •

Mike stood in the hall watching Renee as she leaned against the bar. She made a sucking noise while draining her glass, and there was something sloppy about the way she used her elbow to support herself.

Except for the occasional sound of the glass tapping the bar, the house was quiet. The servants were nowhere to be seen and the front door was unlocked.

He wondered at the ease in which he had entered, undetected. What if he was a thief? Or worse?

He looked at the beige dress that clung to the superb body, at the hair smartly swept to one side, at the diamond earrings glittering like miniature stars on her lobes. She must have been dressed and waiting for hours.

After his meeting with Pete and Buck, Mike had spent time with Trisha, who had come with him to Everman to touch base with Audra Shields and discuss her report on titanium X. Then the three went over every possibility, over every available avenue, and finally Mike agreed with Trisha's decision. Audra was to begin immediate construction and subsequent testing of a titanium X casing on the reactor itself.

He had seen Trisha safely to his helicopter, along with a trusted pilot who would take her to Gibs Town. Mike himself would return tomorrow since he planned to work at the plant most of the night. He had come home only to pick up a few things.

Even now, Buck waited outside in the company car. Since Nolan's death, Pete had insisted Mike ride only in inspected vehicles that were kept under twenty-four hour guard. Cars, Peter claimed, were favorite terrorist targets.

But irate wives could also be dangerous.

Two weeks ago, when he was home last, Renee made him promise he'd take her to the Everman Ball. The mayor of Everman, along with every petty bureaucrat within a hundred miles would be there. He had promised because Renee was persistent.

That was before Nolan's death.

Now, he was in a crisis situation, and balls and petty bureaucrats seemed extraneous. He had tried telling her that on the phone. Even so, she insisted she'd wait.

Renee never relinquished ground gracefully.

As he studied her profile, Mike knew a confrontation was inevitable. He took a deep breath. "Hello Renee. You still here? I thought you'd be at the party by now."

Renee removed her elbow from the bar. "It's about time!"

She had begun using that tone since her return from the Garbys. He assumed it was due to her failure to induce him to go to D.C. and aid Garby's campaign. In a weak moment, she had told him how cold they had been throughout her stay, as though punishing a naughty child. There had been no talk of a return visit; no invitations issued.

The first time she saw Mike after her return she assaulted him with her tongue, screaming he had ruined her and that she'd never forgive him. He guessed that was why she was so anxious to go tonight. Both Senator Garby and Alex Harner would be there, and obviously Renee hoped to redeem herself by bringing him along.

"Look at the time!" she screamed. "You still have to shower and dress . . . we're going to be so late. How could you do this to me! You *promised!*"

"Weren't you listening on the phone? Didn't you hear what I said about Nolan?"

"Yes . . . it's a shame but . . . . "

"But what?"

"Look, I'm sorry about Nolan, really I am. And I don't want to seem callous, but will brooding bring him back? Oh, Michael, this is so important to me! Come on now, hurry and get ready. If we leave soon, we shouldn't miss too . . . . "

"Renee!" Mike's voice cracked like a whip, snapping his wife into silence. "I'm not going tonight. A man has died! My company is in turmoil. There are armed guards crawling all over the plant. I have a schedule to meet, and if things don't go just right I could lose everything. It would be nice if just once you'd take as much interest in my company as you do in the Garbys."

"Michael, stop being a bore. There's a big wide world out there. The sun doesn't rise and set over Patterson Aviation. Now be a good boy and get dressed."

"You haven't heard a word I said. I'm *not* going."

The green cat-eyes narrowed. "I . . . see. Well then, I'll say, 'goodnight.' I suppose I won't be seeing you for another week or two?"

"I suppose not."

"Then . . . a girl will have to find comfort where she can. Won't she?"

"Don't boast, Renee."

"I'm not boasting, darling. You know I don't need to. I suppose you've taken your comfort wherever."

"You'd be surprised at what little solace I have had, in the way you mean, anyway."

"You poor dear. She must be awfully dull, your research girl. That type is. Pious, quaint, old-fashioned, dull."

"What are you talking about?"

"Trisha. It seems that somehow she's converted you. Oh, don't look surprised. I know something's going on between you two. It's the way you say her name, the way you talk about her. So, you see, your secret is out. But I don't mind, though I am surprised, you mixing business with pleasure. And she's not the least bit your type. Not long ago you'd never look twice at a woman who wouldn't put out. Well, I always did say variety was the spice of life. I guess that's what you need, a little change. Call me after you've wearied of your new celibate life, after your knees begin to ache from all that praying you must do together. I mean, what else could the two of you be doing?"

Disgust crept over Mike's face. "You're sick, Renee."

The beautiful redhead picked up her beige clutch-bag from the barstool. "I know. We bring out the best in each other."

Her spiked heels made a clicking noise that echoed through the room as she walked away. It was a strange, lonely sound that seemed to haunt him even after he went upstairs and began rummaging through drawers. But the next sound he heard ripped apart that specter as a loud explosion shook the walls of the house.

"Renee . . . oh, god!" He sprinted down the stairs and toward the explosion.

The four-car garage was a mass of crumpled sheetrock, jagged metal, shattered glass, fire, black billowing smoke and . . . among the debris, two piles of burning, twisted metal: one his car, the other . . . Renee's.

● ● ●

"How was the funeral?" Joshua said, handing Trisha a tall glass of lemon water.

"Sad. But almost the entire plant showed up. I hope that gave Mike some comfort."

"Seems like he's well loved." Joshua noticed a strange expression cross Trisha's face. "Or at least well respected. But all funerals are sad. That's why I thought a little dinner at my place would brighten things up."

He glanced at his brother, David, who sat stony-faced beside Trisha. "Was I wrong?"

"No, it's a lovely gesture and I was happy to come," Trisha said, as she worked up what looked to Joshua like a forced smile. "I've been away so much that it's nice to touch base with friends."

"I know you can't talk about where you go and why, so I won't bother asking." Joshua didn't think his brother looked like he was pleased to be touching base. He shot a glance at Cassy who stood beside the large, carved oak bar in the corner pouring herself a glass of wine. When he caught her eye, he hoped she saw the silent plea for help on his face.

Her nod told him she did.

"All the pundits have declared my uncle president. First time in history, I think, when everyone, even the opposition's camp, publicly voices a winner before the election even takes place." Cassy carried her stemmed glass to one of the elegant silk-upholstered chairs and sat down. "I've never seen anything like it."

Trisha straightened and for the first time seemed to take an interest in the conversation. "I just hope he'll do more than President Baker has about all the rioting. I can't believe the looting, arson and mayhem going on all across the country, even in Everman. It's open season on police now. No wonder they have begun backing off and letting entire neighborhoods burn to the ground. Can we blame them?"

"I've operated on two policemen in the past three days," Daniel said. "And I've treated a half dozen more for injuries."

"All this violence on police is causing a slow motion police strike that's sure to end in even more lawlessness. Now, why would a president not want to stem this chaos by supporting the police?" Trisha sipped her water and shrugged. "I don't get it."

Joshua stood by Cassy's chair and let his hand rest on her shoulder. Follow-up by the Mossad revealed a large camp-like complex complete with barbed wire fencing around the entire perimeter and four guard towers positioned at each corner.

Without exposing his source, he had given Cassy some of the aerial shots in order to convince her uncle of the necessity of coming forward with his information. She was still working on it.

So was he. For the past two days Joshua had tried getting his mind around the "why" of it. Unlike Trisha, he had his suspicions; suspicions so unthinkable he had put off revealing them to headquarters.

But that was about to change.

It was too apparent to ignore any longer. He had already determined that the only logical reason for encouraging lawlessness in a free society was to concoct a reason for grabbing power.

All the pieces were there and beginning to fit.

He excused himself, went to his room, and after closing the door, sent an encrypted text to headquarters: *Riots may be pretext for creating need for Pres B to declare martial law. Internment camps for those who resist.*

• • •

Two days later, Mike knocked on the door marked twelve. When it opened, Trisha stood before him wearing faded jeans and a sweatshirt, her thick, black hair pulled into a ponytail. She looked so beautiful that for an instant he felt his depression lift.

"You just arrive?"

Mike nodded.

"How are you doing," Trisha said softly.

In addition to Mike, all of PA had a hard time coping with the facts surrounding Renee's death. A bomb planted in her car had blown off the side of the house as soon as she started the engine. The explosion had been fierce. Two explosions, really. The bomb planted in Mike's car was set off by the one planted in Renee's when she started the engine. Whoever did the job wasn't taking any chances and had wired both cars.

The explosion was so great that the windshield of the waiting company car was shattered, and Buck needed five stitches in order to close the gash on his forehead.

Renee never knew what hit her.

"Take a walk with me?" Weariness oozed from Mike's request.

It was beginning to grow dark as they made their way to the beach. Tiny crabs scurried over the shadowed sand. Here and there driftwood and shells pockmarked the shore and took on strange new shapes in the dusk.

Trisha stopped to remove her sneakers. They were close to the water and the waves lapped their feet like playful puppies. Mike seemed unconscious of his wet shoes or that they made a squishy noise as he walked.

"My mother died when I was four," he said suddenly, as though in the middle of a conversation rather than beginning one. "I hardly remember her. She was beautiful though. I used to look at her picture when I was young and wonder what it would be like to have a mother like all the other kids." He paused for a second visualizing the photo.

"It left a void when it came to women. I once heard my aunts talking about how my father had married my mother for her money, that their marriage was a business arrangement. I knew my mother had come from a rich family.

"I was in my teens then and I remember feeling shocked. My father had never remarried, and the way he used to talk about mom, well, I just assumed they had loved each other. Maybe they hadn't, I don't know. I never learned anymore.

"My aunts wouldn't talk about it when I asked them. And my father said, 'of course I loved her,' when I asked him. But you know, Trisha, in all these years, I've never forgotten that, and for some reason I never felt the same about my father after that."

"No one's parents are perfect, Mike." Trisha knotted her sneakers together then draped them over her shoulder.

"I know. And I have no right to judge him. I was a terrible husband. I . . . didn't know how to be a better one. Or maybe I just didn't care enough. But I wish Renee could have had better. I wish she . . . ."

"I know," Trisha said softly, slipping her hand into his like a friend offering support. "Come sit with me."

They walked silently, their fingers entwined all the way up the path and along the old cracked airstrip, then along the gigantic hangar. Finally, Trisha stopped by a flat grassy area and sank to the ground. Mike settled beside her.

"Have you been able to sleep?" she said.

"Not a wink."

"Neither have I. So why don't we stay and watch the sun come up?"

He looked at her sideways, at her profile. She looked so beautiful in the moonlight. "I'd like that." Truth was he didn't want to be alone. He didn't want to think. He didn't want to remember that horrible sound of metal and wood and sheetrock all exploding and crashing into a heap.

"When my dad died I was shattered." Trisha slipped her hand over his. "When you're young, you never think about death. It's something that concerns tomorrow, never now, never today. I thought of all the times I should have told my dad I loved him, all the times I should have paid more attention to him, spent time . . . thought of all my neglect.

"I loved him dearly, but you can neglect people even when you love them. I was so busy going to school, studying, trying to get ahead. Always time for everything but him. He loved to play golf and he wanted to teach me. It was something he wanted us to do together. But I never learned. I never had time.

"I . . . cried for months. Even bought a set of golf clubs but never used them. It's funny what we do sometimes. Then one day I realized what was really bothering me was my *guilt*."

Mike nodded. "What did you do about it?"

"I asked God to forgive me for not being the daughter I should have been, that I could have been, that my father deserved, and then I said good-bye to my dad."

"That's fine for you, but I'm not sure I believe in God. I wish I did. Maybe it would make the pain go away. It hurts that I was such a louse and that I can never make it up to Renee."

Mike slipped his arm around Trisha's shoulder and the two huddled in the dark, trying to warm each other while they waited for the sun to rise.

● ● ●

Trisha and Mike walked together into the Sea Breeze looking tired and wind-swept.

"Thanks for staying up with me. The sunrise was beautiful. I really needed a friend." Mike's eyes smiled through heavy lids. Strain and tension and a deep inner sadness marred his face.

"Any time you need to talk, I'm here," she said as they reached room number twelve.

He nodded, the smile gone from his eyes. "Thanks for that. Now, get some rest."

"You too," Trisha said, then put her hand on his shoulder. "Wait here."

She disappeared into her room and within seconds returned with a small, black, pocket Bible which she pressed into his hand. "This will help. There's a 'friend that sticks closer than a brother,' and I pray you'll find Him."

So saying, she squeezed his hand and was gone.

●　●　●

CHAPTER 10

J oshua sat in his comfortable upholstered chair scanning Senator Merrill's spacious Marriott suite. Beside him sat Cassy, her nails unpolished, her hair pulled back in a stubby ponytail, a gray sweatshirt hanging loosely over her slip frame. He thought she looked great but didn't tell her so.

They had flown into Scranton this morning, unannounced, much to the campaign manager's annoyance.

"The senator has a busy schedule and is preparing for an important rally," he had said, his brow furrowed, his lips puckered as though he had swallowed a lemon.

He reminded them that Pennsylvania was a swing state and that Senator Merrill still had a lot of work to do if he wanted to carry it. And for the first time, Joshua was grateful for Cassy's stubbornness because she would hear none of it and insisted she see her uncle at once. The campaign manager seemed acquainted with Cassy's tenacity, for he quickly gave up and said they could have "ten minutes, no more."

Now, they waited for the senator to emerge from the adjoining suite which the campaign maintained for business meetings and press conferences apart from his private quarters.

When the door opened, Joshua rose to his feet, thinking Merrill looked harried. He wondered if it was due to the new death threats he had received, followed by a shot at his car, a shot that shattered the back window but nothing else.

"Thank you for seeing us on such short notice," he said, shaking the senator's hand.

Merrill glanced at Cassy. "I know you well enough, young lady, to believe this is not a frivolous visit. Please tell me I'm not wrong."

Cassy rose, gave her uncle an affectionate kiss on the cheek then waited for him to take his seat before taking her own. "You *must* go to the press with your information." They had received another email claiming a fourth internment camp had been completed and that "time was running out," whatever that meant. "You can't wait any longer, Uncle Phillip."

The senator sighed and shook his head. "Now is not the time. With my poll numbers I don't think Garby has a chance of beating me but I still want to lock up Pennsylvania. There's a lot of anger here in the state, especially in coal country where miners have been shafted, big time, by the current administration. After I finish here I'll consider blowing the whistle on . . . what? I still don't know what this is all about. These emails are disturbing and your photos of that camp west of Everman . . . unbelievable. But what does it all mean?"

Cassy turned to Joshua. "He's the one to answer that."

The senator frowned. "A computer security specialist? If you've brought him all this way to badger me into . . . ."

"He's Mossad."

Merrill's hand dropped limply over the arm of his chair. He looked from Cassy to Joshua, then rose and closed the door to the office suite. "Is this true, young man?"

Joshua nodded. Headquarters had given him the go-ahead to share his credentials with the senator and anyone else he deemed necessary. Joshua had considered Cassy to fall under that umbrella.

"The agency believes you are in danger, as evidenced by those death threats and recent targeting of your vehicle. We want to supply you with additional security guards because we don't know who in the Secret Service can be trusted."

Senator Merrill's face drained. "What are you saying?"

"I'm saying we believe your enemies reach all the way to the White House."

"Go on."

"President Baker can't run for a third term. And the dream of his man, Garby, taking over and continuing his agenda, is evaporating. All the pundits agree it would take a miracle for Garby to win now, even if you don't carry Pennsylvania."

"All the more reason I should campaign hard and once elected, use the full weight of my office to expose whoever is building these abominable camps."

"That's just it, sir, many in the agency don't believe you'll get that far."

"Meaning they'll assassinate me?"

"If they can. If they can't . . . as a way of ensuring the election never happens, we think President Baker will declare martial law under the guise of restoring order to all the riot-torn cities. Either way, they are determined to stop you from becoming the next president of the United States."

● ● ●

Mike was feeling better than he had in weeks. A cool northern breeze had favored Everman and turned their unusually hot day into a perfect stage for celebration. Not since the beginning of the project had there been such merriment. The cause of it was a huge, swan-like object in the middle of the hangar.

Moments ago, the crew had mated the nose or forward-fuselage with the mid-fuselage. And nearby were the rising hulks that would become the aft-fuselage and aft-body. Great accomplishments considering the time frame.

Mike was unusually talkative and had garnered a sizable audience. But his greatest pleasure was seeing Trisha laugh at his jokes and at his often elaborate tales of youth.

". . . and it took all this time to come up with another plane good enough to be called the Patterson II. That's because the P1 was something in its time. It cost my grandfather three thousand dollars; a large sum in 1913 when you consider room and board was fifty cents a day. And he built it in a small garage, nights and weekends, when he wasn't working odd jobs.

"The P1 was small by today's standards, with a thirty foot fuselage and weighing twenty-two hundred pounds. But it could carry two passengers and a pilot. The most amazing thing was its cruising speed of fifty miles per hour and top speed of sixty. In order for you to understand how fast this was at the time, you have to know there were only three designs capable of carrying two passengers, and these could fly only ten miles per hour."

Mike chuckled. "To think my grandfather made aviation history with one tractor propeller and a six cylinder water cooled engine."

"Yes, a Kirkham engine," Trisha said, smiling. "And the cruising speed was actually fifty-one miles per hour, top speed—sixty-three."

Mike laughed. "Do you mind?" He admired her vast knowledge of airplanes. She continually amazed him by pulling up one fact after another, like so many rabbits out of a hat. It was her love of aviation that fueled this appetite for facts—a love that matched his own. "Who's telling this story, anyway?"

"You are," Trisha answered, her lips curling into a crescent. "But you don't want to mislead the audience."

"Well, maybe you can correct all my mistakes at dinner tonight," he whispered as he bent closer and watched her face flush.

● ● ●

Joshua felt something hit the back tire, felt it blow as the car swerved and nearly bounced over the median dividing the busy highway. He and Cassy and Senator Merrill lunged sideways, careening into each other in the back seat. As soon as he righted himself, Joshua pulled out his gun. The security guard in the front passenger seat did the same.

He watched as two white vans closed the gap, one on their right, one in back. The one in back tapped their bumper and would have made their car spin sideways if their Mossad driver hadn't managed to keep it under control. But just as the driver straightened the car, the van on the right swerved and scrapped across their door shearing off the side view mirror. It was obvious that both vans were trying to force them over the median and into oncoming traffic.

As their car accelerated, Joshua felt Cassy's nails dig into his arm, heard the senator curse, then heard the driver yell, "Everyone buckle up!" Then came the squeal of tires as the driver slammed on the brakes, causing the tailing van to rear-end them.

The crash was loud and the jolt so hard Joshua was sure they all had whiplash. But their driver had prepared for the move by turning the wheel to the right, forcing the collision to drive him into the van alongside them and sending it into another lane where it was struck by two vehicles, one a Mac truck.

Without stopping, the driver pulled in front of the three-vehicle pileup and managed an exit off the nearby ramp. Wobbling and limping, and with sparks flying off the steel rim that was bare of rubber and scraped asphalt, the car inched toward the nearby gas station where it finally sputtered to a stop.

Joshua, Cassy and Senator Merrill tried catching their breath while the driver got out and inspected the damage.

"Tire was shot out," he said, leaning into the open window Joshua had just lowered. "I can see where the bullet nicked the rim. I'm calling backup."

Joshua nodded and looked past Cassy to where Merrill sat by the other window, his face looking like it had been dipped in whitewash.

The senator was on his way to a fundraiser. Joshua and Cassy had come along for the ride, hoping to change his mind about going to the press.

Joshua leaned in, past Cassy, and caught the senator by his shoulder just as he was about to keel over. "Ready to go public?"

● ● ●

"Now that we've cleared up all the errors from this afternoon, tell me about your dad. You didn't talk about him at all today." Trisha straightened in her chair, feeling like a schoolgirl on her first date. The broad, handsome man across from her grinned and looked much like a schoolboy, himself. On the table between them were the half eaten remains of a chateaubriand.

"Not much to tell. He was a busy man, like most fathers."

"And?"

Mike narrowed his eyes. For a minute Trisha didn't think he was going to answer. "And. He. Was. Weak." The words came out slowly. "He let everyone manipulate him.

"Granddad began this company after building the P1 on money he earned by giving passengers a ten minute ride for ten dollars each. When he had enough to build a second plane, a twelve passenger seaplane, he formed Patterson Aviation. Then, right before World War I, he got a ninety-thousand dollar naval contract to build a few more single-engine seaplanes. That's when the company took off.

"Granddad made a reputation for himself as one of the best in the field. And in 1946, when most airframe manufacturers were closing their doors, he was still in business. He had foreseen that at the end of the war there would be a surplus of cargo and transport carriers so he developed the EX1, PA's first executive aircraft."

"You're talking about Grandpa again."

"He was an exceptional man, Trisha. I'm proud of him."

"Not like your father?"

"My father ran the company into the ground. His weakness almost bankrupted PA. He consistently surrounded himself with ineptitude. Some of his employees took bribes from competitors to spy and slow up production. My father didn't even fight them. If it wasn't for Uncle Jason bailing him out financially, there wouldn't be a PA today. Even with his help, my father was forced to sell forty-nine percent of the company's stock. I've learned from his mistakes."

Trisha nodded thoughtfully. She was beginning to understand the man across from her. "And Uncle Jason? What was he like?"

"Funny. Clever. Generous." Mike reached across the table and covered her hand with his. "He never forgot me on Christmas or my birthday. His extravagant gifts would be accompanied by long, funny letters." Mike smiled as though thinking of them.

"Humor was a stranger in my house. My father was glum most of the time and seldom laughed. It was hard to believe they were brothers. But Uncle Jason knew how to enjoy life. And with all his money, he never tried to make anyone feel small. I told you he saved the company. According to my father, he never had to ask Uncle Jason. As soon as his brother heard of the trouble, he flew over and gave my father a check. He was that kind of guy. We have a lot to thank him for, too, Trisha, you and I."

"We do?"

"Yes, if he hadn't saved PA, we never would have met."

"I suppose not." Trisha smiled. "Thank you, Uncle Jason."

"Yes, thanks uncle," Mike said, squeezing her hand.

• • •

Audra sat slumped on the bed holding a quart bottle of Corvo wine in one hand and a glass in the other. She emptied the remaining contents of the bottle, not caring that it spilled over the sides as she poured. She hated the Sea Breeze. Hated her room. Hated Gibs Town. Her work was the only thing that made life here bearable.

Seeing the nearly completed mock-up today of the P2 had filled her with joy. The challenge of her work with the NPR910 casing gave her the same kind of joy. But it was a joy constantly marred by fear. Since Mrs. Patterson's death, even the .25 caliber in Audra's purse could not alleviate her fear. Her tension was further increased by the fact that here, there was no Grobens Tavern where a girl could go for some comfort.

Audra tossed the empty bottle onto the carpeted floor. This was her only consolation now; a quart of red Sicilian wine each night. But even this was beginning to lose its charm. It didn't give her that warm, safe feeling it once did. That madman, Kamal—he was to blame; he and the fact that she had turned thirty.

If she could only get her fear under control.

Oh, she had such plans, such dreams for herself! Hadn't her mother repeatedly told her she wasn't this bright for nothing? She was destined to break glass ceilings; destined for something great. So why did her life feel as empty as that wine bottle? Nothing seemed to matter. *Really* matter. Perfecting the titanium X casing would make her famous. And yes, it would make her mother proud. Maybe even fulfill that destiny her mother spoke so often about. But then what? An interview with the press? A Wikipedia entry? Life was as tenuous as the next bomb or hair trigger, and this would only make her a more desirable target for more bombs, more hair triggers.

She thought of Bubba Hanagan. She had never reported the robbery. Not to the police. Not to Michael Patterson.

Why should she?

The way things were going the P2 would never see the light of day. PA was jinxed. Everyone said so. Maybe she should quit her job. Some were. But most were staying.

Yet even as these thoughts flooded her mind, Audra knew she, too, would stay. She was committed to her work. She would play the hand she was dealt. But she didn't have to like it. She kicked the empty bottle and cursed. Maybe if she opened the other bottle of Corvo, the one she had for tomorrow, maybe then . . . .

• • •

For three days all the major news outlets carried the story of secret internment camps sprouting up across America. For three days, all the talking heads theorized what it could mean. For three days accusations and counter accusations flooded the news while scores of reporters descended upon the camp five-hundred miles west of Everman only to find no weapons and a handful of men in camo claiming their camp was nothing more than a fitness facility where young men had the opportunity to endure wilderness training and test their manhood. And it hadn't even opened yet.

For three days, Senator Merrill saw his numbers plummet until he dropped the issue and claimed it was obvious the opposition's campaign had planted this misinformation on his computer to embarrass him.

Then the story faded from the news.

• • •

"Come on," Joshua said, pulling Cassy from her office chair and dragging her to the door. "You've moped around long enough. Your sulking isn't going to make the papers take your uncle's story seriously or generate further interest."

"Stop, Joshua. I'm not in the mood to be cheered up. I'm still frosted over how they made my uncle look like an idiot. And I feel responsible. If I hadn't talked him into it . . . . Boy, all the media seem interested in are starlets getting bust enlargements or getting divorced. What's wrong with this country, anyway?"

"Well, come with me and I'll tell you." Joshua pushed her out the front door of campaign headquarters and didn't stop until they were standing beside his rental.

"Where are you taking me?" Cassy's tone was peevish.

"No place serving hamburgers." Joshua shoved her into the front seat and closed the door. "I know a great taco place near the park." He slipped in beside her and started the car. "Maybe after that we'll take a boat ride on the lake. It'll do wonders for your nerves."

"It's not going to work. You can feed me all day long and paddle me around in a boat till your arms fall off, I'm still going to be mad. I thought for sure at least one enterprising reporter would take Uncle Phillip's story seriously enough to do some real investigating.

"What's happening to us? Do we want to be destroyed as a nation? We're acting like lambs being led to a slaughter. We've cut our military, done nothing about closing our porous borders, refuse to support our allies, and now we don't even care if our country is turning into Nazi Germany complete with internment camps!"

"What do you like? Burritos or tacos? I think their tacos are the best but their burritos are . . . ."

"There are nine countries that have nuclear capability. Iran will soon make it ten. And they're all building intercontinental ballistic missiles. Russia has almost eight thousand nuclear warheads. If any of these were ever sold on the black market and Kamal got hold of them, he'd . . . ."

"Since when have you been so up on current events?"

"I have to keep up with you, don't I? You're always going on about these things. And I'm really ticked off right now that we're letting this stuff happen. Iran's been buying up Russian missiles. Iran—one of Kamal's biggest supporters! It doesn't take a rocket scientist to figure out that ISA would love to add a nuclear war head to their arsenal. And I'm sure you've heard how Iran has been conducting amphibious training exercises under contaminated conditions. Not too difficult to figure out what they've got in mind."

"Where are you getting this info?"

"My uncle. He's furious over what's going on. He's a real patriot. Bleeds red, white and blue. And he says . . . why are you stopping?"

Joshua had pulled the car off the road and put it in park. Without saying another word, he leaned sideways and kissed Cassy.

"Why . . . why did you do that?"

Joshua grinned. "How else could I stop you from talking?"

"Boy are you nervy! I could just . . . ."

"Do I have to kiss you again?"

Cassy leaned closer to Joshua. "Yes, I think you'd better."

•   •   •

Empty coffee cups and a crumpled paper bag that had held sandwiches from the local luncheonette were grim reminders that another dinner had come and gone with Trisha, Mike, and Buck consuming nothing more than bread and cold cuts. Now, all that remained were a few crumbs scattered across the table top and a brown coffee ring.

It had become a ritual, the three of them eating together, sometimes in Trisha's room, sometimes in Mike's or Buck's. Trisha and Mike had not dined alone since the night they held hands over a half eaten chateaubriand.

Hours had whirled into days and days into weeks. Everyone at Gibs Town was keeping a grueling pace, including Trisha and Mike who sat, exhausted, listening to Buck.

"This Najjar Haddad is a character. All his papers are forged: driver's license, social security number, the works. And they're good forgeries, too; good enough to pass his background check. But Najjar Haddad doesn't exist. Even his home address is an empty lot. So I lifted some prints off his tools and gave them to a friend in the FBI. His real name is Azad Hosseini and he is a known member of Islamic State of America. The FBI has him in their sights now and tailing him

24/7. That's straight from Peter Meyers by the way. And the Feds are getting ready to pick him up. "

Buck winked at Trisha who sat staring at him in amazement. "But before they nab Haddad aka Hosseini, I'm going to have a personal interview with him."

"Buck, you're getting too old to play Sam Spade," Mike said. "Why don't you let the FBI or Pete handle it from here?"

"You know how I feel. If you want the job done right, do it yourself. Besides, I'm not that old, *yet.*"

"Okay," Mike chuckled. "But be only as persuasive as you need to. I don't want to have to bail you out of jail for assault."

After Buck left, Mike lingered in his chair. "You need to be careful, Trisha. Until we get this thing figured out and under wraps, I want you to employ the buddy system. Don't go wandering around anywhere by yourself. And another thing, don't drive your car until Buck has checked it out. And I mean each and every day!"

Mike rose and walked to the door that divided their rooms. "I wouldn't like it if anything happened to you."

Trisha followed him. "I'll be careful. Good night."

Instead of leaving, he pulled her closer then kissed her. When he let her go, there was a boyish grin on his face. "You could ask me to stay the night. That's one way I'll know you're safe."

Trisha opened the door between their rooms. "Good night, Mike."

"I'm desperately in love with you, Trisha. I think you know that. But the thing I need to know is do you love *me?*"

"More than life."

"Then be with me, as a woman should be with a man. I've never loved any woman more, or wanted any woman more. And judging by the way you kissed me back I think you want me, too. When Renee was alive I understood that you didn't want to get involved, but things are different now."

"How can I explain? How can I make you understand that what you ask is wrong? That it wouldn't be God's best . . . for either of us."

Mike's eyes caught sight of the cross hanging from her neck. "What's the matter, Trisha, doesn't your God like sex?"

"He's the one who invented it."

"Then I *don't* understand."

"I know," she said, her voice soft. "It's just that sex is supposed to be exclusive between a man and his wife."

"Is that what you want? Marriage? Are you one of those women who use the promise of sex to obtain a piece of paper?" When she didn't answer, Mike frowned. "I'm sorry. That was stupid. I know you believe what you say. I just don't understand it. I've never been much for religion." Mike leaned against the door jamb. "But this is important to you isn't it, this God of yours?"

"Yes."

"So where does that leave us? Do we have a future?"

"I don't know. Two people need more than physical attraction or even common interests to make a relationship work. They need a firm foundation."

"A what?"

"'Unless a house be built upon the Rock, it cannot stand.'"

"Bible talk?"

Trisha nodded.

Mike leaned forward, his face inches from hers. "Don't let this God of yours come between us."

"If you knew how much He loved you, Mike, you wouldn't talk that way."

"I don't know anything about God or His love. I only know how I feel about you." Then with a click, the door closed between them.

●　●　●

Buck knew the Feds were somewhere nearby as he followed Najjar Haddad aka Azad Hosseini down Everman Boulevard and into the Everman City Park. He still couldn't imagine what business Hosseini had here. It was his last chance to confront the creep before his arrest. He hoped if he needed to use a little muscle, the Feds would look the other way.

He passed a long line of pines. Clusters of yucca, candelilla, and guayule were positioned between the trees. And here and there were jogging paths, picnic areas, playgrounds, as well as scores of benches for those who wished to do nothing but watch everyone else. And at the other end of the park was a sizable manmade lake stocked with a variety of fresh water fish. But other than fishermen used it. Lovers would canoe its smooth waters on lazy afternoons, and children would swim in the special section roped off for that purpose.

If Buck wasn't careful, it would be easy to lose Hosseini here.

When Hosseini sat down on a nearby bench, Buck took cover behind a clump of bushes, then pulled out his cell phone. He pressed "video" when he saw another man, neatly dressed in an expensive, gray suit, sit down beside him.

What was Robert Gunther doing here?

"This better be good, Hosseini. Getting me out here . . . . "

"What did you want me to do, go to your office?"

Gunther's pasty face marbleized into hard streaks of anger. "Did you get it?"

"No. The place is under tight wraps. A cockroach couldn't squeeze through! Ever since the helicopter explosion and car bombing it's been like Fort Knox."

"I was told you were the best. Now all I hear are excuses. I'll report this."

"Don't threaten me. People who do, don't live to do it again."

"One week, Hosseini. That's all you have left. Then we'll call in someone else."

The thin, suited man walked away, followed by an agitated Hosseini. Buck couldn't hear the last of their conversation but waited until Gunther disappeared then left his place behind the bushes. "Hello, Hosseini."

The man looked stunned as he realized Buck had been nearby all along. "The name is Najjar Haddad."

"That's not what the FBI says."

Without another word, Hosseini bolted, then Buck after him. And even though Buck had fifteen years on the man, he was able to overtake him with ease. He wrestled him to the ground, then pinned his arms with his knees. Clutching Hosseini's shirt in one hand, Buck's other hand formed a massive fist which he positioned inches from Hosseini's face.

"You have just one chance to answer my questions."

"You don't scare me. You don't know what fear is until you've been around the people I know."

"You mean like your buddy, Kamal?"

For an instant Hosseini appeared frightened. "Who is he? I know no Kamal."

Buck tightened his grip on Hosseini's shirt. "But you know Gunther. Why did he hire you?"

"Why don't you ask him?"

"I want to hear it from you."

"Then you'll hear nothing."

"Here's a news flash. The FBI are waiting to arrest you. But first they said I could have a little talk with you and that they'd look the other way." It was a lie, the part about the FBI looking the other way, but Buck hoped it would frighten the man in his grasp.

Hosseini laughed. "You soft westerners. You think a threat of a beating can break a man. You are women! All of you."

"Well, how about we put you in Fort Leavenworth for awhile, where a lot of soldiers are serving time. But the thing is, most of them had a buddy or someone they knew who died in Afghanistan or Iraq. I'm sure they'd like to ask you a few questions, too. And I wouldn't count on Gunther lifting a finger to help you, either."

For the first time Hosseini's face whitened. "You can't do that. Your law wouldn't permit it. And if anyone lays a finger on me I'll claim discrimination. I'll say you're discriminating against me because I'm a Muslim. It'll rattle the cages of the ACLU and a host of Muslim activist groups. You wouldn't stand a chance."

"Ever hear of paperwork foul-up? It can be done, believe me it can be done. And before anyone knows where you are, you'll have a thousand or so ex-U.S. military inmates as constant companions."

Hosseini's body melted into the ground. "Okay! Gunther hired me to steal specs from the research lab's safe."

"And?" demanded Buck.

"And . . . to relay any information about your secret project."

Buck pulled on Hosseini's shirt raising him off the ground. "And?"

"And nothing . . . that's all!"

"What about the autoclave and the helicopter? What about Mrs. Patterson?"

Hosseini shook his head. "I wasn't hired for that. But don't think I wouldn't have loved doing it and more!" He began laughing. "You think I'm the only one hired? That I'm your only problem?"

Buck released his grip causing Hosseini to fall backward. Then the strong, square man rose to his feet. "Your life won't be worth two copper pennies once the ISA hears how you cooperated with us."

Then he walked away, leaving Hosseini sprawled on the ground behind him.

● ● ●

Mike fingered Buck's phone. "So, Gunther wants our specs. That means someone is paying him. Who and why?"

"Maybe an airline that invested in one of the new planes? The Boeing 737 MAX or the 787 and wants to know what they're up against. Or . . . could be another airframe manufacturer checking out the competition. Then there's always the possibility that he's working on behalf of Tafco Oil. After all, nuclear fusion isn't exactly in their best interest."

"Maybe."

"Would you like me to ask him?"

Mike chuckled. "No." He slipped Buck's phone into his pocket. "I'll ask him myself."

● ● ●

Even from this distance Mike recognized the thin frame of Robert Gunther sitting on the bench. When he phoned Gunther he had insisted they meet in the park. During the call he sensed Gunther's reluctance and was glad. He wanted him off balance, like a teetering Humpty-Dumpty.

With an easy confidence, Mike erased the distance between them until at last he was standing over the pale man.

"Hello, Robert."

The face jerked into a sickly grin as Mike sat down.

"I haven't been here in years. Forgotten how nice it is. And what memories! I had my first fistfight here when I was a kid—a fight between me and Nick Kelsey. I doubt you've ever heard of him. You didn't grow up around here. But Nick was a punk; the number one bully in the neighborhood, and he tried stealing my baseball cards. Then after I beat him, I collected my first kiss, right over there," Mike pointed to a redbud tree in the distance, "from Marylou Turner, the prettiest girl in town. Quite a day."

"I never knew you to go in for nostalgia." Gunther's smile remained frozen, like a lemon wedge, on his face.

"Shows how little we know each other. For instance, I didn't know you had such unsavory friends." Mike pulled Buck's phone from his pocket and played the video.

"What are you going to do?" Gunther asked when it was over.

"What do you think?"

"I'd leave it alone if I were you."

"I can't do that."

"Someone could get hurt if this went any further."

"Is that a threat?"

Gunther's eyes narrowed. "The people I work for have friends, *powerful* friends in high places."

"I have evidence, remember? And this is still a country where one is tried by his peers. I don't think your friends are powerful enough to buy out an entire judicial system. You know, Robert, there's more value in nostalgia than people realize. It shows that the past is not so different from the present."

Gunther rose to his feet. "I'm not Nick Kelsey and the stakes are much higher than baseball cards. You won't find me so easy to beat."

• • •

Mike tapped his fingers on the arm of the velour settee, wishing Abraham Levi would get to the point. Levi had been viewing Buck's video for the last fifteen minutes, playing it over and over. But Mike supposed a man didn't get this rich by being a careless lawyer.

He studied the splendid hand-milled paneling, the expensive oak furniture, the two Tiffany floor lamps, the small Monet on the wall, the plush carpeting, then watched Levi rise from his desk and go to the corner bar and pour out three Perriers. His large diamond ring flashed as he handed one to Mike, the other to Peter Meyers. Then he returned to his desk and replayed Buck's video.

"Well," Levi said, at last, "you don't have a case."

"What do you mean?" Mike shot. "The video . . . ."

"shows nothing except that Gunther knows a creep like Hosseini. And what does Gunther say, really? He never mentions what he hired Hosseini to do. A good defense lawyer would destroy it in minutes. Listen." With that, Levi played the video while they sat silently allowing it to pound home the reality of his words.

"And what about Hosseini's confession?" Mike asked.

"The FBI has him now. They'll want to use him to catch bigger fish. I doubt we'll get any cooperation if we pursue a case against Gunther."

"So what you're saying is that we're going to have to let Gunther get away with it."

The lawyer's wooly-covered head bobbed up and down. "In a manner of speaking. But actually, he hasn't gotten away with anything. Both of Hosseini's break-in attempts failed. You've already tightened security. The thing to do now is keep an eye on Gunther."

"This doesn't sit well, Abe."

"Mike, your company's been bombed, your private helicopter carrying an employee, destroyed. You've lost part of your home, and then of course . . . Renee. You have enough problems. Concentrate on them. We've been friends a long time. Your father and I were friends, and I'm telling you as a friend, don't waste yourself on this. Revenge can be expensive. And in the end you could still end up with nothing."

Mike frowned. "You don't understand. I'm not interested in revenge. I'm fighting for my company's life."

Then he turned to Pete who had not wanted to go after Gunther until they had more evidence. "Don't say, 'I told you so.' But you win. Tomorrow, Gibs Town goes on triple shift. The P2 comes first, and we are going to finish her in record time. Maybe then this madness will stop."

● ● ●

CHAPTER 11

The smoke was so thick Joshua had to cover his face to keep from choking. Flames, fifty feet high, licked the night sky, crackling and hissing as it evaporated buildings a hundred years old. His eyes teared as he maneuvered through the angry mob. Bricks and bottles sailed overhead crashing into storefront windows as gunfire popped in the background.

The chant of *Allah Akbar* rose from bearded young men as they moved through the crowd. Fights broke out among gangs, their affiliations indicated by the different colored bandanas around their heads.

When Joshua saw three men beating a woman unconscious, he fingered the Beretta in his pocket, then realized it was too late to help.

He had gotten all the photos he needed. Best to leave. There was no way to know who to help, anyway. The mayhem was incredible; one faction fighting another, and all tearing the neighborhood apart. Even the police and other first responders were helpless. The streets were too jammed for their vehicles to navigate. The few brave officers who managed to penetrate on foot were now surrounded and forced to use rubber bullets to drive back the crowd.

Joshua was about to leave when he saw Kamal standing off to the side, whipping up the crowd with shouts of "Roast the pigs." The faces around him were frenzied. Terrifyingly so; beyond the point where cold, solid reason mattered anymore.

This time there was no Cassy to worry about. This time he would get his man. He inched his way closer, all the while keeping his finger on the trigger of his concealed weapon. Two more steps and he pulled the gun from his pocket. Another step and he took aim. And when he did, Kamal turned and looked straight at him.

The look was unmistakable. It was one of recognition. Kamal knew who he was though Joshua didn't know how. Kamal signaled two men and at once, Joshua felt something rip into his back. The pain was searing and almost knocked him to his knees.

By the time he steadied himself, Kamal and his men were gone.

Joshua pocketed the gun then inched his way to the car. The back of his sweatshirt clung to him; a heavy, sticky kind of clinging. He was losing blood, a lot of it. He'd go to his apartment where he had a medical emergency kit complete with liquid stitches. Then he'd call David.

The last thing he needed was to be questioned by the police while packing his Beretta.

•   •   •

"What are you doing here?" Joshua said, propping himself against the wall to keep from falling. He scowled at Cassy who stood barring his apartment door. She was the last person he wanted to see now.

"I knew you'd go to the riot! When I saw the coverage on TV I came right over. I've been waiting here for hours." She took the keys from Joshua's hand and unlocked the door. "You look terrible." She turned back to study him closer. "Good grief, Joshua! You should be at a hospital. You're covered in blood!"

Joshua shook his head. "Too many questions to answer." He reached out a shaking hand. "Help me in. I've got some stuff that will stop the bleeding until my brother gets here."

"You could have internal injuries. You could need surgery. You could . . . ."

"For once in your life don't argue. I've seen enough combat to know the wound is superficial. It's not life threatening unless I don't stop this bleeding. Now, will you help or not?"

Cassy slipped her arm under Joshua's and nodded. "Just don't make a habit of it."

• • •

Trisha, are you alright?"

"Fine. Why, Daniel?"

"You haven't heard what's going on?"

Trisha pressed her cell phone tighter to her ear. "No. Tell me."

"Over a hundred people were brought to the hospital last night as a result of the rioting. Half of lower Everman was burnt to the ground. Twenty people are dead, including four police. And the authorities think there could be a hundred more dead in the destroyed buildings. I've never seen anything like it. How could you not know? Don't you get cable where you are?"

"Yes, but I worked most of the night and slept the rest. But are you okay, Daniel? And what about Joshua?"

"I'm fine, just exhausted. And Joshua sends his regards."

"He's there with you? At the hospital?"

"No. His apartment. I just sewed him up. Thirty stitches this time. Someone sliced him with a knife."

"At campaign headquarters?"

"No, the numskull put himself in the thick of things. Seems he was taking pictures of the riot."

Trisha had been making her way to the coffee corner and after reaching it, sat in one of the chairs. "He's going to be alright, isn't he? No internal injuries?"

"Other than being sore from my needlework and the black eye I'm thinking of giving him for being such a fool, he's fine."

"Why in the world did he take such a chance just for a few photos?"

"He's giving me the evil eye and wants me to change the subject so I better. I've been thinking about what you told me the last time you were here. Remember? On the way to Joshua's house?"

Trisha took a deep breath. "Yes. I said I was in love with someone."

"Any changes?"

"No."

"Just asking because I had always hoped that someday it would be me. I guess that dream is dead."

"Daniel I love you like a . . . ."

"Don't say it! *Please*. I guess it was inevitable . . . that you'd find someone who wasn't as safe as me and then fall for him. Someone who'd give you a run for your money. Anyone I know?"

"Daniel, the world is tearing itself apart. Our love lives seem insignificant in comparison. Why are we having this conversation?"

"Because a name will make it more real to me . . . give me closure. Help me get over you. Help me move on. And I need to with what's happening around us. Just give me that, Trisha."

Trisha slumped forward in her chair and closed her eyes. "It's my boss, Michael Patterson." The silence on the other end lasted so long that Trisha thought Daniel had hung up.

"Now, that's the second shock I've had today," he finally said. "And from the two people I love most."

"I'm sorry, Daniel. I never meant to . . . . But what shock did Joshua give you? Are you talking about his knife wound?"

"No. Never mind. Forget I said anything." Then the phone went dead.

• • •

That night, Mike, Trisha and Buck stood huddled around the TV in Trisha's room listening to the press conference President Thaddeus Baker had scheduled for 9 P.M.. They had expected it to be about the recent nation-wide riots that partially leveled three major cities.

They were only half right.

Trisha was the first to collapse in a chair, but Mike and Buck soon followed as President Baker claimed his emergency powers and declared martial law. He then went on to detail how life was about to change; that a nightly curfew would be enforced by armed military patrols, and that the upcoming presidential election, just two short weeks away, was suspended *indefinitely*.

●   ●   ●

Trisha stood off to the side as a gentle zephyr carried the smell of ocean and sent it swirling around the hangar like a dervish dancer. The distant cry of gulls was drowned out by the squeaking of the huge, overhead cranes as they moved the empennage into place and by shouting men running along the scaffolding.

Slowly, the scaffolding and crane slid over the cylindrical body of the P2 like a table over a chair, and a dull thud told Trisha that both empennage and wings were ready to be secured. Then a symphony of air hammers and drills filled the hangar.

Someone shouted, "She's on! She's secure!" And not even last night's news about martial law could dampen Trisha's joy.

The empennage, like a shark's fin, rose high over the sleek bullet-like back, while the wings flared out like two great fans against the sides. The P2 was beautiful and sleek. But she was resilient, too, resilient enough to endure the supersonic speeds that her reactors would put her through, the ones Audra was sure to complete soon, judging by her amazing success so far.

Everything was going well.

• • •

Hours later, after everyone was long gone, Trisha finished her paper-work and left the hangar. It was way past curfew but Peter Meyers, who knew of their crazy hours, had sent a courier with special passes for them to use if stopped by the military patrols.

When she reached the Sea Breeze, she took a detour before heading for her room and tapped on a door she had never entered before. "You in, Audra?"

The door opened in jerks. "Oh . . . Trisha . . . come in." Audra patted her matted hair. "I . . . wasn't expecting company. Excuse the mess." She picked up an empty wine bottle from the floor and hurriedly tossed it into a small garbage pail. Another empty bottle stood on the coffee table. "Sorry I can't offer you anything, but I'm all out."

Trisha smiled. "I guess a lot of people are celebrating tonight. It was wonderful, wasn't it? Seeing the P2 coming together. And we're all so proud of you, Audra."

"Look, Trisha, please don't be offended, but it's been a long day and I'm tired."

"I understand." Trisha felt the familiar disappointment. No mat-ter how much she tried to forge a friendship between them, noth-ing worked; not her invitations to lunch, not her friendly manner or polite conversations. Nothing. It was obvious Audra didn't like her.

Trisha had experienced this before, being disliked without cause. At one time, such unwarranted hostility hurt. And it had puzzled her until finally, in high school, she had asked her father about it. "Trisha," he had said in his customary good-natured way, "you mustn't expect to be liked by everyone." His remark had stunned her and she returned by saying, "But why. *I* like everyone."

She thought of his kind face now, of his response: "You'll learn lass, that people who like themselves tend to like everyone else as well."

Over the years she had come to learn her father was right, and no longer took rejection personally. And being disliked by someone never prevented her from liking them just the same.

Now, as she stood in the doorway she pushed her disappointment aside and smiled. "I'll keep my visit short. I'm here at Michael Patterson's request. He asked me to speak to you."

Audra's face paled as she eyed the empty bottle on the table. "Well, if someone is making a fuss about my going to the liquor store from time to time and getting a few bottles of . . . ."

"It seems that PA has recently been plagued by an industrial spy." Trisha refrained from referring to Azad Hosseini or mentioning Robert Gunther. "We believe the problem is resolved, but Mike wants you to take special care of your notes. Don't leave them or your laptop lying around the hangar or in here, unattended."

When Trisha saw Audra's face grimace as though she was going to heave, she nodded. "I know. That's how I felt when I first heard. But don't worry, Mike is handling everything. Just take precautions."

"I will, Trisha," Audra mumbled almost incoherently. "I . . . I'll be careful."

• • •

Joshua and Cassy sat behind closed doors in the senator's office. Senator Merrill was in D.C. along with his party's chairman and a huge delegation protesting President Baker's martial law. Most of the volunteers at campaign headquarters had quit, but most of the paid staffers were still there trying to figure out their next move or if there even was one.

"I'm in!" Joshua said, smiling at Cassy and secretly pleased he was the first to crack the security code.

She rose from her place on the opposite side of the desk to peer over his shoulder. Her hand briefly touched his as she watched him maneuver through the Tafco Oil database on his laptop. They had been trying to hack into it for the past twenty hours, ever since President Baker declared martial law.

"Don't get too cocky, mister. I was almost there myself." When she tapped his back, he flinched. "Oh, sorry. Forgot about your new trophy."

"Trophy?"

"Your thirty stitches. From playing the hero." Her face was crunched in a frown but there was concern in her eyes. "And I really really dislike heroes."

"I had to do my job, Cassy. And speaking of job, did I say 'thank you' for the great job you did patching me up? As it turned out, it was a good thing you were there. I may not have been able to stop the bleeding myself."

"Well . . . you can thank that little spray bottle of yours. What did you call it, liquid stitches? But don't try to change the subject. I haven't finished my tirade. Just what did you hope to accomplish? You're only one person. One little person against a crowd of out-of-control terrorists."

"King David was only one little shepherd and he killed Goliath," Joshua returned with a smile.

"Well, it's a good thing we're not dating or anything, that's all I can say. Because I wouldn't put up with it. If you think I'm going to walk the floors every night worrying about you, you have another thing coming!"

"Stop babbling and help me out here. There's a file with an added layer of security I'm having trouble accessing so get on your laptop and start . . . ."

"Fine! But let's be clear. I'm not interested in you and never will be. I'll never fall for another hero again." Cassy sat down and began pounding keys. "I'll never fall in love with someone who's in danger all the time." When Joshua didn't answer she added, "So . . . what *was* your girlfriend like?"

Joshua sighed. "I've already told you—beautiful, funny, smart."

"And how exactly did she die? I know Kamal killed her, but what happened?"

"Cassy!"

"Just tell me and I'll never ask again, I swear." She paused and looked up at him. "It's hard competing with a memory, you know. Someone who'll never disappoint you again, never say the wrong things, never annoy you."

Joshua leaned one elbow on the desk and frowned. It still hurt to talk about Rachel. He glanced at the pretty woman across from him and by the look on her face knew she wasn't going to let it go. "Rachel was in Mosul helping an international group set up a school for girls when ISIS attacked. I had pleaded with her to get out long before this, but she didn't think there was any danger. Like I said, she could be stubborn. She thought the Iraqi forces would stand and fight. They didn't. Kamal had just declared jihad on all western teachers and his band had swooped in with the rest of ISIS. That was right before he claimed America as an Islamic state, calling it ISA, and moved his operations here."

"So was she killed in the fighting?"

"No . . . Kamal beheaded her along with every other teacher there. Okay? Now not another peep." When he turned back at his laptop, he was surprised to hear her crying.

•   •   •

Mike had never been so angry. "You can't be serious!" he shouted at the man sitting across from him.

"Don't shoot the messenger," Peter Meyers said, adjusting the collar of his crisp JCPenny shirt. "Since 9/11 every president has been racking up more and more emergency powers. Baker declaring martial law has changed everything. The Constitution has been suspended. No one has any rights, now. Curfews are in place and the military patrol our streets. And the president can, if he needs to, seize private property."

"But why in the world would he want to seize my company!"

"I didn't say he was going to seize PA, I said he *might*. You're now one of the leading companies in nuclear fusion. That should say it all. The government has a right to protect its interests and investments. Must I remind you that startup R&D for your current project was funded by several grants from dear old Uncle Sam? Right now, seizing your company is purely a rumor. I'm just giving you a heads-up."

"Well, I'd like to see anyone try taking PA!"

"Don't be a hothead, Mike. President Baker has the law on his side. Section 201, Priorities and Allocations Authorities gives him the right to 'allocate materials, services, and *facilities* as deemed necessary or appropriate to promote the national defense,' and there's nothing you can do. Just sit tight. The National Continuity Coordinator is the Assistant to the President for Homeland Security and Counterterrorism. I know him well. I'll know before most people if they plan to move on you."

• • •

Joshua held Cassy in his arms as she wept on his shoulder. "What kind of country do we live in?" she said, between sobs.

"Right now, a very messed up one."

"I can't believe they arrested him! How could they? On what authority? On what charge?" When Cassy pulled away, Joshua picked up the box of tissues from the desk and handed it to her. She blew her nose then sat down in her uncle's chair.

"I'll have my people try to find out what camp they took him to. Maybe we can do something then."

Cassy shook her head. "This is unbelievable! Unbelievable! I would never have believed it if I hadn't gotten the call from Uncle Phillip himself just before they took his phone. Can you believe it?"

Joshua stood silent not wanting to tell her that yes he could, that it was poised to happen in the 50s when the FBI created "Plan C" for rounding up subversives, which under the current administration's definition includes anyone "who can influence the lives of the population while undermining the authority of the state"—a broad, scary, open-ended definition.

In the 50s the list of people needing to be interned during an emergency numbered 13,000. Now that list contained over eight million—the "Main Core" it was called.

"Do you think it has anything to do with us hacking Tafco Oil?"

"If it did, they would have come for us." But even as he said it, Joshua was sure there was a connection. Their rooting around in Tafco's database turned up damaging information. Its invoices to dummy corporations provided a trail showing Tafco had made a pact with the Devil. They were paying ISA, through an ISA agent, to protect their oil fields. But that wasn't all. He and Cassy had found proof of government payments to Tafco for building five internment camps, though they hadn't learned what Tafco got out of the deal.

He was sure that one of the reasons Senator Merrill had been arrested was because the enemy didn't know how much he knew or what proof he had obtained from his anonymous emailer.

"Just sit tight," Joshua said, bending over and kissing her on the forehead. "Maybe headquarters can come up with something."

● ● ●

Joshua adjusted his night goggles. In the darkness he could see that Camp No. 3 was well guarded. It was the same camp he and Cassy had found five-hundred miles west of Everman.

Iliab Nahson and Nathan Yehuda hunkered in the dirt beside him; all of them clutching their Uzis. It had always been Joshua's weapon of choice with its compact body and blowback system, its high cyclic rate of fire. It was battle tested and wouldn't fail even in the grime of a desert.

In addition to their Uzis, they each carried a foot-long carbonized dagger clipped to their belts along with four black pineapple grenades each; just in case things got sticky. And satellite surveillance would keep headquarters informed.

He didn't know why, but he always felt better when they had eyes in the sky.

According to the recent text from headquarters, a small contingency of Israeli commandos had already crossed the Mexican border and would be here by zero-one-hundred hours. Joshua checked his black Breitling watch. That was only ninety minutes away.

In the meantime, their task was recon: timing the changing of the guard, determining where they lodged, and, if possible, ascertaining the number of guards as well as how many were interned in the camp by using heat sensitive equipment.

The mission was to rescue Senator Merrill, who, once martial law was lifted and elections held, would become the rightful president of the United States.

It would be a disaster for Israel if anything happened to him.

Yossi Behrman, Israel's Prime Minister, had just ordered his generals to draft plans to strike Russian backed Syrian and Hezbollah forces bent on taking over the new oil fields in the Golan Heights. If possible, Behrman would wait for the lifting of U.S. martial law before ordering the IDF to strike, because after the strike Israel would need a friendly partner in the White House to stem the blowback from Russia.

Joshua just hoped they could get Merrill out alive.

● ● ●

It was over before anyone knew it. The commandos in gas masks moved in swiftly, rendering everyone unconscious by firing pellets of an incapacitating agent into the compound. Joshua's team had determined there were fifty-seven civilians in the camp and twenty guards, and had marked the guard house with his laser. Within minutes Senator Merrill was found and evacuated from the premises.

Their mission did not allow for the rescue of the remaining fifty-six.

Then the commandos, carrying Merrill, disappeared into the night as quickly and quietly as they had appeared. And amid the elation over the success of the mission, Joshua felt disappointment over the fact that he'd be unable to tell Cassy her uncle was safe.

When she was questioned by the authorities, as she would be, she'd have no information to give away.

• • •

CHAPTER 12

Trisha sat across from Mike in a small, dimly lit Gibs Town restaurant and watched the smile on his face grow larger.

"It looks like Audra did it. One hundred successful simulated flights without a single sign of casing breakdown. But we need to keep this under wraps. I don't want to give the government any excuse for seizing the company."

Trisha nodded. Mike had told her about the implications of martial law regarding PA. Peter Meyers said there was no indication of that happening. *Yet.* She tried to push away all the concerns still facing them in order to savor the moment.

"Yes, Audra has done it," she said, smiling, "And now you're going to pay."

"Pay?"

"That's right. This is a celebration and I'm ordering a lobster . . . let's say a three-pounder."

"Do you know how much that's going to cost!" Mike wailed in mock horror.

"I figure I have it coming. With all the overtime I've put in, not to mention the work I've taken back to the room every night, I estimate I've been making about eighty-two cents an hour."

Mike laughed. "What do you want? *Everything?* I did give you the weekend off, remember? And taken you to one of the classiest restaurants in Gibs Town."

"There are no classy restaurants in Gibs Town. That's why I'm wearing jeans."

"After which," Mike continued, ignoring her, "I'll fly you to PA so you can avoid Everman's Friday night rush-hour traffic. And you complain!"

"Make that a four-pounder."

"Okay . . . okay, so I've overworked you a *little*." Mike reached across the table and took her hand, his look tender, his feelings scrawled across his face like an ardent Browning poem. "Before we order, I want to ask you something about your doctor friend. Dave . . . Daniel? Actually about *you* and your doctor friend. You're not in love with him are you?"

Trisha shook her head and laughed.

"What's so funny?"

"I'm thinking about his brother, Joshua."

"You're in love with his *brother?*"

"No. But there's something about him. He reminds me a little of Peter Meyers—secretive, mysterious, like maybe he's . . . ."

"CIA?"

"No, his heart is in Israel."

"That means Mossad."

"Maybe . . . I don't know. How did we get on this subject, anyway?"

"By me wanting to ask you something . . . something *important*. And I had to be sure about Daniel, about your feelings, before I asked. But don't say a word until I'm finished, okay?"

Trisha nodded.

"What I want to know is if . . . *if* we can build on this Rock of yours, *if* it's possible, would you marry me? Right now we have to finish the P2, but when it's done I want to spend time working on us. I love you madly, Trisha."

The familiar fragrance of Old Spice drifted across the table. It was *his* scent and she loved it. It was predictable, unpretentious. So different from his interior which was mysterious, changeful, sometimes arrogant. She had longed to hear him say these words. Had dreamed of them having a life together. But not like this. It would never work.

Convictions couldn't be tied on like a plastic heart.

"I want to say 'yes.' You can't imagine how much."

"But?" returned Mike. His smile faded as he pulled his hand from hers.

"God isn't a convenience. He'll never be real to you as long as you're using Him to please me. Your commitment to God can't be because of me, but because God is, and because He's worthy of that commitment. *Please* try to understand."

The handsome executive settled back in his chair. "I'm trying, Trisha, believe me, I'm trying."

• • •

Audra inserted the key and turned the knob. She could feel the bulge of the .25 caliber in her purse which was tucked under her arm. Her head throbbed. Everman's Friday night rush-hour had been brutal.

She lingered a moment in the open door thinking of Bubba Hanagan and not wanting to go in. But he had taken everything he wanted from her. Why should he come back?

She flicked the light switch by the door before entering. Everything was in place, just as she had left it. Nothing disturbed. She turned on every light as she made her way to the bedroom where she tossed her purse on the bed.

She still hadn't changed her lock. Before she could get a locksmith to come, she had been ordered to Gibs Town. Tomorrow. That's when she'd do it . . . that is, if she could get someone to come on such short notice.

Tonight she was going to Grobens.

There was always Ace Corbet. He would help pass the long night. But first a quick shower and fresh clothes. She rummaged through her drawers wondering what to wear.

This was the first weekend she had off in ages. Strange how she wished she was back in Gibs Town. She hated the place, but she felt safe there. Somewhat, anyway. But Gibs Town was as deserted as the Hamptons in winter. Michael Patterson, in celebration of her achievement, had given everyone the weekend off, with his usual admonition to maintain secrecy. He had also given everyone two hundred dollars in cash so they could have "dinner on him."

As she poked through her drawers, the desire to go out began to fade. The thought of having to drive the streets, to walk down dark pavements beneath the shadow of a thousand dangers suddenly made her queasy.

And did she really want to spend another evening with Ace? Her lifestyle was beginning to make her feel dirty. A strange feeling. An uncomfortable feeling. Was it because she was thirty, now? And one-night stands weren't as appealing as they once were? What she needed was something more wholesome, more substantial.

Maybe she'd just stay home. She had plenty of wine in her pantry.

She shoved her black lace stockings back into the drawer, failing to see the shadow that stepped from the bathroom; failing to see the large, muscular arm as it moved to encircle her. She only noticed a sweetish odor as a cloth was pressed against her face. She felt her legs buckle, felt herself sliding onto the floor, onto a pair of large, tan work boots, and . . . darkness.

● ● ●

Trisha dusted her languid rattan settee, then began wiping down her glass dining room table. She had missed her apartment. It was here she relaxed best, amid the tranquility of muted earth-tones. She should do this tomorrow. It was late. She missed the rush-hour traffic as Mike promised, but they had sat for hours at the restaurant talking. And after landing at PA, and while Buck chauffeured her home, they were stopped by a military patrol and would have been arrested for violating the curfew if it weren't for their passes.

All that took time.

She thought of Mike and the tenderness she had seen on his face. But she had seen confusion and anger, too. She was still thinking about it when the doorbell rang.

At this hour?

Then she remembered Daniel. She had called him from Gibs Town after Mike had given the entire staff the weekend off. She had promised to let Daniel know when she had free time. She was eager to see him, to restore their friendship, if possible, and to find out how Joshua was doing after his thirty stitches.

She glanced at the grandfather clock in the hall. Ten minutes to eleven. Daniel had told her if he finished his last surgery before it got too outrageously late, he would stop by. Apparently, she wasn't the only one working overtime.

"Well, it's not *too* outrageously late," Trisha said, opening the door. But instead of Daniel's face, she saw a dark, scowling man holding something in his hand. Before Trisha could react, he grabbed her then pressed a cloth against her face. A strange, sweetish odor filled her nostrils.

"Oh, God!" she gasped. Then everything went black.

● ● ●

"Any news?" Mike asked. Strands of hair fell into his eyes as he glanced at the man entering his office.

"No, nothing," Pete answered.

It was Wednesday morning. Trisha was not home when Buck came to pick her up Monday and Audra had not shown up for work that day. Neither one had called in. Neither answered their phones, and Audra wasn't home, either, when Buck went to check.

Panic swept through Patterson Aviation and Gibs Town. Homeland Security, along with the Everman Police Department, began an immediate investigation.

But so far, nothing.

No one had seen or heard anything unusual. Neither apartment had been broken into. There were no signs of struggle, nothing amiss.

It was all very strange.

But there was a silent consensus. ISA. Who else would abduct two employees from the same company?

Mike was exhausted. He had slept little since the news. His eyes darted from Pete to the phone. "If it was a kidnapping for ransom, shouldn't we have heard by now?"

"That's what worries me. If it's money they're after, then yes, somebody should have contacted us before this. We may have to face the possibility that they have already been killed."

Mike swallowed hard. "I . . . can't accept that."

Suddenly, one of the DHS agents came rushing in. "We just got the call. It's official. ISA claims responsibility for both abductions."

Mike took a deep breath. "Are they still alive?"

The agent nodded and smiled. "Yes! Both women are alive! And we will be contacted regarding terms for their release."

"Thank God," Mike sighed, as if saying a prayer.

● ● ●

Mike leaned back in his executive's chair, sleeves rolled up, his white shirt, rumpled. His fingers combed through his disheveled hair as he frowned at the pile of papers before him. He had hoped to whittle it down in an effort to keep his mind off the kidnapping. But no matter how hard he tried to hurl it to the peak of that white mountain, it would slide back to the one thing that had made the past few days the most wretched in his life—Trisha's disappearance.

Finally, he opened his desk drawer and pulled out a small, pocket Bible; the one Trisha had given him after Renee's death. She said it would help. He could use that help now. He opened the book randomly and began reading.

"'The Lord is my light and my salvation; whom shall I fear? The Lord is the strength of my . . . .'"

• • •

Trisha sat propped against the stone wall of the semi-dark room trying to get her bearings. The past several days had been like a bizarre Picasso. Hours overlapped, twisted, and ran into blur after blur. She was sure she had been drugged. Her head ached and the bend of her arm was tender. When she looked, she saw a cluster of needle marks.

Whatever the drug, it was powerful.

The fog was lifting only now. She noticed she still wore the same clothes from Friday. She remembered the sinister man at the door, the brief scuffle, the darkness, then a vague recollection of strange faces. Someone fed her, gave her water. There had been a ride in a truck . . . a hot, bumpy ride.

Where was she? She shook herself then breathed deeply, hoping to fill her lungs with mind-sharpening oxygen. It was beginning to work.

She looked around. The room seemed strange, foreign. The walls were whitewashed adobe, the floor hard and covered with straw mats. Aside from the heap in the corner, the room was empty. No furniture, no wall hangings, nothing. On the opposite wall was a closed door. The room was dimly lit. The single source of light came from a small, glassless window that only a tiny child could squeeze through.

It had to be near sunset because even as Trisha watched, the light grew fainter. She'd have to get her bearings quickly. She struggled to her feet then staggered to the window, pushed her face through the opening as far as she could, then squinted in the twilight at the barren landscape, the dusty streets, at the adobe-like dwellings—all flat-roofed and clustered together. To one side, a large adobe oven belched smoke while women gathered nearby, wearing black robes and head coverings.

She breathed deeply. The air smelled of dung, grain, fodder, all mixed together to make one singular odor that was neither offensive nor pleasing. From her vantage point it looked like they were surrounded by mountains. A few scrubby-looking trees dotted the embankment on the right.

Suddenly, a loud, eerie wail floated overhead and Trisha knew it was the *muezzin* calling the faithful to prayer. But instead of a minaret, she saw a stubby adobe tower where the sound seemed to emanate.

Impossible. This couldn't be the Middle East. She shuddered and hugged herself. Then all was silent and dark, and Trisha stood frozen by the window. Her mind was sharper now and had begun grappling with the gravity of the situation. She was sure she was no longer on U.S. soil, but didn't believe she was in the Middle East, either. So where was she? Mexico? South America? The village didn't look Mexican but then again it did.

"'In thee, O Lord, do I put my trust; let me never be ashamed: deliver me in thy righteousness,'" she whispered, trying to push back the blade of fear that had begun cutting through her courage.

When she heard a low, muffled sound behind her, she stiffened. "Who's there?"

The only response was a moan. How was that possible? The door had not opened. No one had entered. When the moan grew louder, Trisha moved in the direction of the sound. It was then she remembered the heap in the corner. The moaning continued until it turned into words.

"Ooh . . . ooh . . . where am I . . . what . . . what is this . . . ooh . . . I'm sick. Please . . . someone help . . . ooh please . . . somebody."

It took Trisha a while to recognize the voice. She groped her way in the darkness until reaching the quivering mound.

"Audra! Audra it's me! Trisha!"

"Ooh . . . I'm sick . . . help."

Trisha cradled Audra in her arms. She was sure Audra had been drugged, too. But in addition, she appeared ill and was both perspiring and shaking.

"It's okay. You're going to be alright," Trisha said softly, all the while hoping someone back home knew where they were. She thought of Mike and wondered if she'd ever see him again.

Throughout the night, Trisha held Audra while trying to doze against the wall. In the morning, when she awoke, Audra was still feverish.

"Are you injured?" Trisha asked, keeping her voice low so as not to alarm anyone on the other side of the rough, wooden door.

"Ooh," was the reply.

Trisha scanned Audra for signs of a wound and found no blood stains.

"I need a drink," Audra muttered. "Please."

"Audra, try to understand. We're prisoners. We've . . . ."

"Please! Help me. *Please* give me a drink."

Trisha studied the quivering woman for a second. The symptoms were beginning to make sense. She had seen them at a mission where she used to volunteer when she had had more time. They were the same symptoms she had seen in other alcoholics who staggered, shook and begged for a drink or the money to buy one.

Trisha's hand stroked the perspiring head knowing this was a real crisis. The withdrawal process could be excruciating and sometimes even deadly.

"Audra I have nothing. We are . . . prisoners." She scanned the room. Both sun and noise now streamed through the narrow window as the village awoke. She wanted to see if she could spot something that would tell her where they were, but she dared not leave Audra.

"Help me," Audra whispered through chattering teeth.

Suddenly, the door flew open, hitting the wall with a loud bang. Two men in baggy khakis stood in the entrance. One was dark, lean, and tall, with black, threatening eyes. Two bandoleers of ammunition formed an X over his chest. In his hands he cradled a Russian automatic rifle whose barrel was pointed at Trisha's head.

The man beside him was also dark, but shorter, and stocky. Though he, too, looked menacing, he wore neither bandoleers nor carried a weapon. Without being told, Trisha knew they were in the hands of ISA.

"Up!" growled the man with the bandoleers, in English. "On your feet! Get up, slut!"

"My friend is ill," Trisha said. "I don't think she can move."

Ignoring Trisha, the gunman came over and nudged Audra with the toe of his boot causing her to moan. "Bring the *daya*!" he shouted when it became obvious Audra couldn't rise.

Moments later, a woman wearing a black burka and head covering stepped quietly through the door. Her face was unveiled and she looked to be in her sixties. Her large, doe eyes stared shyly at the two strangers, but they were filled with gentleness and compassion as though they had seen their share of suffering. And for a brief moment they shone with an understanding, as though in some way she identified with the two captives. She was the *daya* or mid-wife, and Trisha would learn that aside from delivering babies, she often tended the sick women in the village.

The *daya* examined Audra while she still rested on Trisha's lap. When she was finished, she said something in Farsi to the gunman whom she called Mustafa. Her words caused him to explode with laughter. When he tired of the joke, he bellowed another order which seemed to displease her. She made a feeble attempt to argue, but in the end nodded and left.

"The *daya* has seen this sickness before, in Russian soldiers." His voice was cold, hard. "It is the curse of the drink. Allah, in his wisdom, forbids Muslims to partake of this poison and the *daya*, a true believer, didn't want to defile herself by handling it. But I have sent her for some. What is it to us or Allah if infidels want to pollute themselves?" He gestured with his rifle toward Audra as though he was gesturing toward a rodent.

Trisha had been praying silently. A supernatural peace had settled over her. It was as though God had woven together all her insecure threads, forming instead iron that braced and strengthened her for whatever was to come. Fear no longer prevailed. She had settled the question of death. Her life was not in Mustafa's hands, but in God's.

Her steady gaze seemed to anger Mustafa. "Lower your eyes!" he screamed in English. Trisha obeyed. There was no point in needlessly provoking him.

All the while the other man, whom Mustafa called Nabil, stood watching. "Infidel pigs!" he said in English, making a spitting noise. After sufficiently purifying his mouth, he released a string of vile obscenities just as the *daya* returned carrying a bottle of Russian vodka.

Mustafa took it and barked an order. Again, the woman disappeared, returning moments later with a small, shallow clay bowl. Mustafa handed his rifle to Nabil, then poured vodka into the bowl and placed it on the floor across from Trisha. Then he walked over, and after taking his rifle from Nabil, used the butt to push and prod Audra until her eyes opened and she sat up.

"You want a drink?" Mustafa said in English, looking like a sadist about to pull the wings off a fly. When she didn't answer, he held up the vodka bottle.

Audra, who looked like she could barely focus, managed a nod.

Mustafa pointed toward the bowl across the room and bellowed, "Then get it!"

Audra looked confused, not sure what she was supposed to do. When she tried to rise, Mustafa's foot shoved her to the floor.

"No! Not walk, but crawl like the dog you are."

Trisha tried to hold her back, but Audra pulled away then slowly made her way on all fours, to the saucer of vodka twelve feet away. When she was about to reach for it, Mustafa's boot pinned her hand against the floor.

"Lap it, infidel!"

Without a word, Audra lowered her face into the bowl and began lapping up the liquid.

Unable to watch any longer, Trisha turned her head and wept.

"It is well that you cry, whore," Nabil said, seemingly pleased by her tears. "For Allah has reserved a most fitting fate for all infidels."

Then the two men and the *daya* were gone.

●　●　●

"It's been five days, Pete. Five days since we've been contacted by ISA." Mike looked rumpled and out of sorts. "This waiting, the not knowing anything . . . it's hard. And my employees are being affected. Several have quit, others are threatening to. Everyone is afraid. They wonder who will be next. My staff has tried portraying calm, but if mass hysteria sweeps through PA, it's going to leave an empty plant."

"Your R&D people don't seem to be panicking. They appear more angry than anything else."

"That's because they're taking this personally. Two of their co-workers have been kidnapped. They're pretty mad. And that's saying a lot because most of them are the brainy-pacifist type."

Pete nodded. "I can't blame them. And the waiting is always the hardest part. That's when time seems like the enemy."

"I don't like sitting around doing nothing." Mike had left his desk and paced the room.

"Believe me, everything is being done."

"I'm not faulting you, Pete. But I was sure ISA would have called back by now. Still . . . something doesn't sit right. Why would ISA want the women alive? They killed Nolan. I thought the idea was to stop our nuclear fusion project? It doesn't make sense. What are they after?" Mike felt his chest tighten. "You don't think they've gone ahead and . . . killed . . . them, do you?"

Pete drummed his fingers on the arm of his chair. "I'm sure the women are safe, for now anyway. Had ISA wanted them dead, they wouldn't have bothered abducting them. Maybe they're holding back communications to make us more desperate, more receptive to their demands."

Mike stopped pacing. "You don't pull any punches."

"Would you want me to?"

"No. That's why I trust you. And Pete . . . you know I don't pull any either."

"What's that supposed to mean?"

"Just this: I want Trisha back, and I'll do whatever it takes."

• • •

Hours later, Mike stood ringing the bell of a posh Everman condo. Within seconds, the door opened, revealing a tall, lean man with delicate hands. "Dr. Daniel Chapman?"

"Yes."

"I'm Michael Patterson from Patterson Aviation. I've come about Trisha Callahan. I need your help."

• • •

CHAPTER 13

Trisha peered out the small, glassless window and surveyed the strange, dusty village below. She had come to realize that her dwelling was higher than most, being built on the side of a mountain, and this afforded her a good view. After endless days of gazing through this opening, she could recall every detail with her eyes closed: the whitewashed adobe houses with their flat roofs where clothes were dried; how the houses were clustered together; the village square; the two large beehive-shaped communal ovens; the stubby tower where the muezzin's wail called the faithful to prayer five times a day; the training ground in the distance where men rolled and tumbled across the ground, lifted concrete blocks as weights, climbed wooden barriers or fired their rifles into human-shaped targets.

The men wore Arab head coverings or *kuffiyehs*. Some were dressed in black loose fitting trousers but most wore mismatched baggy clothes. The men far outnumbered the women. Some had wives or perhaps they were women captured from other villages and taken as slaves, the *daya* had been unable to make that clear.

The women wore black burkas and head coverings, and appeared to be a solemn lot; washing clothes in large metal tubs or baking in the communal ovens. They never seemed to rest.

Not like the men.

Whenever they weren't training, the men appeared idle; toting guns and milling around the village square, talking, arguing, laughing. Many spent hours drinking *finjans* of coffee.

By night, they gathered in the square, lighting smudge pots to drive off insects, then lighting their own pipes filled with crumpled hashish. Before long, the music of reed horns, *tambours* and the *dhamboura* filled the air. Then eight or ten males would begin the *dabkah,* a dance only for men. At first, they moved together, bodies rigid, arms draped over the next man's shoulder. But it would end wild, frenzied, with maniacal war cries and knives slashing the air.

During the times when the guards allowed her and Audra to go to the outhouse, Trisha scrutinized every detail. And whenever she could, she's prod the *daya* for information. Surprisingly, the woman was eager to talk. In broken English, she had revealed these details, including the fact they were in a Mexican village the jihadists had taken by force. The *daya* also told her, with evident pride, that there were at least three other ISA settlements scattered across Mexico.

Trisha wondered at the *daya's* devotion to her cause and at the hatred she saw in the male faces whenever they looked at her. How had the world gotten here? How had tradition, superstition, and fear brought it to this? How had the sperm of hostility reproduced itself throughout the centuries, shaping the basic canon of these people's lives? This offspring was enmity; brother against brother, tribe against tribe, and all against the infidel.

Yet, if a villager was asked why this was so, why the Quran ordered him to kill all those unlike himself, Trisha doubted he'd be able to explain, any more than a salmon could explain why it swims upstream.

All this hostility made her long for a friendly face. Audra rarely spoke. Three times a day a saucer of vodka was prepared, and despite Trisha's pleas, Audra obliged her captors by crawling on all fours across the room.

But Audra's shame manifested in a prickly and quarrelsome manner. Often she'd instigate groundless arguments with Trisha. It made

Trisha pray more earnestly; storming heaven with pleas of deliverance from addiction and God's tilling of Audra's heart to enable her to receive the seeds of His love.

And it was beginning to happen.

"Look," Trisha said, "here come the peddlers."

It was market day again and the entire village bustled with noisy confusion as scores of peddlers arrived in their trucks, protected by three jeeps fitted with machine guns. The trucks carried wares stuffed in enormous clay jars except for the one carrying meat which hung from racks.

In the jars were medicines for every known ailment; amulets to ward off evil spirits; combs and mirrors, cloth, used clothing, and shoes. There were jars of beans and rice, corn meal, condiments and spices, sesame seeds, pistachios and pecans.

Other peddlers sold their services; grinding knives, scissors, and gardening tools; repairing everything from pots and pans, to guns and rifles. Still others dealt in luxuries; glass beads for necklaces, perfume in alabaster jars, gilt-handled daggers. There was even a craftsman who made tiny objects out of gold or silver.

"I wonder where they come from?" Trisha said. The jeep mounted guns made her think they were somehow associated with the drug cartels.

Audra struggled to her feet, then walked to the window and peered out. "It's been two weeks since they were here last. How many more market days will we see, do you think? I just wish we knew what this was all about and why we've been brought here."

Trisha had wondered that herself. Neither she nor Audra had been interrogated. And other than the cruelty with the vodka, they had been well treated. A large clay jar had been brought into the room and filled with fresh drinking water, daily. Outhouse privileges were frequent. And though they still slept on the floor, blankets were given to each of them as a buffer against the chilly evenings.

In addition, the *daya* brought them beans and rice twice a day. Only once did this vary, and that was on the last market day when they were given *falafels* or deep fried balls of crushed wheat and chick peas, steamed grape leaves filled with pine nuts and currants, and two pieces of roasted chicken covered with *couscous*.

It was a feast, and Trisha had had that uneasy feeling she might be eating her last meal. "Remember that wonderful dinner we had on market day?"

"I'm trying not to. I don't know how many more meals of beans and rice I can stomach. If . . . we ever get out of here I'll never eat them again."

"Well, I certainly wouldn't recommend this restaurant." For the first time since their captivity, Trisha heard Audra laugh.

"At least we never have to wonder what's for dinner."

Now they both laughed, and so hard—like a corkscrew popping a tension-filled bottle—that tears rolled down their faces. And as they laughed their hands reached out to each other and held fast until the door suddenly flew open.

Mustafa stood in the entrance, the same bandoleers of ammunition across his chest. As he pointed his finger at them, Trisha knew their three-week routine was about to change.

"You," he shouted, "come with me!"

Audra squeezed Trisha's hand so hard her fingernails turned white, but neither one of them moved because neither knew who Mustafa was summoning.

"I said *you*, come here!" Mustafa's blazing eyes exploded with fury as he saw his command go unheeded. He strode across the room, then gestured toward Trisha. "I mean you."

Trisha nodded and tried to leave but Audra won't release her. "It's okay, I'll be back," she said, not convinced of the statement herself. But it seemed to persuade Audra because she let go. Then Trisha followed her jailer.

Mustafa's office was a room much like the one they had just left. The walls were whitewashed adobe, the floor covered with straw mats. But attached to the far wall was a long, mud brick bench upon which the stocky Nabil half sat, half laid. A gray, metal desk dominated the center of the room.

Mustafa pointed to the cell phone on the desktop as he slid onto his chair. "I have just received orders to begin interrogations. And I'm authorized to use any force necessary. Believe me, sooner or later you'll tell me all I wish to know."

He opened one of the drawers and pulled out a large knife with a rough, wooden hilt. He smiled as he placed it on the desk.

"What do you want to know?" Trisha said calmly.

"She is proud, this infidel!" Mustafa growled.

Nabil rose from the bench and began encircling her. Today he was armed with a revolver which was holstered and strapped to his waist. "Yes," he said with a hiss. "We may have to teach her some manners."

"We know the company that employs you is owned by Zionist pigs," Mustafa said with an air of authority. "We also know that you are building a secret super plane which your employers will use to slaughter thousands of innocent Muslim women and children."

Trisha's eyes grew wide, and before she could stop herself she blurted, "That's ridiculous."

"By Allah's beard, how this infidel lies!" Mustafa shouted, thumping the desk with his fist.

Nabil nodded. "Has not the Quran warned us about nonbelievers, especially the dirty Jews? The *surahs* wisely caution us against befriending Jews for they are corrupt and untrustworthy. It is unfortunate for this daughter of a camel that she doesn't know the wisdom of our holy book."

"Jewish entrails will be used as fertilizer!" shrieked Mustafa, picking up the knife. "Their eyes will be torn from their sockets! Their skulls will be used as kick-balls by our children! May the Prophet strike us blind if we do not exterminate every living Jew who breathes the air of Allah's earth!"

Trisha watched madness sweep over Mustafa as his voice grew louder. The blue, bulging veins on his neck formed a roadmap pattern. Herein traveled his hot, flowing hatred, pumped into every cell of his body.

"You will give us the details of this super plane," Mustafa said, replacing the knife on the desk. "Every minute detail."

When Trisha said nothing he rose from his seat.

"Are you deaf, whore? I said you will give us the details of this airplane. And you will write it on this paper." The lean guard poked a pad of yellow paper with his finger.

Still Trisha remained silent.

"Well!" shrieked Mustafa, the veins on his neck bulging again.

"I can't do that."

Mustafa convulsed in amazement. "Has there ever been such an evil, treacherous woman? We give her the chance to repent, to strike a blow against the Zionist pigs, thereby endearing herself to Muhammad the Great Prophet, the Ultimate Messenger of Allah, and she insults us! We who have shown her Allah's compassion! It is her Jewish friends. The scum have defiled her beyond redemption. It would be a just act, indeed, to spill her blood with this knife." Once again Mustafa picked up the weapon.

"Not yet," returned Nabil, putting up his hand. "This whore is proud. Perhaps all she needs is a lesson in humility. Perhaps we can still make her see the truth and justice of our words." Nabil stopped circling, then slowly, almost ceremoniously, he pulled the revolver from his holster. "You will disrobe, and in shame and humiliation kneel before us, ask our forgiveness, and beg us to spare your life."

The look on Nabil's face told Trisha he was prepared to kill her on the spot. She shook her head no, then held her breath. She was not afraid to die. She just hoped it wouldn't be painful. She prayed for a swift end.

Nabil pressed the barrel of the revolver against her temple. "You will do as I say or die!"

Trisha closed her eyes. Her legs shook and in an effort to stave off fear, she began singing in a low, quivering voice, "'Jesus, Jesus, He's as close as the mention of His name.'" As her fear began to dissolve, her voice grew louder. "'Jesus! Jesus! He's as close as the mention of His name!'"

She waited for the sound of an explosion. There was only silence. When she opened her eyes, she saw Mustafa looking at her with a gaping mouth. She began singing again, and the louder she sang the more Mustafa's mouth dropped. Finally, his shrieks silenced her.

"Majnun! Majnun! Majnun!" he shouted, as he backed away from the desk. "Demon. She has a *majnum*, a demon. She is possessed! See how crazy she is! Remove her! Take her away!" Mustafa had backed as far away as he could and stood pressed against the wall.

Nabil appeared cautious, but not convinced. "It's best that I kill her," he said, the revolver still pressed against Trisha's temple.

"No! Are you so foolish? She may have many demons. And you know how they work. If she dies, the *majnuns* will jump from her body and take control of one of us. Away with her! Take her away!"

Nabil's face revealed his disapproval but he slipped the revolver into his holster, then without another word led Trisha out the door. Once in the adjoining room, Nabil ordered Audra, who crouched against the wall, to follow him. She quickly rose in obedience.

When they entered the office, Nabil slammed the door. His scowling face was red. "I know your company is the tool of Zionist pigs. Do not deny it!"

Audra stared blankly at her interrogator. "I . . . I don't understand."

"May Allah the Merciful grant me patience!" bellowed Mustafa from behind the desk where he had returned to sit. "We are dealing with another lying whore."

"No . . . please. I really don't know . . . ."

"Silence!" Mustafa screamed. Then, looking over at Nabil who was once again sprawled across the mud brick bench, he added, "This one is worse than the last. She is of no more worth than a camel chip. See how uncooperative she is!"

Nabil pulled out his revolver. "Then let me dispose of her at once. It's obvious that Jewish depravity has infiltrated these women completely. They are impossible. One is crazy, the other is a liar and thief. She doesn't want to return to us what is rightfully ours. I say, kill her."

Audra's bottom lip quivered. "I do want to cooperate."

Mustafa smiled. "Ah! Perhaps she is not as depraved as you thought, Nabil. Perhaps there is hope. Maybe the light of Muhammad's truth can still penetrate her blackened soul."

"Yes . . . I'll do whatever you ask. Just . . . tell me what you want." Clusters of tears worked their way down Audra's cheeks.

Nabil slapped the black pistol against his palm. It made a dull, sickening noise, and for a moment Audra thought she was going to throw-up all over Mustafa's metal desk. She clutched her stomach.

"We do not want to hurt you," Mustafa said. "It was never our desire or intention. Do you take us for your cut-throat Jewish friends? Well, do you!"

Audra shook her head.

"Of course not. And if you cooperate, you will continue to be treated as an honored guest."

"Alright," Audra stammered.

"We know that your Zionist owned company is building an airplane which they intend using to slaughter our people. Because of this evil intent, they have forfeited their right to it. We claim this plane for ourselves. It is, by the will of Allah, ours. You can see that this is so, can you not?" questioned Mustafa.

"I . . . I suppose . . . ."

"Good. Excellent. Then you will furnish us with the details of this airplane; *all* the details."

"I . . . don't think I can."

"May Allah make my teeth fall from my gums if I show this whore such mercy again!" Mustafa bellowed. "We are getting nowhere. Kill her, Nabil and be done with it."

"What I mean is . . . I don't know if I can remember everything without my notes. I . . . could try."

Mustafa's lips curled into a smile. "On your knees then. Beg for mercy and forgiveness. And maybe, if Allah wills, I shall allow you to give us that information."

Fear buckled Audra's legs. As she knelt before the gray, metal desk she whispered, "Forgive me."

"What did you say? Speak up!" Mustafa barked.

"Forgive me," Audra said louder, choking on the words that tasted like vomit in her mouth.

"You will demonstrate your sorrow by kissing our boots," Mustafa returned, his piercing, hate-filled eyes drilling through any will Audra had left.

Audra struggled to keep back the tears as she crawled, first to Mustafa, then to where Nabil sat on the mud brick bench. By the time her lips touched the stocky guard's dusty, black boots, she was convulsing in uncontrollable sobs.

"We must forgive her, Nabil," Mustafa said. "It is our nature to be merciful. Can we fight against our own nature?"

"It would be most unwise," returned the stocky guard.

"That's it then. We forgive you, golden-hair woman!"

Audra sobbed into her hands.

"Ah! She is overwhelmed with gratitude!" Nabil cried. "That is good." So saying, he took his boot and shoved her onto the ground. "And now I think we can make her even more grateful."

There was a questioning look in Mustafa's face as he watched Nabil unbuckle his holster. "Yes, it would be an honor for her to service us," he returned, as the realization of what his friend was about to do, became obvious.

Audra watched in horror as Nabil moved towards her. "She is, after all, only a whore."

• • •

For the next week Audra was called into Mustafa's office every day. The routine never varied. Her progress was questioned. It was always poor. Audra had lost, temporarily at least, the ability to think clearly. Her notes were disjointed; her diagrams incomplete or inaccurate.

The guards, lacking the knowledge to interpret the accuracy of her report, were unaware of Audra's impediment. But her slow progress infuriated them. They viewed this as defiance. So everyday Nabil waved and pointed his gun. And everyday there would be loud cursing and name calling, accusations, and threats. And always, always it would end with one or both of the guards shoving her onto the floor saying, "She is, after all, only a whore."

Those times on the floor especially, were times Audra tried to block everything out. Survival was, after all, everything. Maybe if she didn't resist, maybe if she did all they asked, they would eventually release her, and she could go home.

Her thoughts of home were fuzzy. At times it was difficult to recall the color of her kitchen or how the living room was arranged. In her more lucid moments, she'd think of Tom Halleron. He had loved her once and even proposed. Maybe life in suburbia with kids and a SUV wouldn't have been so bad.

But there was one bright spot. She didn't have to take her vodka from a saucer anymore. The guards had tired of that game. Instead, they gave her half a bottle a day, to drink whenever she wanted.

Audra thought she would have gone mad if it were not for this one comfort. She especially needed it after her daily interrogation. When it was over, she'd go to her side of the room where the bottle was kept; drop down onto the straw mat and take one large gulp. After that, she'd take five or six sips, then cap the bottle for later.

It was only then that she was able to turn and look at Trisha Callahan.

She had grown to hate this woman with the thick, black hair and chocolate colored eyes. That brief moment of friendship, when the two held hands, was long forgotten. After the first day of interrogation, Trisha had never again been called into the office. *She* was not shouted at or scratched by a gun barrel or threatened or pushed to the floor and used as a whore.

And Audra hated her for that.

"Was it bad today?" Trisha asked softly.

"I keep telling you to mind your business!" Audra snapped, pushing back the honey blond hair that hung in tangles around her face. She fingered the rip in her blouse. Nabil had been exceptionally vicious today, and in demonstrating his power over her had torn her sleeve. "And stop staring at me!"

"I just want to help. We need to stick together. Don't isolate yourself. If you'd only come to know Jesus. He could . . . ."

"Shut up! Just shut up!" Audra screamed, her face looking like a hernia ready to rupture. "Stop preaching to me. I can't stand it! I don't need you or anyone! Do you hear that! I don't need anyone!"

● ● ●

CHAPTER 14

Joshua sat in Michael Patterson's paneled office watching the handsome face of Peter Meyers contort in an array of emotions. He was flanked by his brother, Daniel, and Mossad agent Iliab Nahshon, a man of shadows with a lethal reputation.

"I've been told of your efforts to track down Kamal and other members of ISA." There was a smile on Peter's face, the kind that was as plastic as an iPod cover. "And all *without* the aid of the DHS or CIA or FBI. But I suppose we should be grateful."

Joshua met the blond agent's fierce stare and shrugged. He refused to engage in a verbal war over turf like a bulldog marking his territory.

"But I don't mind telling you that when Mike told me he had gone to see your brother, Dr. Chapman, I was pretty ticked off. And actually furious when he told me it was because Trisha suspected you were working for the Israeli government in some clandestine capacity." The muscles of Peter's face tightened. "I figured you for a corporate spy. I never imagined you were *Mossad*."

Peter fingered the lapel of his dark blue suit. "Do you know what Mike said when I told him to let DHS handle things? He said he was having trouble believing DHS could handle a bus transfer across town."

Joshua stifled a laugh. No use insulting the agent. Besides, he had been at the other end of this stick and was still embarrassed by his own failure in his last Middle East mission involving Kamal—the mission where the Mossad had Kamal in their sights but lost him due to his miscommunication, a snafu that forced the agency to send Iliab Nahshon to America.

Joshua eyed Peter with sympathy. The women had been missing for twenty days. It was only in the last forty-eight hours that any intelligence on their whereabouts had been gathered. And that information had been gleaned, not by DHS but by the Mossad.

"Your concerns are noted. But I think we need to put aside our differences and work together. Illiab, here, has come up with a plan." Joshua gestured with his chin toward the man on his right. "I'll let him explain."

"First, understand that this is not an unselfish act on our part," Iliab said with a thick accent, the gentleness in his deep voice contrasting the scarred, rugged face.

Joshua had learned a few things about this enigma of a man since working with him. And aside from the scars on his face, Joshua knew a network of scars also plated his body; some obtained in combat but most while in an Arab prison.

"We are hoping these efforts on our part will encourage greater cooperation between your agency and ours."

"I understand," Peter said, "but you must know that any commitment I make now is strictly unofficial."

"Must we play these silly cat-and-mouse games when lives are at stake?"

"I don't make policy. The bureaucrats in Washington . . . ."

"Politics don't interest me," Iliab snapped. "And quite frankly, there are many in the Mossad who no longer trust your government and do not wish an alliance between us. Fortunately, there are more who do. But we all have a long memory and still mourn our martyred Mossad brothers."

Peter blushed. "Our agency had nothing to do with that fiasco. That was well before our time."

Joshua tensed. He hoped this wouldn't get out of hand. Iliab, like many in the Mossad, still resented the former secretary of state who, while trying to bring Arafat to the peace table, had given the PLO, as barter, the names of three top Mossad agents, agents who had infiltrated two different terrorist groups. It cost the agents their lives, and with no real peace to show for it. That same secretary of state continued to be a curse word among many in Israel.

"What is it you want?" Peter asked, his forehead creasing.

"It goes without saying that relations between the U.S. and Israel have been strained of late. President Thaddeus Baker is decidedly pro Arab. And as long as martial law is in effect, nothing will change. I don't believe your countrymen want to live under a dictatorship. We have certain facts in our possession that could remedy this; facts damaging enough to warrant congress impeaching President Baker and force the lifting of martial law."

"What information?" Peter pressed.

"We're not prepared to go there," Joshua said hastily, seeing the impatience on Iliab's face. Lacking diplomatic skills, Iliab would be more than capable of pressing Peter to the wall. A counterproductive move. "Once the mission is over, we can discuss this aspect."

"Fine, but what do *you* hope to gain from the lifting of martial law?"

"A new president," Joshua said. "One who will protect us in the UN. One who will veto the continuing efforts by the Palestinians to declare themselves a state without first renouncing their terrorist activities and acknowledging Israel's right to exist. One who will not allow Russia to steal our oil and gas rights.

"We also want the U.S. to stop twisting Israel's arm to give up land for peace. We've done that. And where is the peace? Tensions are higher than ever. The area is a tinderbox.

"And finally, we want you to stop threatening to cut off our weapon supplies as a means of pressuring us to do your bidding. We're allies. Your best friend in the Middle East. Your *only* friend right now. Stop treating us like the enemy.

"If we pool our intelligence, our resources and efforts, we'll be able to defeat terrorism. Alone, we'll accomplish a fraction of what we actually could."

"That's a tall order," Peter said, pulling his chin. "You're pretty much asking for carte blanche. We may be allies but we don't always see eye to eye."

Joshua nodded. "That's because your current president is weak on terrorism and we are serious, often unconventional, and strike hard. We're in this to win because that's our only option. The world hates terrorism, but all too often has no stomach for doing what is necessary to stop it. But we cannot fight global terrorism alone. We need you as a partner."

Peter twisted the bulky West Point ring on his finger and Joshua wondered if it was to remind himself that he was trained in tactical warfare as well as negotiations. "I understand," he said. "And I agree, off the record, of course. But again why me? What makes you think I can do anything for you or have the clout or connections needed to begin impeachment?"

"You have powerful friends," Iliab said, curtly, then smiled when he saw the surprised look on Peter's face. "We do our homework. Under the current law we know where the power has shifted and that you are connected with one of your country's most influential men; a man we don't think supports President Baker."

"I suppose you're talking about my friend, the National Continuity Coordinator?"

When Peter didn't answer, Mike leaned forward. "I don't know what there is to think about. Terrorism is not just a Jewish problem. The sooner we all get on board this train, the sooner we'll win. And I want to *win*, gentlemen."

Joshua glanced at his brother who sat glum and silent. What was he thinking? Joshua already understood that Daniel had lost Trisha to this man who built airplanes, a man not willing to sit idly by while someone he loved was in danger. Still, he was proud of his brother for not hesitating to help. The heart was a strange thing, and not all who had been spurned would be so inclined.

"Well, what do you say?" Joshua said, brushing his hand over his brother's shoulder as he settled back in the chair.

"If your information is all that you imply, then it could be dangerous for me and anyone else I share it with."

"It is," Joshua said, without emotion. "But if you want your country back, you'll need it."

Peter gnawed his lips. "What you're implying is that there are some in my government I'm not to trust."

Iliab leaned forward. "Exactly." He extended his hand to Meyers. "Do we have a deal?"

"Yes," Peter said, taking his hand and shaking it. "Now, tell us about this Seco Polvo where they're holding the women."

Iliab's lips arched into a thin smile. "Seco Polvo is a small Mexican village about a hundred miles from the U.S. border. It's one of several villages taken over by ISA; where all the men and children have been killed and the women kept as slaves. It was obviously chosen for its inaccessibility—being surrounded by desert and rough, mountain terrain. We also believe it is Kamal's North American home base."

"I understand you have been contacted by ISA," Joshua said, looking at Mike. "Once to claim responsibility, the second time with demands."

"Yes. They want one million dollars before releasing the women. I'll be contacted in three days for my answer, along with further instructions."

"You cannot pay," Joshua said. "Once you do, they'll kill them both."

"Then what are our options? What can we do?"

"We can go to Seco Polvo and get the women out."

"How?" Mike returned, leaning forward in his chair. "You'd need an army."

"Yes, it would take an army if we wanted to conquer the village," Iliab said. "And the terrorists would kill the women before we reached them. That is why we will use only four men."

Mike, who seemed to be appraising the Israeli, tented his fingers. "You're a man of few words. I like that. I'm not interested in boastful claims or false bravado. You say you have a plan. Let's hear it."

"Seco Polvo is partially built into a mountain on one side, surrounded by desert on two. The fourth is flanked by a treacherous gorge. Strategically placed sentries patrol twenty-four hours a day. Impossible to penetrate without immediate discovery. And we have already discussed the hazard to the women once the village is alarmed.

"But Seco Polvo has market day every two weeks. It, as well as the other terrorist camps in Mexico, is serviced by the drug cartels. On market day peddlers come to sell their wares. Surprisingly, many are Middle Easterners, some even members of the cartels. And all give a portion of their proceeds to them. The day is filled with confusion. It would be easy for us to slip in during this time."

"Maybe," Peter said, looking unconvinced. "But wouldn't four strange faces arouse suspicion?"

"There is a risk," Iliab responded. "But only two of the men would be new. The other two are Mossad agents who have entered Seco Polvo many times. One agent poses as a peddler of precious metals, the other as his assistant. Being a terrorist village, Seco Polvo is rich compared to the average small Mexican village. Money flows like the Euphrates from the coffers of Iran, Libya and Syria to fund them. Believe me when I say our silver and gold peddler does a good business."

"Fine. But how are you going to get the other two men in undetected?"

"The drug cartels provide armed escorts for the peddlers. But once those peddlers, not directly linked to the cartels, leave the caravan they become easy prey for desperados laying in wait. A peddler of precious metals is an even greater target. We'll stage a fake robbery of our agents; let the word get around. Then, when they show up with two heavily armed bodyguards, no one will question it. In fact, they'll expect it."

"Alright, so you can get in. But how are you going to get the women out?" Peter asked.

Iliab frowned. "That is the hard part. We know the exact house where the women are being held, and the number of guards with them. Our peddler agent was able to obtain that information the last time he was in Seco Polvo. These terrorists love to boast of their conquests."

Iliab paused as though thinking of the perilous journey. "It will be difficult, but you must leave the rest to us. Understand this, if I didn't think it was possible, I wouldn't attempt it."

"Then you'll be one of the bodyguards?" Peter asked.

"Yes." Iliab looked over at Joshua. "And my young companion here will be our back-up. He and a team of men will wait for us in the gorge."

Peter compressed his lips. "Is rescuing the women your first priority? Or killing Kamal?"

"Can I not do both?"

"I don't care who you kill," Mike said, "as long as you get the women out. My only question is when . . . *when* will this rescue take place?"

"In eleven days the peddlers are due to return," Iliab said.

"Nearly two weeks. So *long*?" Mike said with a frown. "The terrorists will contact me in three days. What should I say?"

"You must stall," Iliab returned. "And you must be convincing. If the terrorists suspect anything, your women will be killed. Do you understand?"

Mike nodded. "I understand."

● ● ●

"Mr. Patterson?" asked an accented voice over the phone.

"Yes." Mike jerked his head telling Peter Meyers that contact had been made.

"Are you prepared to deliver the one million dollars?"

"No," Mike replied, sounding calm. He had rehearsed his answer a thousand times until he could say it matter-of-factly. But he couldn't keep his palms from sweating.

"*What?*"

"These women have few family members. And they are not wealthy. But then, you knew that, otherwise you wouldn't have contacted me." Mike paused to give the caller a chance to comment. When he didn't, Mike added, "Therefore, I have assumed responsibility and am, even now, in the process of liquidating some of my assets."

"Do you think this is a game and you can make up the rules as you go!" snapped the accented voice. "Perhaps you need evidence of our serious intent. A finger or toe of one of the women delivered to you in a package should convince you that *we* dictate the terms!"

Mike's heart pounded at the prospect of Trisha being maimed. But if he panicked now the outcome could be disastrous. "Do you expect me to pay for damaged goods!" he shot back. "These women aren't family! They are valuable to me as employees. But everyone is expendable. If you're so eager for bloodletting, I can't stop you."

"Then . . . you do not care what happens to them?"

"Of course I care, in the business sense. I assumed you were a businessman as well; that we could come to equitable terms."

"You have a proposal?"

"I do. In nine days I will have liquidated enough assets to pay your ransom. In addition, I am prepared to pay you twenty thousand dollars a day interest, beginning today, until everything is settled."

There was a long pause and Mike hoped it was because the man on the other end had understood the obvious financial benefit. The ransom price was one million dollars. Anything over that amount could be pocketed and who would know?

"I will call you in nine days," came the reply which sealed the agreement. Then the phone went dead.

Peter had been listening to the conversation on another line. "You handled it well, Mike. You kept a cool head. Now, there's nothing more we can do."

In eight days Iliab Nahshon and his men would be in Seco Polvo. In eight days Trisha would either be rescued or killed. "We can pray," Mike returned, tapping the black pocket Bible on his desk.

"Don't tell me you've gone and gotten religion?"

"I'm trying to keep my balance here, Pete. If you have a better suggestion, then let's hear it."

The DHS agent just sighed and shook his head.

• • •

After driving up and down the streets of the Cherokee community for twenty minutes, Mike finally stopped and asked directions to the home of Mrs. Paddy Callahan. He followed the prescribed route, then parked in front of a modest brick dwelling with green shutters and a green door.

Large, clay flower pots, clustered here and there on the porch, formed little rainbows of color. A wooden rocker, with a calico blanket thrown over one arm and an open sewing basket on the seat, looked like it belonged on the cover of *Better Homes & Gardens*. A red brick path, lined with shrubs, led from the porch to the street. All this on a back-drop of lush green grass that carpeted the front like a short, shag rug.

If nothing else, the house beckoned people to enter, with the promise that they would find a warm welcome inside.

He had not known what to expect. Trisha rarely talked about her mother or her life outside Patterson Aviation. He suspected it was another way of keeping her distance, of not getting too close to a man she had yet to fully trust.

The green door opened and out stepped a middle aged woman in jeans. When she waved and smiled, then walked down the porch steps, Mike got out of the car. He had sent Mrs. Callahan a telegram after Trisha's abduction. Now that the Mossad had gotten involved and there was the possibility of a rescue, Mike thought he should give her this news in person.

Before he could take a step, Mrs. Callahan was beside him. He noted she was an attractive woman, but not a beauty like Trisha.

"Mrs. Callahan?"

"Yes. How can I help you?"

Mike was taken back by her wide smile and sparkling eyes. He was a stranger. He could be anyone yet she greeted him like a friend. "I am Michael Patterson, from Patterson Aviation."

Mrs. Callahan took his arm and led him towards the house. "You must have news about Trisha. It's best we go inside."

"It's good news," he said quickly as they headed for the porch.

Mrs. Callahan eyed him. "That's kind of you to want to relieve my fears. And yes, I was taken back when I saw your car. A stranger's car. That's how it was when my Paddy died, you know. Someone came to the house to tell me."

Once inside she made him sit down at the butcher-block table while she slipped a K-Cup into her Keurig. As he listened to it gurgle and pump coffee into a glass mug, he looked around.

The living space was one great room where kitchen, dining and living area all opened into each other. Everything was clean and tidy and color-coordinated in various shades of blue and green.

Mrs. Callahan's tastes appeared simple and practical, yet pleasing, too.

"You have a nice place here," he said, trying to make idle conversation.

Mrs. Callahan placed the steaming cup of coffee in front of him then prepared a small plate of assorted cookies before sitting down.

"Tell me about Trisha," she said.

Mike told her about Iliab Nahshon's plan to rescue the two women.

"It sounds dangerous," she said when he finished.

"I won't lie. It is." He had already determined not to sugar coat his message. If Mrs. Callahan was anything like Trisha, she'd see through it in a flash.

"My daughter is in big trouble."

"Yes," Mike said, again not blunting his answer.

"But she serves a big God. Nothing is impossible."

Mike looked into the pleasant face, at the large, hopeful eyes, and watched as a bright smile appeared. He wished he had such faith.

"I've seen her in my dreams, you know. She's weary, but holding up. And she prays often. As do I. But you don't believe." Mrs. Callahan searched his eyes as she covered his hand with hers. "It's a sad thing to face trouble alone." Her tender gaze seemed to penetrate his soul.

In truth, he had never felt so alone, so desperate. These past weeks he had struggled to hold onto some firm ground, something that did not ebb and flow with the tide. Instead, he had been tossed back and forth, like a bobbing cork. The tide could be cruel, bringing you just short of land, then dragging you out again. This time, even Buck's friendship wasn't enough to anchor him.

"Michael, you are a man in authority. A man used to controlling events and people."

"Trisha wrote you about me?"

"No. Your name tells me this. Michael Patterson, of Patterson Aviation. You are the owner? The president?" The executive nodded. "It's often difficult for a person of position and power to surrender, to give his life to God. To say, 'I'm tired and weary. Take what I have, what I am. I give it all to you, Lord.' But if you want peace, the peace that only God can give, then you must surrender. It's the only way."

"Trisha has talked to me about God, but quite honestly, Mrs. Callahan, I don't believe. I want to. I've tried but I just can't seem to take that leap of faith."

"It doesn't take a leap of faith but the sincere cry of a longing soul. Search the scriptures with an open heart. When you do, you'll come face to face with Jesus."

"Trisha gave me a Bible. I've tried reading it, but it doesn't penetrate. It doesn't make sense to me."

"When you're ready to humble yourself before God, that's when you'll find Him. God stands, as a loving Father, with outstretched arms, waiting for us to leave our folly and turn to Him."

"You make it sound so simple."

"It is."

Mike pulled his hand away then took a sip of coffee as he studied the woman in front of him. He could see Trisha's depth and warmth mirrored in her mother, and couldn't help but like the woman.

"Well," he said, at last, putting down the cup, "I just wanted to come in person and let you know what's going on. I'll let you know the minute I hear anything new."

Mrs. Callahan nodded and smiled. They remained this way for several minutes, Mike fingering his coffee cup, Mrs. Callahan smiling and staring with a strange expression on her face.

"What are you thinking, Mrs. Callahan?" Mike finally asked, leaning across the table.

"I am thinking how fortunate you are to have Trisha's love. And how fortunate she is to have yours."

● ● ●

CHAPTER 15

The battered Ford pick-up and the two heavily armed men on horseback who flanked it, kicked up a large mushroom of dust as they entered the village.

"May Allah and the Great Prophet curse the scorching heat," shouted the stout gold and silver peddler through the open window as he pulled in beside another parked truck in the caravan.

One by one, assorted trucks, and even a few donkey carts, stopped and uncovered their wares. While his assistant rolled back a dust-covered tarp, the gold and silver peddler stood up and addressed the villagers.

"Warm greetings and all manner of blessings on your head," he shouted into the crowd. "All gratitude and thanks to the merciful Allah, God of the seven heavens, for once again guiding me safely into your blessed village. I, Izzat, merchant of precious metals am your humble servant and await your pleasure."

So saying, he climbed onto the truck bed, seated himself on a stool, and began picking over the items laid out by his assistant. Then, with incredible dexterity he worked a tiny piece of gold foil. With a gas flame and quick, expert movements, he twisted cobweb like filaments of gold into a miniature Islamic crescent that could be attached to a chain or weapon.

The villagers had seen him do this dozens of times, yet they looked on in amazement. Meanwhile, the peddler's assistant held up shiny, silver worry-beads for their inspection. Within minutes he sold one. The uncertain life of a terrorist was best dealt with on the beads.

The two guards mingled among the crowd. Their presence had caused no alarm. Everyone had heard how Izzat had been robbed; how both he and his assistant had been left with good size lumps on their heads and an empty truck. And everyone agreed that the shrewd Izzat always got his money's worth. Were there any fiercer looking guards in all Mexico with their Arab headdress, black baggy shirt and pants, and fully packed bandoleers of ammunition crossing each chest?

And what of the splendid rifles slung over their shoulders? Or their large daggers, with highly polished rhino horn hilts, lashed into scabbards on their waist?

As Iliab Nahshon and his companion moved through the square, admiring eyes followed them. They allowed the villagers to satisfy their curiosity, taking pains not to appear rushed, but stopping here and there inspecting the different wares on other trucks or donkey carts. Iliab even purchased a new harness for his horse from the leather merchant then made a point of showing it to one of the cartel's armed guards.

As the novelty of Iliab and Nathan's presence wore off, the pair moved further away from the square.

"I didn't see him, did you?" Nathan said.

Iliab compressed his lips into a tight line and shook his head, trying to hide his disappointment. As Peter Meyers guessed, Kamal *was* his primary target. Iliab was to help Nathan and Izzat and the other Mossad agent get the women to safety, then after retrieving his sniper rifle from a hidden compartment in Izzat's truck, he was to return and take out The Blade. Now, it looked as if that would have to wait for another day.

He and Nathan stopped at the village perimeter and studied the topography, committing its layout to memory. They whispered in low tones devising their strategy. Both agreed that exiting to the right of the square was the best route. That way, there were only three walls to scale though they'd have to pass through a small animal courtyard and a long alley which, from what Iliab could see, would take them to the base of the mountain and another cluster of houses.

There were at least twenty in that cluster, most of them attached by twos and threes, and rising steadily like giant stairs, three tiers high. The last row was butted into the mountain rock itself, with one house rising slightly higher than the rest. This house was their target; a difficult objective. The danger of being spotted by the half dozen lookouts positioned on the overhead rocks was great, not to mention the cartel's own armed men who prowled everywhere and had Russian open-bolt PKMs mounted in their jeeps.

The pair returned to the crowded square where vendors shouted exaggerated claims and villagers scrambled for a bargain or an exhibition. Again, they appeared unhurried, and Iliab even stopped to allow one of the fighters to inspect his rifle.

Finally, they were able to make their departure to the right, then into the animal courtyard and alley, and over the three stone walls, keeping close to the sides of the houses as they moved. From time to time they stopped, huddled against the mud brick, and listened for sounds of alarm.

There were none.

Slowly, they moved forward. Twice Iliab had to get his bearings because the alleys formed a labyrinth. But his eye always found a landmark that he had previously etched in his mind. Then the journey continued, now up the tiers of houses. One tier, two tiers. Iliab signaled Nathan to stop.

Still no sound of alarm.

So far they had not encountered anyone. It seemed all the villagers were in the square. Next, the third tier and finally the very door of the house. They pulled out their daggers, then entered.

Large jars and tins, used for fetching well water, cluttered one side. Nathan's foot barely missed knocking one over as he passed. They were in the kitchen now. There was no fire in the open hearth where the cooking was done, but the room was well stocked. Lined against a wall were clay jars full of coffee, salt, cornmeal. To the other side were clay bins of nuts and dried fruit. On the third was a closed door through which male voices could be heard. Izzat, the peddler, had told them only two men guarded the women.

Iliab raised his dagger. He would only have one chance to get his man. Nathan's dagger would have its own target. When Nathan conveyed his readiness with a nodded, Iliab put one hand on the knob, then twisted and pushed. The door flew open, and both daggers sailed through the air, hitting their marks with a sickening thud.

At once, Iliab and Nathan were upon the prone bodies, withdrew their daggers then used them to slit the guards' throats. It was not an action born of blood lust or barbarity, but out of caution. An injured man could still sound an alarm or even bury his own dagger in an unsuspecting back.

The agents wiped their knives clean and slipped them into their sheaths. Nothing must be amiss when they returned to the square.

That done, the pair moved toward the second door. It was Iliab again who opened it. In the heat-laden room were two women. He had not been certain in what condition he'd find them. At first glance, they appeared well. One woman, with black hair twisted into one braid down her back, stood peering out a small window. The other woman, with matted blond hair, sat in a corner holding a bottle.

The blond saw them first and drew the bottle closer to her chest.

The dark haired woman turned from the window and stared in amazement. The men had penetrated the house so quietly it was obvious neither woman had heard them enter.

"We're here to rescue you," Iliab said in English.

"I saw you coming . . . from the window." Trisha quickly introduced herself and Audra. "I've been watching you and your friend darting by the houses and over the walls. I'm so . . ." her voice broke, "so glad you're here!"

"If she saw us, then perhaps others did too," Nathan said. "Maybe one of the guards on the cliff."

"Not likely," Trisha returned calmly. "On market day they smoke hashish in the shade. Even now I can smell it drifting from the cliffs."

Iliab nodded when he recognized the spicy smell. "Even so, we must move quickly." He pulled a black dress and scarf from his loose shirt, not noticing he had pulled out his new leather harness as well, and that it fell to the floor. "Put this on." He tossed the clothing to Audra while Nathan took a duplicate outfit from his shirt and handed it to Trisha, who nodded in understanding.

Without a word, she slipped the dress over her clothes and covered her head. Then she pulled Audra to her feet. "Come on. You must wear these."

Audra looked terrified but offered no resistance.

"Okay. We're ready," Trisha said, covering the last strand of Audra's blonde hair with the *hijab*, the head scarf.

Iliab led the group through the room where the two guards lay dead, then into the kitchen. He stopped by the large tins and shook them until finding one that was full. In the meantime, Nathan pulled goatskin pouches from his shirt and filled them with dried food from the clay bins. He tied them and handed them to Trisha, while Audra stood clutching her vodka bottle.

When that was done, Iliab ushered the group out the door and onto a steep, narrow path. He would find a cave to hide the women until he could return for them that night.

The terrain was rough, and Audra slowed them down. As the sun moved further west, Iliab realized he couldn't take them as deep into the mountain as he had hoped. He would have to find a cave soon. There were many in the area and the men scouted several before choosing one.

When Iliab's eyes grew accustomed to the darkness, he noticed a ledge high off the ground. If a person lay flat and against the far wall, he would be impossible to see from the ground. It was a perfect hiding place.

Iliab explained his plan to the women. Then, after promising he would be back for them that night, he and Nathan lifted, first Trisha, then Audra onto the ledge, followed by the food and water.

"Make sure you eat and drink your fill. After this, you'll be on rations," Iliab said.

Then the men were gone.

• • •

The ledge was littered with rocks that dug into the women's skin as they squirmed to find a comfortable spot in the darkness.

"Why have they left us here?" Audra's shaky voice bounced off the ceiling in eerie, hollow echoes.

The platform was close to the cave roof making it impossible to sit upright. All Trisha could do was hover over Audra and pat her back as if she were a colicky child.

"Hush. It's going to be alright."

• • •

Iliab and Nathan trudged silently through the mountain. The climb downward was quicker than the ascent, and the two men made good progress. Along the way, Iliab's mind sketched the terrain, the pathways, the shape of the boulders, the position of the village below. He would have to know these things when he returned for the women.

When they arrived at the outskirts of the village, near the house where the women had been imprisoned, all was quiet. So far, no one had discovered the dead guards. The pair moved along the shadows of the buildings. Their most vulnerable position was still over the three walls. They scaled the first, the second, and were about to scale the last when Iliab noticed that some of the villagers were drifting away from the square.

"Do exactly as I do," he whispered. In one fluid motion, he dove over the wall, propped himself against the mud brick and pulled a pipe and bag of hashish from his shirt. He filled the pipe bowl, lit it, and took a drag. Nathan had followed him over the wall, and now sat beside him.

"*Allah Akbar! Allah Akbar!*" Iliab said in a loud voice as he passed the pipe to Nathan who took a quick puff.

"Join us! Join us!" Iliab said laughing, as two men approached. He searched for signs of hostility and found none. They only appeared hopeful of being invited to share the pipe. At once, Nathan offered it, and each man took his turn before passing it to Iliab.

"*Allah Akbar!*" Iliab roared again.

"*Allah Akbar!* Allah is great!" they all repeated.

"So this is where you have gone," said the younger of the two. Iliab recognized him as the one who had inspected his rifle. "I wanted my friend to see your beautiful weapon."

"By the Prophet! It's a day that man must find shade or die!" Iliab gestured for the men to sit in the shadow of the wall. They quickly obliged. "I am honored that you find my unworthy weapon of such interest." He handed the man's friend his rifle.

"Unworthy!" cried the young terrorist who had already seen it and who even now looked at it as though it was a beautiful woman. "It's a most wondrous instrument, a most magnificent instrument!"

Iliab's weapon was a Russian SR3M automatic assault rifle used by many in the Russian secret service or Special Forces. Not always easy to get. Its balance and precision were impeccable. In addition, he had added some ornate features. The entire rifle butt was overlaid with a latticework of sterling silver.

"Unworthy!" repeated the young man.

"Perhaps to the eye, it pleases. But it has yet to be used to end the life of a single Zionist. Does not the Quran, in *surah* fifty-seven, tell us of the punishment due unbelievers? And does not *surah* twenty-two tell us that because the Jews were led astray from Islam they must be humiliated in this world?"

The other three men nodded. "Yes, it is so," they all agreed.

"Ah! So you see, this unworthy weapon has yet to humiliate one Jew! It has only been used to protect a gold and silver peddler from the poor unfortunate men brought low by the Zionist pigs and their capitalist cohorts. Do not the Jews ruin the whole world with their greed? And because of this, aren't the desperados who rob along the roadside, forced by their regrettable circumstances to squeeze out a living from someone else's pocket? A thousand curses on the dirty Jews! It is they who steal Muslim land, rape Muslim women, butcher Muslim children. It is they who have forced our brothers to live in squalor! By Allah's beard, I swear I will kill a thousand with this rifle before I'm through!"

The young terrorist holding Iliab's firearm nodded. "It is our duty to relieve the earth of all Jewish scum. You are correct. This is an unworthy weapon," so saying, he handed it back to Iliab.

The scarred-face man waved it high in the air. "*Allah Akbar!* Death to the Jews!" The three joined in with similar shouts, pausing long enough to drag on the pipe as it was passed. When the last ember in the bowl went out, the two terrorists departed, somewhat unsteadily on their feet. Not so, Nathan and Iliab, as they had been careful not to inhale.

Without further incident, they reached Izzat's truck. The gold peddler was already packed. Several other trucks were, too, but Izzat prudently waited for them to leave before pulling out. Iliab and Nathan followed on horseback.

As the wheels of the truck again churned the desert dust, Iliab resisted the impulse to look back. He envisioned an angry mob behind him. But when he listened he heard no shouts or foot-falls or gunfire.

Their deed still remained undiscovered. And only the crunching of dirt and the whining engines of the departing caravan filled the air.

The peddler's assistant had, by previous instruction, made a small puncture in one of the tires. The disability was of no consequence for they had with them the means to quickly repair it. About half an hour into their journey, the sabotaged tire finally flattened.

This created excitement among the other drivers as word of Izzat's distress traveled throughout the caravan. There were offers of help, but Izzat refused. He had three able-bodied men, he insisted. There were wails of protest and feigned distaste at leaving the gold peddler, but in truth, all the drivers were anxious to be off. No one wanted to be caught in the desert at night. So, after invoking Allah's blessing and protection upon Izzat and his companions, everyone hastily departed, including the cartel guards.

The tire was repaired, and two more rifles were pulled from a secret compartment in the truck. Within twenty minutes they were moving again, not south as the other trucks had gone, but eastward, toward the ravine.

At a designated spot, the truck stopped, and Iliab and Nathan dismounted. Izzat and his assistant would remain here until early morning with the horses. They would cover the other two men. If anyone followed, it would be up to the peddlers to stop them. Ten miles away—the nearest place a truck was able to drive in the gorge—Joshua Chapman and two other agents waited. Iliab was to meet Joshua with the women in three days.

Now, taking his rifle, a canteen of water and his hashish pipe, he led Nathan up the mountain and back toward the village.

Iliab didn't mind the rough terrain. As a youth, he had spent hours exploring the Judean wilderness. He was a tough, disciplined man who had mastered the art of surviving in a hostile land.

Born in Jerusalem and weaned on firearms, he could take a rifle apart and put it together in minutes by the time he was ten. By eighteen, he was in the Israeli army and had seen a dozen border skirmishes.

By twenty he was captured and imprisoned in an Arab jail where he spent the next five years being tortured until the Mossad rescued him.

He came out bitter and with a thirst for revenge, and found an outlet for them both as a sharpshooter for the Mossad. He had killed many and had buried his share of friends who, in turn, were killed.

But now at forty-one his interest was no longer revenge but the survival of Israel. He was certain Israel was the last hope for world Jewry.

He and Nathan trudged along until they reached the outskirts of Seco Polvo. They were on heightened alert, now. Sentries were posted all around, and the fading light made seeing even a few feet in any direction, difficult. From their position, shouts and angry cries could be heard as sporadic rifle-fire pierced the air.

It was obvious that the bodies of the dead guards had been discovered. They would have to reach the women before the terrorists took action and formed search parties. As Iliab studied the terrain in the moonlight, he knew the cave was nearby. In spite of the poor visibility, he was still able to follow the path he had memorized earlier.

Within minutes, they were inside the dark interior. Using a torch was out of the question. Its light would certainly attract the sentries. Iliab fumbled in his pocket and after finding his matches, lit one. The radius of light was no more than two feet in diameter and dwindled rapidly as the fire burned down the stem. But that was enough time and enough light for Iliab to determine that the ledge where he had left the women was a yard to his right. He took a few steps in that direction then lit another match.

"Miss Callahan," he said. "It's Iliab." The match went out. Not even the sound of breathing could be heard overhead. Iliab struck another match. "Miss Callahan! You must come quickly! We need to leave at once!"

A face peered over the ledge, and before the match went out, Iliab recognized the beautiful, dark haired engineer.

"Leave the tin of water. It is too cumbersome to carry. But throw down the bags of food. Then Nathan and I will assist you in getting off the ledge. But quickly, ladies. You must move quickly!"

Trisha tossed over the bags. "We have a problem. It's Audra. She's unconscious."

"What happened?" Iliab whispered.

"She didn't believe you were coming back and tried leaving on her own. I had to stop her. We struggled, and she hit her head on a rock. I'm sorry. I know this makes things more difficult."

"What is done, is done. No time for regrets. Quickly! Roll Miss Shields off the ledge," Iliab said. "We'll catch her."

Trisha maneuvered the limp body to the edge, and after saying a quick prayer, rolled Audra off, hopefully into four waiting arms. There was a groan as Audra's legs struck Nathan in the face, but even in the pitch black, the men managed to keep the unconscious woman from landing on the ground.

"She's fine," Iliab said as they laid Audra down. "We have her. Now, lower yourself, feet first. We'll catch you. Have no fear."

Trisha obeyed and when Iliab and Nathan had a firm grip, she let go, and in seconds stood beside them.

"Gather the bags of food," Iliab order, lighting another match.

Nathan and Trisha crouched on the ground and retrieved all but the one that had split open.

Iliab struck another match and moved to where Audra laid. When the light went out, he stooped down and slipped one arm around her torso, and lifting her into the air, deposited her, like a sack of grain, over his shoulder.

"We must move together," Iliab ordered. The three inched toward the faint glow that marked the entrance, holding onto one another until they were out of the cave.

The moonlight seemed bright in comparison to the darkness of the cavern. Even so, the path was difficult and treacherous. At times it became so narrow the trio had to pass in single file. Progress was measured in inches, and was exhausting. As they rested a moment against the huge rocks, the night air was fractured by voices overhead. Instantly, they shoved themselves into a large crevice.

"May Allah choke me with my own spit if I don't kill the scum!" said a loud, angry voice. A small group of villagers had gathered and one of the more zealous was talking to the guard positioned on the cliff.

"Yes, word was passed earlier to be on the lookout, that the women had escaped. By the Prophet! I pray they will be my bullets that bring down those daughters of a camel!"

Iliab recognized the voice as belonging to the young Muslim who showed interest in his rifle. He must have taken his place at guard duty before the bodies of Nabil and Mustafa were discovered.

"We are sure there are others," added the zealous terrorist.

"Others? But who? No one entered our village that was unknown."

"Surely you cannot believe that two frail American women could overpower and kill our glorious fighters?"

"No . . . of course not. Impossible!" replied the guard. "Why, it would take five such women to equal even one of our females. And everyone knows that even one of our women, even if she is a *shaheed* herself and has died a martyr's death, is not equal to any of our males. But . . . who then assisted these women in their crime?"

"We're not sure. It's possible Izzat's two guards had a hand in it."

"Izzat?" returned the young guard. "The gold peddler? But I myself spent time with his guards. We smoked the pipe together. I inspected one of their rifles. We cursed the dirty Jew. No . . . they can't be the ones."

"We found a new leather harness in Mustafa's house. Someone remembers seeing one of these men purchase such a harness from the leather merchant."

"Those deceiving pigs!"

"Stay alert now! And may Allah give you the eyes of an owl to see into the night and bring down the traitors."

"*Allah Akbar!*" screamed the young guard. Then the group of villagers moved onward, themselves screaming and waving their weapons in the moonlight.

When they were a good distance away, Iliab gave a series of signed commands. Immediately, Nathan rested his rifle against the boulder, removed the dagger from his sheath, and disappeared. It was obvious what had to be done. The position of the guard overhead made it impossible to progress undetected.

Iliab listened for an alarm. All was quiet except for the distant trailing voices of the terrorists moving from one checkpoint to another.

Suddenly, there was the sound of footsteps and small pebbles skittering against the boulder, then scuffling noises. Moments later, Nathan stood before them clutching his chest. With his knife, he cut cloth off the bottom of his shirt and stuffed it under one arm.

His entire right side was soaked with blood.

"Is it bad?" Iliab asked, his voice devoid of emotion.

"Yes." In faltering words he told them how he had not taken the guard by surprise. Just as he was about to strike, he lost his footing and instead of a quick, clean kill, a scuffle had ensued. In the end, Nathan got his man, but not without a price. He was certain his right lung was pierced. Breathing was painful and difficult.

"She will dress it for you." Iliab pointed to Trisha.

"No . . . it's no use. Go. I will cover you. If anyone follows, I'll stop them."

"I won't leave you," returned Iliab in a harsh whisper, his feelings finally working their way to the surface.

"You must not jeopardize the mission."

Iliab gestured to the limp body of Audra still slung over his shoulder. "If only this woman were able to walk . . . I could carry you."

Nathan struggled to pick up his rifle, then propped himself against the boulder. "But she is not. Now go. This is a good spot. They won't get past me here." He was protected on all sides. And the side facing the pathway offered him a good view. From here, he could stop anyone who tried to follow his companions.

"*Please*, my friend! Go quickly!"

Iliab stooped and deposited Audra on the ground then removed one of the bandoleers of ammunition. Without a word he draped it over Nathan's left shoulder, picked up Audra and left.

For three hours Iliab labored under the burden of Audra's limp body and his own heavy heart. Progress was slower than he had hoped. Finally, in utter exhaustion, he searched out a suitable cave. They needed rest. It was while helping to settle the women that he heard a faint, far-away sound coming from the direction of Seco Polvo.

"What is it?" Trisha whispered.

"Rifle fire."

The two stood by the cave entrance listening until the popping noise stopped and all was quiet. And both knew that Nathan Yehuda was dead.

● ● ●

"Get away from me!" Audra shrieked. Her blond, matted hair stuck to her dirt-smudged face as she pointed at something neither Iliab nor Trisha could see. "Keep it away." She dove into Trisha's arms.

"It's gone," Trisha whispered softly.

"You said that before but it keeps coming back."

"It won't if you sleep." She led Audra to the rear of their small cave. "Lie down and rest."

Large drops of perspiration streamed from Audra's face. "I'm so cold." Although the heat of the day had begun to penetrate the interior of the cave Audra's body shook, her teeth chattered. Trisha removed the black dress Nathan had given her and covered Audra with it.

"Will she be all right?" Iliab asked, a look of both concern and disgust on his face.

"She has the DTs, delirium tremens." Trisha pushed her hair from her face as she watched Audra convulse. "If she goes into shock we could lose her."

"What does she need?" Iliab barked. "Besides a drink?"

"A sedative, and she needs to be kept warm."

Iliab removed the pipe and small bag of hashish from his shirt which he had told Trisha he carried when on a mission posing as an Arab. He claimed it proved invaluable as a bribe or for loosening a stranger's tongue.

She wondered if it would prove equally useful on Audra's behalf.

He filled the pipe, lit it, then handed it to Trisha. "Make her take several puffs." Then he removed the bandoleer and his shirt.

Trisha was startled to see wide scars plating his chest. Other scars covered his back and sides.

"Use this to keep her warm," he said, handing her his shirt. Then frowning, he added, "Are all American women as spoiled and self-indulgent as that one?"

Trisha looked away. She knew what he was thinking; that Nathan had given his life to rescue two self-centered Americans. For although Iliab had not said it, Trisha was sure that in his mind he had included her with Audra.

"Make sure she is ready to travel by nightfall!" he growled, taking up the bandoleer and his rifle then moving once again toward his post by the cave entrance.

"Iliab," Trisha said softly, causing the scarred man to turn towards her. "I'm sorry about Nathan."

● ● ●

CHAPTER 16

Trisha struggled to help Audra over the dark, rocky path. They were traveling by moonlight again. The ever-present patrols made day travel too dangerous. But the rough terrain and ISA fighters on their trail weren't their only problems. Water was another. It was rationed. And right now, dust and grit coated Trisha's mouth like wallpaper. No one had thought to take Nathan's canteen. That left only Iliab's.

One canteen for three people.

Already, too much of it had been used. During the worst of Audra's DTs Trisha had persuaded Iliab to give the metallurgist extra helpings. Now, they were critically short. There would be enough food, although only handfuls of it were doled out at a time. It was rationed, too. But water, that was the real issue.

They were less than ten miles from where Joshua waited with fresh supplies but it would take another two days to reach him. Travel was slow going and the mountain so treacherous they often had to backtrack, then go forward, then backward in a zigzag pattern. It could take hours to move forward one mile.

"I'm so thirsty!" Audra grumbled. The danger of shock had passed, helped by Iliab's hashish which he had given her in small amounts. "I can't go another step unless I get some water!"

"Lower your voice!" Iliab said between clenched teeth. "There's danger all around. I've warned you of this before! Why are you such a foolish woman?"

"I'm doing my best to cooperate, but I'm *so* thirsty."

Iliab unscrewed the cap of his canteen, took a small sip and handed it to Trisha.

"Wait . . . what about me!" Audra's voice started to rise again.

Trisha was about to hand the canteen to Audra when Iliab stopped her. "No! *You* drink. One sip, like I took." Trisha obeyed, then returned the canteen to Iliab.

"We must ration the water," Iliab said, looking at Audra. "And you've already had more than your share."

"Just a sip! One sip, *please!*"

Iliab held his fist within inches of Audra's face. "If you speak loudly again I won't hesitate to silence you."

Audra compressed her lips, and for the remainder of the night didn't utter another sound.

Just before sunrise, Iliab directed them to a cave where they stayed the day discussing the journey ahead or dozing or eating their ration of dried fruit and nuts.

There was enough hashish for one more pipe and Audra smoked it sparingly, trying to make it last. It seemed to improve her mood. The sore spot was still water. They were allowed two small sips for the entire day, and one small sip during their travel at night.

"The ISA fighters are still searching for us," Iliab said, slipping on the bandoleer and slinging his rifle over one shoulder. The women had already gathered up the goatskin sacks containing their food and tied them to their belts. The cave was black now, and the three stood by the mouth waiting for the last trace of sun to disappear.

"How far away are they?" Trisha asked.

"Half a day, judging from their dust." It was Iliab's practice to spend part of the daylight hours scouting. "It's a small group, maybe four or five men. But there must be dozens more all over the mountain, and their advantage is they travel by day and cover more ground than we do. Even so, we can escape detection if we're not careless. They cannot see us in the dark."

That night the three pushed harder than ever, spurred on by the thought of the trailing ISA fighters. But it was not without incident. The jagged rocks and sudden drops made the hike treacherous. Sometimes the trail was a narrow ledge. Other times there was no trail at all and ground was covered by crawling over boulders.

Night travel would have been impossible if it were not for the full moon. But even with it, every step was one of chance and danger. It was while rounding one of those narrow ledges that Audra lost her footing and fell ten feet into a chasm. Retrieving her was difficult, and valuable time was lost.

After that, she limped and began complaining again. "I can't walk! Don't go so fast!" she repeated like a stalled recording until Iliab threatened to leave her behind. For the next three hours Audra traveled in silence. But by the time Iliab began looking for a cave in which to spend the day, her ankle was swollen to twice its size and she dragged her foot as she leaned on Trisha for support.

By daybreak they were in their new cave. While Trisha and Audra rested, Iliab scouted the area. When he returned he told the pair they were not as close to where Joshua Chapman and the other agents waited as they should be. If they didn't reach their destination by tomorrow morning Joshua had orders to pull out, and with him the two transport trucks as well as fresh food and water.

Audra cried when she heard the news.

Trisha prayed. She was sure their only option now was day travel, and wasn't surprised when Iliab's order came.

"Sleep now. In another hour we move out."

"I can't sleep," Audra said with a moan. "My ankle hurts too much."

"Then rest. But rested or not, we all leave when I say."

"I'm sick of you telling me what to do!"

"Keep your voice down!" Iliab barked.

"And if I don't, what will you do? Kill me?" Audra was becoming hysterical.

Without another word, Iliab walked over to her.

"What? Stop that! Let go! What . . . what are you . . . ." Then she went limp.

"Did you hurt her?" Trisha asked with a frown.

"No. Just rendered her unconscious."

Trisha looked down at Audra's sprawled body. "I'm sorry."

"Why are *you* sorry?"

"Because you've risked your life, and lost your friend, and we seem to give you nothing but trouble."

Iliab shrugged. "I've been on worse missions. And this is what I am now. I suppose I'm no longer suited for anything else. Perhaps that's why I'm so callous."

"No, not callous. You forget I was with you when Nathan died."

• • •

Mike sat on a patch of grass and leaned against the corrugated wall of the hangar, listening to the distant sound of pounding waves. This was the spot where he and Trisha sat after Renee's death. He'd give anything to have Trisha here now. He could think of little else. Even the progress of the P2 mock-up didn't alter his mood or relieve his agony of mind.

He had never felt so alone.

Buck was away, too, somewhere over Mexico heading for a secret CIA landing strip. If the rescue was successful, Buck would fly the women home. Flight plans and rendezvous points had been furnished by the Mossad and cleared by DHS. Still, it was a civilian who had to go. If anything went wrong, DHS didn't want any of their team found in Mexico.

Mike had wanted to be the one flying that plane, but he had been overruled by Peter Meyers. The P2 project had first priority, he was told. A fusion powered airplane had military applications and the government was too invested in PA to have something happen to Mike now. While Pete and the government were covering their backsides, Mike stood to lose not only the woman he loved, but his best friend.

If anything happened, how could he bear losing them both?

He pulled a black, pocket Bible from his shirt. It had been important to Trisha. Carrying it around made him feel closer to her. When he opened it, a crumpled paper fluttered to the ground. He picked it up. Trisha's bookmark? Or had she meant for him to find it? It was her handwriting. He quickly read it.

What is the praise of men
But grains of sand that shift
With every passing breeze,
To form small, barren mounds,
First here, then there.

He felt a dull ache in his chest as the words sank in. Everything seemed unimportant now. Even the P2. He carefully folded the paper and slipped it back into the Bible as he thought of what Mrs. Callahan had said.

Nothing was impossible with God.

She made having faith sound easy. But it wasn't easy. Not for him. *Just the sincere cry of a longing soul,* that's what she had said it took.

"Oh God, why? *Why* did You allow this to happen to the only woman I've ever loved?" His eyes narrowed. He had read the Biblical story about how Jacob had wrestled with God. Well, he could identify with that. If that's what it took, he would wrestle with Him, too. He opened the Bible. "Are you real, God?" He looked toward heaven and shook his fist. "I swear, I won't leave this place until I find out!"

• • •

"Wake up! Come on! Wake up!" Iliab said, shaking the two women who lay sleeping near each other on the cave floor. "I've been keeping watch and we've got one, possibly two patrols on our tail. According to all the maps I've studied, the safest place for a descent is up ahead. That's where we'll scale down the mountain to the gorge. And *she* better not hold us up!" Iliab gestured toward Audra who sat rubbing her face.

"I'll try my best, but it's not my fault I can hardly walk."

Iliab bent down and inspected her ankle.

"Ouch! Stop pressing it! Can't you see it's swollen?"

Without a word, he cut a long strip of material from his shirt then wrapped it around Audra's ankle.

Her eyes narrowed as she watched him. "What did you do . . . before . . . ?"

"I used a three-pressure point technique, to quiet you down."

"It felt more like a karate chop. You belted me right behind the ear, didn't you?"

"Stop it, Audra," Trisha snapped. "Iliab isn't your enemy. He's doing everything he can to help us."

"Who asked you, you *prig*?" Audra's eyes flared as though remembering how day after day Mustafa had called her and not Trisha into his office. "I'm sick of everyone telling me what to do."

Iliab grabbed Audra's shoulder. "Get hold of yourself! If you lose it, so help me I'll knock you out again and leave you! There's an armed patrol on our heels, not even an hour away. The terrain we must cover today is the most difficult yet. Eat something. And be ready to go in five minutes or stay behind!"

Audra bit her quivering lip as she unfastened the bag of nuts at her waist. She shoved a handful into her mouth then spit them out. "I can't eat this. I'm so dry I'll choke."

As Iliab reached for Audra, Trisha grabbed his arm. "Please, Iliab. Give her my water."

"I'll not let her drag us down. Either she cooperates or I'll kill her myself."

Audra jutted her chin. "If I thought you meant it, I'd tell you to go ahead. But you'd leave me behind, for *them,* for the terrorists to find, wouldn't you?" With a shaking hand she tied the goatskin bag to her waist as though trying to tie together the raveling ends of her nerves. "But I'll not give you the satisfaction. Keep your ration, Trisha. I don't want it. I can manage."

Iliab studied Audra, not even trying to conceal his doubt. "Let's move," he finally ordered. But his look said he would be watching her closely.

• • •

Three long and painful hours later, Audra stood by a steep, jagged drop thinking she should throw herself off and be done with it. The pain in her ankle was unbearable. And relentless. It radiated throughout her entire body, making her want to vomit.

She could think of nothing else.

Now, she was faced with having to scale down the side of this rugged bluff. Trisha and Iliab had helped support her along the mountain. But even that would be impossible. It would be every man for himself. She didn't see how she could make it. It would be easier to just sail through the air and onto the rocks below, mercifully dead.

The view was hypnotic. And just when she was ready to let go, she saw a pair of tan boots step toward her and stop.

"You can do this," Iliab said. "It will be difficult, but you can do it."

Audra continued staring at his boots.

"Miss Shields, we must start now. I will go first, then you, then Miss Callahan. I'm putting you between us and we'll try to help you as much as possible."

"Tan boots. He wore tan boots!"

As Iliab studied her, Audra knew what he was thinking. In a few minutes they would be hanging over the precipice. If she became hysterical it would mean disaster. She could pull both him and Trisha down with her.

"We must go!" he said sharply.

"You don't understand. Tan work-boots! I know who kidnapped me. It was Bubba Hanagan!"

"You'll have time to deal with your kidnapper later. But now you must concentrate on the task before you."

"Bubba. Bubba Hanagan," Audra mumbled. She failed to see Iliab's hand move for his dagger. "Bubba Hanagan," she repeated. He was the one responsible for those weeks of degradation in Seco Polvo; the one responsible for the nights spent sleeping in dark, uncomfortable caves; for eating out of goatskin sacks like an animal; for trudging over this hostile, rough mountain; for her terrible thirst; for her painful, swollen ankle; and now, for having to dive off this cliff in the hope of putting herself out of her misery. *Bubba Hanagan!*

Waves of hatred rolled over her like a tsunami, filling her, inflating her.

"Iliab!" The sound of Trisha's frightened voice jolted Audra. When she saw the dagger in his hand, she knew what he was about to do.

"I cannot leave her for the ISA fighters to find. It would be too cruel." Iliab took a step closer.

"Don't do it," Audra found herself saying. A moment ago she would have welcomed it. But the adrenaline of hate had pumped her up, revitalized her. "I'm alright. I can make it. I'm sure I can."

Iliab's dagger moved toward Audra's throat. "She's a risk and could get us all killed." He stopped when he saw her hate-filled eyes and squinted as though deciding what to do, then he sheathed the dagger. "Okay, I'll take the chance. I go first, then you."

The descent was slow. Once, Audra stopped and cried from the pain. She needed to use her leg with the bad ankle for balance. Often times it would have to support her entire weight as the other foot probed the rocks for the next safe foothold. More than once she was tempted to give up. But then she'd probe again with her good foot and the group moved further down the incline. The jagged rocks ripped their skin and clothing as they went while Iliab pressed the women to move faster.

When he reached level ground, he removed the rifle from his shoulder and positioned himself behind a boulder. He didn't have to wait long for suddenly four men appeared at the top of the ridge. He opened fire, drawing attention away from the women who were still exposed as they maneuvered the last several feet of the crag. Then noise, like firecrackers, exploded in the air as the four terrorists responded.

A bullet grazed a rock next to Trisha, slicing off a tiny stone chip, as sharp as a razor, and cutting her hand. As she wiped it on her jeans, Trisha saw the body of one of the fighters fly past her. By the time she reached level ground, another body had fallen. Now, there were only two fighters left, and they would have to scale the same precipice.

To the side of the boulder where Iliab crouched was the dried gorge that cut between the mountains. Somewhere ahead, Joshua and his men waited. "It will be an easy trip, now. We should reach Joshua before the two fighters scale the bluff. But other patrols must have heard our gunfire and will be coming, so we must move quickly."

He looked at the two women squatting next to him. Audra's cracked lips were bleeding. Her body was bruised and cut, her blouse, shredded. Large tears streamed her pale cheeks as she clutched her ankle. The climb had all but finished her. Trisha sat beside her, her lips and body equally battered; her left hand caked with dried blood.

"Up! Get to your feet!" Iliab said gruffly.

Audra began to sob. But when she looked at Iliab's boots she wiped her cheeks with the back of her hands, and with Trisha's help, rose to her feet. Then leaning on the engineer's shoulder, she slowly moved one foot in front of the other.

"Come on! Come on!" snapped Iliab. And throughout the rest of their journey he drove them like cattle, whipping them with his tongue. "Faster! Move!"

"I hate you!" Audra blurted, half crazed from pain and thirst and exhaustion.

"I'm not concerned with your feelings, Miss Shields. So, don't waste your energy on such useless words. Now . . . move . . . quickly . . . quickly!"

And so it went, until Trisha spotted a pair of trucks nestled between two boulders framed by rifle barrels. When they were recognized, Joshua and his men were all over them, half carrying, half dragging the women to the trucks; laughing and congratulating Iliab as they went. For Trisha, there were added displays of affection from Joshua as he hugged and kissed her.

"Where's Nathan?" Joshua said, looking around.

"He didn't make it." Iliab's tone was emotionless, but for a time, the laughter and chatter stopped.

As the women guzzled water from fresh canteens, Iliab looked backward at the path. "We need to go. There are sure to be one or more patrols on their way here. If we get a head start the fighters won't be able to catch us on foot."

He ushered Audra, then Trisha, onto the truck, and slipped in beside them. Within seconds, he pulled ammunition from his bandoleer, reloaded his rifle, then positioned it for laying cover fire.

Audra was already sprawled on the truck bed. She had never felt so battered or in such pain. She tried ignoring Trisha, who was praying as usual. The praying irritated her, though Trisha prayed silently and off to the side.

"If we travel the rest of the day we can reach the airstrip where a plane awaits you. You are almost home," Iliab said.

"Yes, but at such a great price!" Trisha responded.

"In this world, everything must be paid for, one way or another," he returned dryly.

Audra rolled onto her side. Yes, that was the very thing she was thinking. And she was determined to extract payment.

● ● ●

CHAPTER 17

J oshua sat in Mike's office watching agent Peter Meyers turn various shades of red.

"This was not authorized!" Peter shouted. "The Mossad never cleared this with DHS! You spoke of a better partnership between us. Is this what it looks like?"

"Our agency knew you wouldn't want your fingerprints on it, so we took the initiative. You should be glad there's one less terrorist camp in Mexico," Joshua returned calmly.

"One less terrorist camp? You've got to be kidding! Seco Polvo was incinerated!"

"To everyone's satisfaction. Even the Mexican government. Why else would they have their newspapers write it up as a drug war between two rival cartels?" Joshua's lips formed a crescent.

"Yeah. According to their news, two unmarked helicopters swooped down on Seco Polvo and pulverized them with what the reporter believed were ATAS, air-to-air Stinger missiles. Stinger missiles? For crying out loud, talk about overkill!"

Joshua leaned forward. "This is war, not a polite parlor game. We don't take short cuts or do half measures. That's why we'll win. The Mossad is thorough. Besides, we wanted to send a message."

Mike thumped his desk. "Where is the argument? Joshua is right. The mission was accomplished. The women are safe. We should be rejoicing. It's a victory for the good guys. And I agree with Joshua on the message part. ISA will think twice, now, before trying to kidnap one of ours."

"How are the women by the way?" Joshua said.

Peter slid down in his chair like a petulant child, but his countenance told Joshua the verbal tongue-lashing was over. "I haven't seen them since their debriefing. Right now Trisha is staying at a motel in Everman under heavy DHS security and Audra is still detained."

"Trisha looks thin," Mike said. "But her color is coming back and her lips aren't bleeding anymore. She still looks pretty banged up, though." He frowned when he saw the look on Joshua's face. "What?"

Joshua still felt sorry for his brother for losing Trisha, but like anyone who had loved and lost, he'd get over it. Hadn't he gotten over losing Rachel? Or . . . almost? At least he was working on it. "And Audra? How is she?"

Mike appeared embarrassed for having forgotten her. "I hear she's doing okay. After her debriefing, she was forced to check into Everman City Hospital under an assumed name for further observation."

"Regarding her mental stability?"

Mike nodded.

"I'm not surprised," Joshua said. "She seemed pretty fragile on the trek home."

"But this whole thing still doesn't make sense," Mike said with a frown. "What did ISA hope to gain? As much as I hate saying it, if they wanted to stop the P2 wouldn't they have been better off killing them both? But a kidnapping for ransom? That doesn't add up."

"The Mossad agrees," Joshua said, feeling a familiar rage come over him. "Believe me, if destroying your project was Kamal's purpose, you'd have found the women dead in their apartments. He has no qualms in murdering anyone, no matter their sex or age."

He glanced at Peter. "Our agents have learned that while Tafco Oil was interested in stopping the P2 project, Kamal was interested in obtaining the specs."

Peter shook his head. "No, your boys are wrong this time. Both ISIS and ISA want to stop all use of alternative energy. They want everyone using oil so they can control it and its revenue as a means of crippling the industrialized west and filling their war chests."

Joshua picked up one of the brown envelopes sitting on the desk in front of him and handed it to Mike. "Here's proof that Kamal and Robert Gunther made a deal with Russia to obtain your specs, unbeknown to ISIS or ISA, or even Tafco Oil, and for a large sum. When the attempts failed, Kamal decided to take the women, instead.

"It's not clear whether Gunther was privy to this part of the plan. At any rate, when they didn't succeed, Kamal settled on the idea of a ransom, maybe figuring a little money was better than nothing. So he made the demand reasonable, just a million dollars, something doable for you. But we don't think Kamal's men at Seco Polvo knew he was operating on his own rather than under orders."

Mike tossed the envelope onto his desk. "So what part did Tafco Oil play?"

"The part that involved sabotaging your project in hope of stopping it. Robert Gunther, on the other hand, wanted to profit from it personally by selling the specs to the Russians. Right now the agency is inclined to believe Gunther was acting without permission, and in sole collaboration with Kamal."

"I never did trust him! But this! It's beyond the pale."

"Tafco Oil has other sins to answer for," Joshua said as he watched Peter drum his fingers on the arms of his chair. After a brief hesitation, he slid the second, even larger, brown envelope across the desk. "Here's the proof you'll need, Peter, to get your country back."

Peter tapped the envelope. "Something tells me this is trouble."

"Plenty of it. It shows how President Thaddeus Baker used government funds to pay Tafco Oil to build five internment camps in preparation for when he declared martial law. In exchange, Baker was to push Israel to relinquish their oil holdings in the Golan, after which Tafco would be paid to extract the oil. Baker was even prepared to back a Russian-Syrian invasion to accomplish it. Apparently the three of them, Tafco, Russia and Syria were to share the spoils.

"It's also obvious that declaring martial law was Baker's plan all along. The report details how he did it by enlisting the aid of imams and members of American based Islamic groups, as well as elements of the Islamic Brotherhood to foment riots in major cities and start an anti-police campaign. Then, when lawlessness spiraled out of control it would set up the perfect scenario for establishing martial law.

"It's possible he wouldn't have followed through on the plan if his puppet, Senator Garby, had a chance of winning the presidential election. Having Garby as president would enable Baker to essentially conduct a third term behind the scenes, much like Vladimir Putin did with Medvedev. But when it became obvious it was not going to happen, Baker settled on Plan B—a forced takeover of the country."

Peter's fingers rested on the envelope. "This is explosive stuff. If it's true, if your so-called proof holds up, it makes it dangerous. People have died in the riots, many more taken to internment camps under the guise of maintaining law and order. What makes you think President Baker will stop at that? What's my life, or the life of anyone else worth if it threatens to thwart his plans?"

"Nothing. That's why you must share this with people you trust. I suggest you begin by leaking it to the press, a press not sympathetic to Baker or they'll squash it. I would be lying if I said Israel isn't anxious for you to do this. President Baker has begun what we call the 'Hitler Plan.' He's blaming Israel and the Jews for the rise in world terrorism. He's doing what Hitler did, making us the scapegoat. It's also one way he can justify martial law. Between the riots at home and the increasing terrorist threats, people will continue to be tolerant of his takeover. When citizens are afraid, it makes them more willing to give up their liberties."

Peter picked up the envelope and slipped it into his briefcase. "Only the president can end martial law and reinstitute our constitutional structure. Impeaching him may be impossible. Many powerful leaders in congress support him. And even if we could impeach, it would all be for naught if we don't have an honest candidate to fill the presidency.

"No one has seen or heard from Senator Merrill in weeks. No one knows where he is. It's rumored he's been arrested and taken to one of the internment camps. Is he alive? Or dead? No one knows that either. And if he's dead and we manage impeachment then the lifting of martial law and new elections, what do we gain if there's no one but Garby on the ballot?"

Joshua smiled. "Don't worry about that. If and when you're able to hold elections, you'll have your honest candidate."

"Don't tell me your boys have him?" Peter said, frowning.

"This debriefing is over, gentlemen." Joshua rose to his feet. "I've given you the number where you can reach me. And use a secure line when you call. It's not just your necks on the line. We have several there as well. But considering President Baker's 'Hitler Plan' I don't know how much longer we'll be able to work together."

Mike's intercom buzzed just as Joshua turned to go. "I told you I didn't want to be interrupted. *What?*" Mike motioned with his hand for Joshua to wait. "Are you sure? What did he say? All right . . . put him through." Mike's face tightened as he picked up the desk phone. "It's for you, Joshua. The man claims to be *Kamal*."

Joshua took the phone. "Yes." He listened to the familiar voice identify himself. "What do you want?"

"Payback. It's coming. You took my property. Those women were mine. And you incinerated my town, killed my men. Now, it is time for you to lose something. Perhaps your brother or your new friend, Cassy. I haven't decided which. Maybe both. But you shouldn't mind so much, me removing Cassy's head from her shoulders. She's not as beautiful as your Rachel was. But I can make sure it is more painful. Whatever I do, whoever I do it to, it will be painful, rest assured of that." Then the phone went dead.

Joshua hung up his end, then pulled his cell phone from his pocket and began punching numbers.

"Was that really Kamal? Peter asked. "What did he want?"

Without answering, Joshua bolted out the door.

● ● ●

Joshua pressed hard on the door bell. Even from his position in the hall, he heard the annoying ring that pulsed nonstop at the command of his thumb. His other hand was on the Berretta tucked behind his back. No telling if ISA got here ahead of him. He released the gun when the door opened and he saw Cassy.

"Well," she said, folding her arms across her chest, "I didn't expect you to be *this* anxious to see me. Not after you leave town without a word and don't even bother calling. Am I supposed to be all flustered and excited that you've decided to pay me a visit?"

Without a word, Joshua shoved Cassy inside then closed and bolted the door.

"Easy lover-boy. If you think it's going to be that simple you've got . . . ."

Joshua grabbed her and kissed her. "Now, will you stop talking and listen?" he said, releasing her. "You always have to get the last word, and there isn't time."

He told her about Kamal's threat and watched color drain from her face. "You must be taken to safety. Two Mossad agents will fly you to Tel Aviv where you'll stay in a safe house, under heavy guard."

Cassy pursed her lips as she shoved her growing bangs behind one ear. "I don't want to go to Tel Aviv."

"It's only for a little while. Until we get Kamal."

"And how long have you been on his trail? Two years. Isn't that what you told me?"

"Yes, but . . . ."

"I'm not leaving my apartment or my work for that long. Besides, this is your opportunity, Joshua. You have him where you want him. He's desperate to hurt you. To extract revenge. Use that against him. Let me stay and be your decoy. Let's finish him once and for all."

When Joshua looked away, Cassy tugged on his arm. "That's what they want me to do, isn't it? The Mossad wants me to be their decoy."

Joshua nodded. "I told them, no. We're not dealing with a man but a devil. Without a conscience, and capable of anything. And Kamal promised that whatever he did would be painful. Not like last time when he killed . . . ."

"Finish it, Joshua. When he killed Rachel?"

"Yes. And I can't let that happen again to someone I . . . ."

"to someone you like, respect, find funny . . . what?"

"You really want me to say it?"

"Yes."

"To someone I like a lot."

"You mean in the way you like baseball a lot or bubblegum a lot or . . . ."

"Love . . . I should have said love, ok? And I can't go through that again. I can't let that butcher do it again."

"Well, thank you. That's the first time you've actually used the word 'love'. And if I didn't love you, too, I'd probably take that vacation you offered me in Tel Aviv. But the problem is, I do love you, Joshua. And Kamal has made this *our* fight. And together we can beat him."

● ● ●

Hours later, Joshua showed up at his brother's apartment accompanied by two men in black suits. "Pack your things," he said. "You're going on a trip."

• • •

"How reliable are his sources?" Trisha asked, outwardly calm, but inwardly seething.

Mike handed her a baloney sandwich and settled in a nearby chair. "Not the best accommodations," he said, looking around the small motel room. "Can't DHS do better than this?"

"I'm supposed to be keeping a low profile, remember. Not splashing around a grand pool at the Ritz. But let's get back to Joshua. Did he really prove that Tafco Oil, or at least Robert Gunther, was behind the abduction?"

It had been a week since she left Nathan Yehuda in the mountains. The remainder of the trip to safety and the days that followed were, for Trisha, almost as much a blur as her initial abduction. Buck had been waiting at the airstrip. There was the flight home. Then came a trip to a giant, gray-green fortress—a military installation of some sort—for a physical and a battery of questions. And finally, the reunion with Mike. He had come often to see her but this was the first time he had come here, to the motel, the first time they had been alone, without doctors or nurses or secret service body guards, though two guards stood outside their door.

"It appears that Gunther was the mastermind behind the Russian deal. Then things took a turn when he was unable to steal the specs. We're not sure Gunther ever intended for you or Audra to be abducted but certainly once he found out he went along or at least didn't stop it.

"So far, the news of your rescue has not been made public. But Pete has scheduled a press conference for early evening. An official DHS statement will be given. He also wants a brief statement from you. Audra won't be there. They say physically she's healing nicely, but questions have been raised about her mental stability."

Trisha took a bite of her sandwich. Though she had been given a clean bill of health not all was well with her, either. Resentment and anger continued to gnaw at her. Since her return she had thought of nothing but her ordeal and the people responsible. She found it difficult to pray, and was moody. And Iliab's words haunted her.

Everything was bought with a price.

God had paid an awesome price for her. He had paid with His Son. The price she must pay was to surrender to His will. She would have to forgive. "Well, how reliable are Joshua's sources?" she repeated.

"Reliable as any bribed information can be."

"So you're saying that while Gunther was trying to steal our specs, Tafco was trying to sabotage the project, to stop the P2. I guess I can understand that, in a way. At two hundred fifty dollars a barrel of oil, Tafco stands to lose a great deal of future revenue if our plane is successful. As long as ISIS and ISA continue to wage war, oil prices will continue to soar. And the war could last for years. It also means that Tafco is not only responsible for the autoclave explosion, but Nolan and . . . Renee's death."

"Yes. And do you know the worst part? They may get away with it."

"What about Joshua's proof?" Trisha asked almost desperately. Forgiveness was easier if it came with a pound of flesh.

"I'm not sure it would hold up in court. Understand that this information was bought in a back alley or extracted by torture."

Trisha felt her stomach knot. It couldn't end like this. Surely justice would be served. But even the man who had abducted her had not been found, despite her detailed description. He had disappeared without a trace. "What about this Hanagan . . . Bubba Hanagan that Audra claimed kidnapped her?"

"During her debriefing she told Pete about the incident on the bluff. But she swore she was mistaken; that she had temporarily snapped under the pressure. She claims he's just a former boyfriend who jilted her. That could account for her hostility. But DHS will check him out. And Pete will also investigate Alex Harner and Gunther."

Trisha placed her sandwich on the paper plate. "I've lost my appetite."

Mike leaned over and took her hand. "When the dust settles and we have more time, I want to hear all about what happened out there, at Seco Polvo and in the mountains. Every detail. We've had a page ripped off our calendar, an entire month stolen from us, and we need to try and get it back. And I have a lot to tell you, too. I've been reading that Bible you gave me and stumbled on the story of Jacob. And I guess you could say I had a fight with God, too. And it changed me."

"Can't you tell me now? I'd love to hear about it."

"No. We need to rehearse what you're going to say at the press conference. You'll be facing a battery of cameras and have to be prepared."

Trisha swallowed her disappointment and nodded. Yet she knew that even when they had the long hours to share their experiences, it would only be shared in part. There would be fragments, pieces of that month, which could never be fully explained or understood by the other.

And in a strange way, that made her sad.

• • •

Audra still had a slight limp as she walked down the corridor of a dilapidated apartment building. She scanned the numbers on the doors and stopped in front of number twenty-four. In her mind, she had stood before this door a hundred times. The past week was all a fog. She remembered few details. The only consistent and clear memory was the scenario she was about to enact. It had been the one overriding imagery filling her mind. And she had managed to be very clever when DHS questioned her about Bubba Hanagan. She was not going to allow them to mess things up.

But getting out of Everman City Hospital, undetected, had been tricky. DHS had already retrieved some clothes and shoes, and even her purse from her apartment so she didn't have to wear those hideous hospital gowns—all in an attempt to make her feel less a patient and more like the "guest" they insisted she was.

They hadn't fooled her. Their agents were everywhere, watching her and making sure she didn't escape. Still, she managed it by climbing out a three story window.

Audra chuckled to herself as she thought of it. The experience in the mountains had proven useful after all. She was able to shinny down the drainpipe with ease. After that, she had stopped at her apartment to pick up the .25 caliber.

DHS had removed the one in her purse.

She also picked up the key which she now carried in her hand. She inserted it into the lock. No, DHS wasn't going to rob her of her revenge. It was for this that she had managed to survive the descent on the ridge, the painful trek in the gorge. It was for this that her will to live had been restored.

She removed the gun from her purse then turned the knob and entered the apartment. It was dingy and ill kept, with newspapers and empty snack bags of chips, pretzels and the like littering the floor.

He was such a slob.

She moved through the cluttered living room toward the kitchen where a radio blasted a country-western tune. And there was Bubba Hanagan, standing by the counter making himself a ham sandwich and singing off key.

"Oh little darlin' I knowed you'd leave me some day-a."

She pointed the silver .25 caliber at his face. She knew what a bullet could do to human flesh. She had seen it in Mexico. One blast could render it unrecognizable. That's what she was going to do to him. "Your little darlin' has returned," Audra said with a sneer.

Hanagan's massive body recoiled. "How in the world . . . ?"

"I'm going to kill you, Bubba!" Audra shrieked. Her eyes were wide, fierce. In one blast she was going to erase the memory of her crawling on straw mats, the vodka bottles, the trips to Mustafa's office. They were going to be gone, all gone, wiped away like a bad dream. And she was going to wake up and be Audra Shields again: brilliant, hard working, respected.

"Well, hello there, sexy!" Bubba said, straightening. "Now, don't tell me you're still sore because I walked in on you and that dude? You never did forgive me for that. But live and let live, I always say." He moved toward her as he spoke.

"Stay where you are! Not another step!"

Hanagan smiled boyishly. "Okay, I'm easy." Even so, he continued walking.

"I'm warning you . . . ." Audra's hand shook.

There was a popping noise as the gun went off. The bullet grazed Bubba's shoulder, but still he kept coming. Audra had time to squeeze off one more shot. The bullet lodged in his upper left arm making him wince with pain. In one swift motion, his muscular right arm swung away from his chest, back-handing her and knocking her to the ground. The gun flew out of her hand and skittered across the floor. Then Hanagan picked up one of the metal kitchen chairs and smashed it across Audra's body, and she went blank.

"Look, Gunther, I need money and I need it now!"

Audra opened her eyes and saw a blurred figure of a man talking on a cell phone. When she tried to move she almost blacked out again from the pain. Breathing was difficult. She felt wet, then realized she was lying in a puddle of her own blood. She remembered the encounter with Bubba and realized she was still on his kitchen floor. Obviously, Bubba thought he had killed her. She dared not move. She closed her eyes and took short, shallow breaths.

". . . Don't tell me to keep calm! The cops will be looking for me, not you! And remember, if I fall, I won't fall alone!"

". . . You could call it a threat. You owe me."

". . . Yeah, I know you already paid me for the job. But you told me this bimbo had a one-way ticket, that she was never coming back, and the next thing I know she's standing in my kitchen with a gun."

". . . Don't con me. I didn't bargain for this. There's a dead broad in my apartment and I need to get out of here, fast. I'm just asking you to do right. That's all. Just asking for enough cash to get out of town and carry me until this thing blows over."

". . . Mexico? Sure, I'll go there. The further away from here the better. And by the way, I need a doctor to get a slug out."

". . . That's right, the bimbo shot me."

". . . No, I'll live, but I can't travel like this."

". . . Okay. I'll meet you at the usual place in thirty minutes. And Gunther . . . thanks. I knew you'd come through."

The pain made Audra lightheaded, and for a moment she blacked out again. When she came to, she heard drawers slamming as Bubba pulled clothes out of his dresser. She had heard enough of his conversation to know he was preparing to leave town. She held her breath when she heard footsteps approach, then stop next to her.

She dared not move a muscle.

She was lying on her stomach; her face partially covered by her right arm which was wet with blood and so painful she was sure it was broken. If her breathing was shallow enough he'd still think she was dead. It was her only hope.

Her eyes were closed so she didn't see Bubba raise his foot, but she felt the tan boot smash into her ribs. The crushing jar to her body caused her to bite her tongue. Hot, sticky liquid ooze between her lips. Audra heard his footsteps as he headed into the dingy living room and out the front door.

Then everything went blank.

• • •

"They've just brought Audra Shields to Everman City Hospital," said an agitated Peter Meyers, powering off his phone. He had joined Trisha and Mike at the motel. Two hours ago his agent had reported Audra missing. Since then, DHS had been raking the city and this was the first news they had of her.

"What happened?" Trisha asked.

"I don't know," Pete said, the muscles of his face clenching. "And she's in no condition to tell us, either. She's unconscious, and by the description my man gave, has taken quite a beating. She might have broken bones, possibly a concussion, and who knows what internal injuries. My man said she's a bloody mess."

Mike shot an anxious glance at Trisha. "It's not ISA again, is it, Pete?"

"No. Doesn't look like it. Audra left the hospital on her own, and, for whatever reason, didn't want us to know about it."

"Where did they find her?" Trisha asked.

"Some dumpy apartment. One of the tenants heard gunshots and called the police. When they arrived, they found the apartment door ajar and Audra on the floor, but no one else."

"Until you know more, I want Trisha to have extra protection," Mike said.

"I've already taken care of that. And I've moved the news conference up a few hours. It will be held at Everman Hospital. I want to talk to the press before this news about Audra gets out."

● ● ●

CHAPTER 18

A t four o'clock sharp, a black, unmarked SUV pulled behind Everman City Hospital. From it, stepped Mike, Trisha, and Peter Meyers. They were followed by two heavily armed men in black suits. A back door was opened by a DHS agent dressed as an orderly in a white uniform. The man led the five down the hall, onto a freight elevator used by hospital personnel, then into a large conference room on the fourth floor.

When the group entered, members of the press strained to see the heroine who had escaped the tentacles of ISA while DHS agents strained to detect any sudden or erratic movements.

"Ladies and gentlemen of the press," Peter's clear, crisp voice rang out over the microphone. "I'm sure you're all eager to hear Miss Callahan's story and how she survived her hellish ordeal. And, you'll have your chance. But first, I'd like to open this press conference with a statement. The other survivor of this ghastly kidnapping, Miss Audra Shields, now lies in critical condition right here in this hospital. It appears that another attempt by ISA was made upon her person. When she resisted, she was brutally beaten and left for dead. The doctors don't know if she'll make it. As you are all aware, we live in perilous times; times of uncertainty and tension. And we at DHS . . . ."

As Peter droned on, a heaviness fell over Trisha. The reporters had packed the room in hopes of hearing a titillating, perhaps gory story of violence and terror. Certainly Peter was priming them for that. And he had briefed her on what to say. There was not to be the slightest hint of Tafco's involvement. She was to give them what they came to hear: the agonizing ordeal of the kidnapping, the brutality of her captors, the hardships endured throughout her escape. When it was finally her turn to go on, she took a deep breath before stepping up to the podium.

Well, they would all be disappointed, all except Peter. He'd be angry.

"I'm grateful to be home," she said, speaking slowly into the microphone. "I thank God for my safe return. Truly, He went before me always. I also wish to acknowledge the brave Israeli fighters whose efforts were primarily responsible for my escape."

The room exploded with chatter as everyone spoke at once. Cameras clicked while reporters scribbled on their pads, Peter's face reddened, and Mike's eyebrows arched in interest.

"And last of all," Trisha continued, "I want to remember Nathan Yehuda, the Israeli who laid down his life so Miss Shields and I could escape."

As Trisha left the platform, dozens of reporters shouted out questions, creating pandemonium and causing DHS agents to surround her while others cleared a path for an exit. A flushed and bewildered Peter Meyers jumped in front of the podium and shouted into the microphone. "Ladies and gentlemen of the press, I'm sorry, no more questions . . . no more questions, please . . . that's quite enough. Thank you. No . . . I'm sorry . . . this press conference is over."

● ● ●

"Why did you do it, Trisha?" Peter asked as he paced back and forth in one of the doctor's lounges that had been sealed off for their use.

His face was still flushed, and his cheeks puffed in and out like two fanning billows.

"Why did you lie about Audra?" Trisha snapped.

Shortly before the news conference, DHS had learned in whose apartment Audra Shields had been found. It didn't take long to figure out the reason she was there. A Raven .25 caliber hand gun had been found on the floor when the apartment was searched. The serial number was registered to Audra. The blond metallurgist had lied to Peter and the other DHS agents regarding Bubba Hanagan. It was clear she had gone to his apartment in hope of extracting revenge. In light of this intelligence, Peter had deliberately falsified his information at the press conference.

"I didn't intend to embarrass you," Trisha continued, her voice softening. "But this entire story is becoming muddled. And when it's finished being told and retold, it won't resemble the truth at all. If I had given them what you wanted, the news media would have buried the public with an avalanche of gory details. No one would ever know about Nathan Yehuda or the other brave members of the Mossad. And they deserve more, especially now, with all the anti-Semitic fervor President Baker's crowd is whipping up. He didn't . . . he isn't . . . for heaven's sake Pete, Nathan didn't even get a decent burial!"

Peter's cheeks stopped billowing and he sat down. "I suppose you did what you thought was right, but now I'm going to have a lot of explaining to do. Many in my department are in lock-step with Baker and they're pushing the so-called 'Hitler Plan', too."

Trisha nodded. She already knew about this plan from Mike. "I'm sorry. I didn't think. That was selfish of me, putting you in a bind that way."

"Okay, so the partnership between DHS and the Mossad becomes public," Mike said, shrugging. "What's the harm? If people understand how valuable the Mossad is to us, maybe it will do some good; stem the tide of anti-Semitism here in the U.S.."

"Maybe."

Mike chuckled. "Let's face it, Pete, you'll turn out to be a hero, and in a few months they'll give you a promotion."

"Well . . . ."

"How does U.S. Secretary of Homeland Security sound?" Trisha teased.

"Here, here," Mike said, laughing.

"Well, as head of DHS I would be in a better position to expose Tafco Oil."

The smiles disappeared from everyone's face. The chances of bringing Tafco Oil to account for sabotaging PA and for Nolan and Renee's death were slim.

And they all knew it.

The remaining hope was that Peter, using the evidence he had regarding the collusion between Tafco, President Baker and various Islamic groups, could bring down Baker and martial law.

"I guess the important thing now is to get our country back and put an end to Baker's dictatorship," Mike said with a frown.

"I'm working on that and so far it's giving me nothing but insomnia. It's going to be an uphill climb." Peter shrugged. "I'll work it out. But now, let's check on Audra and see how she's doing."

Before anyone could move, a DHS agent appeared. "Sir," said the well-groomed agent, "Miss Shields has just died. We were unable to get a statement. She never regained consciousness."

● ● ●

Joshua sat in front of a bank of monitors and watched Cassy move from one room of her apartment to the other, making silly faces. She knew he was watching and it irritated him that she was trying to make light of the situation. He wished she'd stop trying to be so brave. She was a decoy, a sitting duck, a lure to bring in one of the most vicious terrorists he had ever encountered. And though DHS had set up headquarters in the apartment right next to hers, and her apartment was wired with the most sophisticated surveillance system known to man, he still knew there was plenty of danger, and no guarantee she'd come out of this in one piece.

Since their setup, he had not taken a chance on visiting her. Kamal or one of his men could already have her under surveillance. He was glad he had made his brother leave the country. At least he didn't have to worry about him, too.

"Row, row, row your boat gently down the stream," Cassy sang in a squeaky, off-key voice. Though she couldn't hear him, he could hear her. But at times like this, he wished it weren't so.

For the past forty-eight hours he had learned a lot about her. She was an early riser, worked long hours on her new assignment for DHS—which involved hacking into various Russian and Chinese systems—kept a neat apartment, ate terribly, mostly chips and soda and little frozen hamburgers that she nuked in her microwave.

His cameras covered every inch of her apartment except the bathroom, and he had even argued for that because it had a window. But reluctantly, he conceded the inappropriateness of the thing. He had no wish to be inappropriate. He just wanted to keep her safe.

If anything happened to her . . . .

"A hunting we will go, a hunting we will go," Cassy croaked.

"Oh, zip it!" Joshua mumbled as she continued singing. He was relieved to see her stand in front of the large picture window, throw up her arms in a stretching motion, then settle down at the computer desk beneath it. She never sang while working. That at least was a consolation.

He was about to go to the kitchen for coffee when he noticed a shadow moving across her wall. At first he thought it was the slant of the sun until it stopped, lingered in one spot, then moved again. And it came from the direction of the *bathroom*.

He studied the monitors covering the kitchen and bedroom. Nothing seemed amiss. When he leaned closer to the one panning the living room his heart stopped. No mistaking it—the shadow was that of a man.

He pulled the Beretta from his belt, grabbed Cassy's key and headed out the door. Within seconds he was standing by the over-turned desk chair and staring into the dark, maniacal eyes of Kamal the Blade. Cassy stood motionless. One of Kamal's arms was locked around her ribcage; the hand of the other pressed a large, curved knife against her throat.

"Put the gun down!" Kamal shrieked. "Or I'll kill her right now, in front of you."

"Nothing doing. Then you'll kill us both." Joshua pointed his gun at Kamal's forehead. "And which do you think will be faster? My gun firing a bullet into your head or your knife across Cassy's throat?"

"If you drop it, I give you my word I will be merciful. I will kill her quickly. If you don't, I will take my time. You have no out. Any second my men will come through that door and disarm you. And you'll die with the knowledge that Cassy will live long after you, and suffer greatly."

Joshua moved to his right forcing Kamal and Cassy to move closer to the desk. "If you're talking about the two men in black T-shirts lurking in the hallway, forget it. My friends have already taken care of them. The building is surrounded, Kamal. There's no escape for you." He prayed he was convincing. The thought of Kamal carving a crescent into Cassy's forehead and then . . . .

"I got in, undetected. I'll get out the same way. Do you think I didn't know you had an apartment next door? Or that you had these rooms under surveillance? You didn't count on that, did you? Me knowing. And I saw only two of your men outside while I have at least four others you know nothing about. If I don't leave soon, they will kill your men and come for me."

Joshua cupped his extended hand, the one holding the Berretta. "You'll never get out alive. Even if more of your men come, I'll kill you before they get me." He continued moving slowing to the right, forc-ing Kamal to move directly in front of the desk. And just when Kamal's face broke into a cruel smile and Joshua was sure he was going to use his knife on Cassy, a bullet whizzed through the window glass and struck Kamal in the back of his head. Within seconds, he was crumpled on the floor, dead, and Cassy was crumpled against Joshua's chest.

"I was beginning to think Iliab was never going to take his shot," Cassy said, trembling."

Joshua held her as he kicked the knife away from Kamal's hand. "I guess *he* didn't count on Iliab being the real triggerman, not me." He signaled to the apartment window across the street, where he knew Iliab was still positioned with his sniper rifle, telling him he had hit his mark. Then he looked down at Kamal's lifeless body. "He was a coward to the end, hiding behind a woman. He was brave only when it came to killing the defenseless and unarmed."

Cassy continued shaking. "I . . . I . . . I'm glad it's over."

"Come on, sit down." Joshua led her to the couch. "You were terrific, you know. I've never seen anyone braver."

"Well, you took your sweet time getting here," she said through chattering teeth. "I saw the beast coming in from the bathroom and tried warning you with my last song. Boy are you dense!"

"You mean 'a hunting we will go'? That one?"

Cassy nodded.

"How was I supposed to know? You should've told me in advance that this would be your signal."

"I was thinking on my feet."

"And by the way, you're a lousy singer."

"But you're crazy about me."

"Totally."

Cassy appeared calmer now and leaned her head on Joshua's shoulder. "So what are you going to do about it?"

"Why don't you come with me to Dimona? The Mossad could use someone like you in their cyber warfare department."

"Would I have to use a gun? I don't do guns."

"You'd have to learn how to use one—go through rigorous training. But I doubt you'll ever have to fire it for real."

"Well . . . I guess I could do that. But where would I live? I hear rent is a killer; very expensive."

"You could always bunk in with your uncle."

Cassy's eyes grew wide. "You mean *you* have him? He's *safe*?"

Joshua nodded, glad he was finally able to tell her. That was one of the conditions he had set up with headquarters. If Cassy did this, played the decoy, when it was over he'd tell her about her uncle.

She took his hand and squeezed it. "Thank you."

"So what do you say? About Dimona and your uncle's apartment?"

"Dimona sounds good. But I'm not liking the idea of sharing an apartment with Uncle Phillip. He's a vegetarian and my burger habit would drive him up a wall."

"You could always come live with me."

"You mean like your concubine or something?"

"Concubine? Nobody uses that word anymore."

"Well . . . like what then?"

"Like my wife."

Cassy sat upright. "Are you telling me you're over Rachel?"

"As much as I'll ever be, just like you're over Chad as much as you'll ever be. I'm not one to fall in love easily, Cassy. In fact, Rachel is the only woman I've ever loved . . . until you, and I don't want to lose you now. I know we can make a future together. Only one thing—no more singing, ever."

"We'll see about that," Cassy said, kissing Joshua and ignoring the two Mossad agents who had suddenly burst into the room.

● ● ●

CHAPTER 19

"Come on. Let's go to the hangar," Mike said as he opened the door of the Sea Breeze. "Everyone will be arriving soon." His large, powerful arm extended outward, and Trisha walked towards it. When she was near enough, the arm wrapped around her like a shawl. "They're going to love her. The P2 will be a huge success."

Trisha slipped her arm around Mike's waist as they walked toward the car. It had been three weeks since the press conference at the hospital; three long and difficult weeks of dodging curiosity seekers and persistent reporters. Much had gone on during her captivity. Mike had driven himself and his people almost to the breaking point. The result was that the P2 mock-up was way ahead of schedule.

During the past three weeks, Trisha had kept in touch by phone, and remained abreast of things through briefs and Mike. This meant more separation for them since he had to be at Gibs Town so often. But both agreed with Peter that Trisha needed to stay in Everman, and while shielded somewhat from the press, be visible enough to keep interest focused on her and away from what was going on in their hangar by the sea.

Now, that was no longer necessary.

The P2 mock-up was complete, and another press conference, so different from the one three weeks prior, had been scheduled for this morning.

"She's as wonderful as we think, isn't she, Mike?" Trisha thought of the terrible cost of it all.

"A stage mother's jitters? Yes, Trisha, the P2 is as wonderful as we think, and more. All Patterson Aviation should feel proud today. She's their 'special child' and the world will love her. We've done the best we could, now it's time to let go."

Trisha's eyes teared. "Letting go is harder than I thought."

Mike drew her closer. "Yes, but we're going out there now, like proud parents and cut the string."

"You mean cord, don't you," she said, smiling now. "The expression is, 'cut the cord,' as in umbilical cord."

"No, I mean string, as in purse string. It's time for the whelp to go out and make money for us!"

Rich, throaty laughter cascaded from Trisha's lips as she gazed at the man next to her. It seemed like ages since she had laughed. She almost forgot how good it felt. "Then, by all means, let's cut the string."

● ● ●

Trisha breathed in the fragrance of fresh flowers that obscured the smell of ocean. "How lovely," she murmured, as she stepped from the car. She scanned the large, white tent set up by the caterers. It shaded several tables holding huge arrangements of cut flowers. Around them were placed copious platters of hors d'oeuvres.

To one side, and away from the tent, folding chairs were arranged in neat rows. And at the end of each row was an urn of red and white roses, pink and yellow carnations, red and purple gladiolus.

In front of the chairs stood a bulletin board on which were tacked large sheets of paper.

The guests had yet to arrive. Those milling around the airstrip were employees belonging to PA or to the catering outfit Mike had hired for the day. And mingled among them were the ever present DHS agents.

Trisha whistled softly. "Impressive. Very impressive. It proves everyone is expendable. You have managed quite well without me."

"You'll never know how poorly I've managed." Mike's dark eyes searched hers. "And today you'll be indispensable." He pointed to the podium. "I hope you approve of your stage, madam."

"Seems a bit elaborate. You do remember that my presentation is short?"

"That's all I want. You're just a hors d'oeuvre, meant to whet the appetite."

"Well, thanks. You sure know how to keep a person humble." She slipped her hand into his. "Come on, let's say 'good-bye' to baby."

As soon as she entered the hangar, Trisha felt the charged atmosphere as people scurried to finish their tasks. The excitement on each face was obvious. Now, she brought fresh excitement as the hangar exploded in greetings. Most knew her well. Many had been deeply affected by her abduction. It was with genuine joy and love they greeted her now.

Trisha responded with her own smiles and waves, with handshakes and hugs. When the commotion died down, she was free to make one last greeting and farewell.

Impatiently, she dragged Mike closer so she could study the P2. Her eyes settled on the pointed beak-like forward fuselage. "She's beautiful, Mike! More beautiful than I ever imagined!"

She walked around the P2, her eyes taking in everything; the graceful, downward slope of the forward-fuselage merging into the mid-fuselage, the expanse of the sculptured wings fanning outward over the wide underbelly, the sleek aft-fuselage and aft-body where the tall, fin-like empennage rose high into the air.

There were tears of joy she wanted to weep over her. A mother had so few occasions in which to be truly self-indulgent. A child's "coming out" was one of them. But the time for self-indulgence was cut short, for suddenly someone shouted, "They're coming! They're coming!"

"Looks like you're on," Mike said, unable to conceal his pleasure.

Trisha didn't move. Her eyes kept sweeping over the P2, caressing it here and there with soft, lingering stares.

"Hey you two, come on! Everyone's here. What a turnout! They all want to see the plane. I keep sending them to the tables, but it's like trying to stop a herd of stampeding bulls with a red handkerchief. Trisha, you better give them that presentation before they storm the hangar!"

Mike nodded at Buck. "We're coming." But before he moved, he looked once more at the P2 and then at Trisha. "Yes, she is beautiful," he said, his eyes melding into hers.

Outside, parked cars and helicopters dotted the airstrip. Most of the airline executives and PA board members had come by helicopter. The cars belonged to the host of reporters who had all arrived in keen anticipation, made keener by the wave of terrorism that had plagued PA these past several months.

A cacophony of sounds shattered the air like splintering glass, and Trisha experienced a moment of uneasiness as she realized that most of it was aimed at her. But presently, she relaxed, until she saw *him* standing by the tent.

Gunther!

How did he have the nerve to show his face here? She moved to the podium as Mike quieted the crowd and invited them to take their seats. All the while Trisha's eyes remained on the thin, pasty-faced man. She prayed silently trying to deflate the rising feeling of bitterness that had become all too familiar, a feeling heightened after Bubba Hanagan's body was discovered in a garbage dump.

Hope of bringing the guilty parties to justice was quickly evaporating.

When everyone was quiet, Trisha began speaking. "Ladies," she paused to smile at the handful of women, mostly reporters, the others, members of the catering staff, "and gentlemen. You have been invited here today to experience a revolutionary new aircraft, an aircraft of many firsts, the Patterson II or P2—a commercial passenger SST, the first aircraft ever powered by nuclear fusion."

A buzz arose from the audience as people talked among themselves. Trisha stood quietly, allowing the initial impact of her words to subside. While she waited, she watched Gunther and noticed a redness creep, like an inch worm, over his face when he discovered he was being observed.

He turned away.

"My aim," she continued, "is to provide you with a brief description of the P2 and its propulsion system. Further details as well as a 'question and answer' session will be provided during the tour to follow. Also, those who wish to look at sketches of the P2 may do so." She pointed to the bulletin board beside her.

"To begin, the P2 is a wide bodied SST; the only SST in service since the retiring of the Concord. It has a variable sweep wing design with unlimited range, which means, in plain language, it can fly nonstop to any city in the world, at speeds of over 2,000 miles per hour, and at altitudes above 60,000 feet. The propulsion system consists of four mini-reactors or NPR910s; each eight feet in diameter, roughly the size of the Rolls Royce RB211 engine built for Lockheed."

She spoke for several minutes, further describing the plane and its propulsion system, along with their use of deuterium and Nolan's contributions and breakthroughs.

"I'd like to end this briefing by mentioning that use of new composite materials increased payloads by 10% over other passenger aircrafts of equal size. Some of these materials may already be familiar to you. However, the one most revolutionary is the new composite, titanium X, created by a former employee, Audra Shields." Here Trisha paused to allow the swell of the murmuring voices to shrivel. There was still public furor over Audra's death, and her name continued to make good copy in the press.

"Without titanium X, the NPR910 would not be a reality," Trisha continued. "Because of it, our engines are capable of withstanding the tremendous heat of a repeated thermonuclear explosion. In over 200 simulated flights the NPR's titanium X casing has not shown the slightest sign of corrosion or breakdown. We have, for your pleasure, prepared the NPR910 for such a simulated flight.

"Now, our staff awaits your inspection of both the NPR910 and the P2, and will be happy to answer your questions. So, without further fanfare, I'll close by saying it has been a pleasure to address you today. Thank you for coming."

Trisha left the podium to sounds of applause. It was obvious that those who had come were not disappointed. The P2 was years ahead of any aircraft in existence. But the applause and the victory became secondary as Trisha moved toward the thin, nervous-looking man beneath the tent. Already the crowd was shuffling in the opposite direction toward the hangar, making her move against the flow.

Gunther had not gone with the others but stood in place as though expecting her to seek him out. "Your disclosures were most interesting, Miss Callahan, if not startling." The pale, pasty face twitched as he forced a smile.

"They were meant to be. Precautions were taken to ensure they would be." Trisha felt the familiar anger fill her. She had to make a choice. There was always a choice. She could forgive or not.

"I had no idea you'd be so successful," Gunther said, the plastered smile still on his face.

"I guess we've both had a shock."

"What do you mean?"

"I mean, *I know*."

"I don't understand."

"We all know: Mike, Pete, all of us."

"What are you talking about?"

"Perhaps you have fooled the law and will escape punishment here. But there's a higher law which you cannot escape, and someday will face. So I release you to that law now and I . . . forgive you." She smiled, feeling freer and happier than she had in weeks.

"I assure you I haven't a clue of what you're talking about."

Her smile deepened.

"Miss Callahan, really! I . . . I'm not . . . ."

"Goodbye, Mr. Gunther," Trisha said, walking away and leaving him standing with his mouth open.

●　●　●

Once more Robert Gunther found himself with his mouth open as he stood before the committee.

"We are quite grieved over you, Robert," boomed a deep, masculine voice from the head of a long, rectangular table.

Two dozen wealthy and influential men were gathered in the room. Bankers, newspaper editors, politicians, business executives, as well as Alexander Harner and Senator Garby were present.

The meeting was taking place in an old, meticulously kept mansion belonging to the Chairman—a heavy set but impeccably dressed man; one of the most powerful bankers in the western world. He leaned against the high back of his mahogany chair. As a young boy he had watched his father conduct business in this very room— the great room—he called it, and around this same magnificently carved twenty-foot long table. Years later, after his father's death, the Chairman began having his own meetings in the great room and had been doing so for over twenty-five years.

The Chairman took a puff of his cigar, and with the other hand thumped the newspaper that lay open before him. "This," he said, striking the front page picture of the P2, "is most disappointing,

Robert. You know how I hate inefficiency. And from what I can see, you've bungled this assignment from beginning to end."

The pasty face turned red. "I . . . I tried my best."

"That's the point. Even doing your best, you failed miserably. I gave you carte blanche. You were to use every means to stop the P2. Your efforts were unimpressive, impotent. For heaven's sake, Robert, you couldn't even kill Patterson."

"How was I to know that someone else was in his private helicopter? I hired the best and . . . ."

"Still failed."

"Well, Mr. Harner didn't do much better!" Gunther blurted, as beads of perspiration dotted his forehead. "He was supposed to 'buy' Patterson; win him to our side." Gunther turned to Harner. "The autoclave would soften him, you said."

Alex Harner shrugged and smiled sheepishly. "We weren't all that confident about turning him. We figured we'd win him or kill him, whatever came first."

"Never mind that," shot the Chairman. "The primary mission was given to you, Robert. And the fact remains that all your efforts failed. In addition, you were foolish. You compromised Tafco Oil by contracting the jihadists through our Syrian branch. Good grief, man, do you know what that's going to cost! I'll have to call in a lot of favors and line dozens of pockets before I quell this thing. The plight of those women has aroused public sympathy. And the one that got stomped by your muscle bound idiot has become a national heroine."

"There was a million to one chance of these women ever leaving Seco Polvo alive. And the trail to Tafco was well covered. Only a handful could have exposed it. Am I to blame if one of them got greedy and sold out?"

"But you sold us out, too, didn't you, Robert? You and Kamal wanted to make a little money on the side. Without consulting us. Without our consent. And that has cost us dearly. Now, the papers are interested in us. Word has leaked out about our part in creating the climate for martial law. Even as we speak, forces are moving against us. Against President Baker. We've worked years behind the scenes to amass this type of power, this type of takeover. And now it may prove difficult to hold onto. And all because of your greed."

"I'm sorry. I never intended for it to thwart any of your plans. I thought that since all our efforts had failed, what was the harm in trying to get a little something for our trouble?"

"The harm!" The Chairman slammed his fist against the table. "I can't begin to tell you all the harm that has been done! Because of you we were forced to eliminate many in order to erase the trail leading to us. In other words, to tidy up *your* mess."

The Chairman paused to puff on his cigar. "Like I said, Robert, you were careless. And normally I'm a forgiving man. But this time there's too much at stake. You know how hard we've worked to get Senator Garby into position. When all our opposition is destroyed or detained in the internment camps and martial law is lifted, he'll be the only viable candidate left standing. You know our objectives, Robert. You know there's more at stake than Tafco Oil or you or me or even Senator Garby. It's a whole new world order we're talking about; an empire of unimaginable power; a new Tower of Babel if you will, based on economics, *our* economics. He who rules the gold, rules the world. And this time neither God nor man will stop it."

The expression on the Chairman's face became dark. "Your name has shown up in too many DHS reports. Your inefficiency and stupidity have caused a cloud to hang over Tafco Oil. You've left a trail that had to be erased because we can't have some wide-eyed reporter trying to make a name for himself by doing an expose´ on you or Tafco. In short, Robert, you have become an embarrassment. And you know we never leave embarrassing loose ends."

Gunther's face reddened. "You're not seriously . . . ."

"I am most serious! In our organization we do not fire. We do not demote. We *eliminate*. You understood that from the beginning."

"Yes, but . . . but surely . . . ."

"We are all expendable. Building a one world government, a new world economic system, necessitates thinking of the larger picture. We cannot quibble over one life, more or less. And if we didn't spare Senator Garby's wife, what makes you think we'll spare yours?"

The Chairman glanced at the senator. "Bad business when a wife betrays her husband. Her emails to Senator Merrill regarding our internment camps were inexcusable. But you didn't hear Senator Garby protest the necessity of removing her. Her massive stroke relieved the senator of his liability, and in fact made him a most sympathetic and attractive candidate. Who doesn't feel for a grieving widower? I'm sorry, Robert. But you are no longer an asset, and have, in fact, become a liability."

Gunther's red face paled. He understood the significance of the Chairman's words. He had one chance left. Always in such cases, the committee had the right to overrule. If enough voted on Gunther's behalf, his life would be spared.

"Before sentencing becomes official," the Chairman continued, "is there anyone who cares to cast a contrary vote?"

Frantically, Gunther looked around the table. Not one hand was raised. His eyes rested on Senator Garby. The senator shrugged as if to say, what can I do? Then Gunther turned to Harner. "Alex? Alex!"

The barrel-chested Harner squeezed out a weak laugh, "I'm sorry, Bob."

Robert Gunther dropped his face into his hands, and instead of the sobs everyone expected to hear, there arose peels of laughter. Trisha Callahan had been wrong. He had not escaped anything. The irony of it seemed overwhelmingly funny.

Twenty-four hours later, Robert Gunther was found with a bullet in his head in the same dump-sight where Hanagan had been discovered. The press buzzed for days about the murder of one of Tafco Oil's leading executives. Then finally the mystery was solved. EPD received a phone call from ISA claiming responsibility.

The case was closed and life continued as before.

• • •

Mike studied the man who sat across the desk drumming his fingers on the arms of a chair. He had never seen Pete look so tired or rumpled. His blue suit was creased, his blond hair stood up in back as though he had just gotten out of bed.

"You look awful, Pete. What's going on?"

"I've come to say goodbye. I'm being transferred to the Syrian refugee safe zone set up by the coalition. I'm 'mission support' for the medical team and other humanitarian aid we are sending."

"*What*? How could that happen? I thought you were in tight with the National Continuity Coordinator?"

"Guess not. He said I'm making too many waves, and that Syria may do me good, though I haven't the faintest idea what he means by that. I've turned the package Joshua gave me over to him and he says it'll take time to rectify the situation. But I'm doubtful he'll do anything with it. How could I have been so wrong about a person? How could the Mossad have been so wrong?"

"Maybe President Baker got to him. Bought him off or is holding something over his head or his family's head. It happens, Pete."

"Yeah, but the laugh is on him. What he doesn't know is that I've also given a duplicate to a reporter working for an independent newspaper. He's already leaked bits and pieces, but with all the crackdowns by President Baker, it might be just a matter of time before they identify him as the leaker and shut him down.

"They're already cracking down on independent tabloids and even internet use. Now, you have to obtain a special permit to run a newspaper. And soon they plan to do the same for internet use, restrict it for the average Joe, allowing fuller access only to those who obtain special permission. You won't believe the number of people disappearing every day. And I mean prominent people, important people! It looks as if President Baker is systematically eliminating every dissenting voice.

"You better watch your back, too. Baker isn't thrilled about your fusion reactor. Remember his jihad buddies don't want alternative energy. But right now you're such big news he can't move against you. Too many people interested in your P2. So for awhile at least, you're fine. But don't trust anyone. Not even my replacement." Pete rose from his chair. "I have to go pack." He smiled sardonically. "What are people wearing in Syria these days? Do you know?"

Mike had also risen. "I'll always be grateful for your part in getting Trisha safely back. If you hadn't been willing to work with the Israelis I don't know what would have happened." He extended his hand. "I'm sorry it caused you problems." He gestured toward the small, black Bible on his desk. "I'll keep you in prayer."

Pete shook Mike's hand. "I'm not sorry. It was the right thing to do. And once we stop doing what's right, once we go over to the dark side, it'll be all over. I still love my country even though it resembles more a banana republic than the America I grew up in. I don't know what's in store for me in Syria but now that you've found God, yes, I'd appreciate your prayers."

● ● ●

Bodies pressed together, like tissues in a box, along both sides of the newly paved Gibs Town runway. Heads bobbed, straining to see the P2, the great silver swan complete her first test flight, then descend for a perfect landing as TV cameras and newsmen recorded the event.

The success of the flight insured the P2 a place in history as the first nuclear powered SST in the world. It also insured national and international prominence in the here and now, for it would revolutionize air travel in particular and transportation in general. The P2 would be the forerunner of all that followed. In the not so distant future, it would fly people from New York to LA in two hours, and from D.C. to Paris in three. It was doubtful that even President Thaddeus Baker himself could turn back the P2 now.

Away from the crowd, Mike and Trisha stood holding hands as they watched Buck descend the gangway. Trisha tried to imagine his pride, his exhilaration. He had flown the P2 well. Now he was the first to have carnal knowledge. He alone could answer those important questions regarding pitch control, trim, airfoil efficiency and auto-landing so critical to a pilot. She watched reporters corral him like a prized stallion. The moment was his now and the P2's.

Trisha and Mike were content to watch from a distance.

Eight months had passed since Robert Gunther's murder. Everything had changed and nothing had changed. Audra Shields had become a folk hero. There was even talk of a movie. Her story had been told and retold, embellished and changed so many times that little truth remained until she emerged as a female counterpart of Rambo. Peter Meyers had been killed by terrorists while serving in Syria. The attempt to impeach President Baker had failed. But it had extracted a promise from him that new presidential elections would be held in four months. The sticking point—Senator Garby would be the only one on the ballot.

Peter's replacement was a company man, loyal to Baker, and Mike followed Pete's advice about trusting him. His guard was never down around him. And there was no contact between Pete's replacement and the Mossad, either.

Baker continued ratcheting up his anti-Semitic campaign and had broken with Israel in the UN by spearheading a UN resolution mandating Israel to return to their 1967 territory—an untenable position since it not only returned the Golan Heights to Syria but left Israel with indefensible borders.

In spite of the break between the U.S. and Israel, Joshua Chapman corresponded periodically. He even sent pictures of his and Cassy's wedding. The couple lived in Tel Aviv, and both were employed, Trisha suspected, by the Mossad.

Daniel was dating a dermatologist and seemed happy.

And Mike . . . he finally shared his Jacob-experience with Trisha. They had wept together that day. Since then, he continued growing in the Lord. A wedding date had been set. They had even visited Trisha's mother and gotten her blessing. In a few short months Trisha would become Mrs. Michael Patterson.

Now, she rested her head on Mike's bulky shoulder, her heart swelling with joy as she looked down the runway at the P2 and sea of reporters. The world was full of violence and uncertainty but Trisha was at peace. She and Mike had put themselves in God's hands. They were determined to live day by day under the umbrella of His protection. And however long or short their lives, they purposed to make their days count.

"I feel God smile as He looks at what we've made," Mike whispered.

"Yes . . . I feel it, too," Trisha returned. "We make a good team, the three of us."

Mike laughed. "That we do. But it's been a wild ride. I'll be glad to get back to normal, to have things quiet down. The most exciting thing I want on the board is next year's new interior colors for the EX4."

Trisha wrinkled her face. "We can do better than that. I have an idea of what we should do next. I was doodling the other day and came up with a sketch I'd like you to see."

"Oh, no," Mike groaned. "This sounds familiar."

"What I had in mind," Trisha continued, ignoring his remark, "was a new type of cargo carrier."

"Cargo carrier? Our C101 is doing well."

"Yes, I know, but I'm talking about a totally *new* cargo carrier, a VTOL . . . ."

"VTOL? Explain to me why a cargo carrier needs to take-off and land vertically?"

"The world is in trouble. Think of the many places where only a helicopter can go because there's no airfield. But a helicopter is limited. It can't haul really huge cargoes. Half the famine in the world could be alleviated if we could just get the food to them."

"No. The answer is no."

"And not only could it deliver goods to inconvenient places, think of its rescue value."

"This is crazy, Trisha."

"You could airlift an entire village, livestock, personal possessions."

"Trisha!"

"Suppose you had to remove the inhabitants from the path of an oncoming hurricane or flood or . . . a war?"

"Out of the question."

"I thought we could begin with a stretch version of the C101 and . . . ."

"How many engines?"

"Well, that's the really exciting thing because I figured we would use just two NPR910s with . . . . "

"Why two?"

"Because I think we can achieve double the fusion capability of each engine by altering . . . ."

The End

CHARACTERS

Abraham Levi: Mike Patterson's lawyer

Ace Corbet: bartender and one of Audra Shields' lovers

Alexander Harner: head of Tafco Oil

Arie Katz: Mossad agent

Audra Shields: metallurgist working for PA

Bubba Hanagan: one of Audra Shields' lovers

Buck McNight: test pilot and mechanic for PA, long time friend of family

Cassy Merrill: Senator Merrill's niece and database manager for his presidential campaign

Dr. Daniel Chapman: highly respected surgeon in Everman Hospital; brother to Joshua Chapman

Iliab Nahshon: Mossad agent

Joshua Chapman: A Mossad agent with dual U.S. and Israel citizenship; a computer security specialist; Dr. Daniel Chapman's brother.

Kamal: called The Blade; terrorist; head of ISA, the Islamic State of America

Michael Patterson: President of Patterson Aviation (PA)

Mrs. Callahan: Trisha's half-Cherokee mother

Mustafa: terrorist

Nabil: terrorist

Najjar Haddad aka Azad Hosseini: terrorist working undercover at PA

Nathan Yehuda: Mossad agent

Nolan Ramsdale: nuclear engineer for PA

Peter Meyers: DHS (Department of Homeland Security) agent

Rachel: Joshua Chapman's fiancé

Renee Patterson: wife of Michael Patterson

Robert Gunther: on board of PA; affiliated with large oil company

Senator Phillip Merrill: U.S. senator running for president

Senator Garby: U.S. senator running for president of the United States in Merrill's opposition party

Thaddeus Baker: president of the United States

Tom Halleron: Audra Shields' college beau

Trisha (Patricia) Callahan: head of Patterson Aviation's Research and Development Department

Yossi Behrman: Israel's Prime Minister

GLOSSARY

albondigas: meatballs

artesonado: an inlaid wooden ceiling with gilded, painted or carved panels

dabka: a dance only for men

daya: midwife

dhambora: musical instrument

DHS: Department of Homeland Security

DTs: delirium tremens; a disorder found in habitual users of alcohol

couscous: coarsely ground pasta made of wheat

empanadas: stuffed pastry or bread, fried or baked

enrollados: dough filled and rolled with either meat, cheese or vegetables, or combination of all; can also be a desert filled and rolled with sugar, nuts, etc.

falafel: deep fried balls of crushed wheat and chick peas

finjan: small containers for serving coffee

jihad: Muslim "holy war" against infidels

jihadist: a Muslim who participates in jihad

garbanzo salad: salad made from garbanzo beans and a variety of other ingredients

gazpacho: chilled vegetable soup

hijab: woman's head scarf

IDF: Israel Defense Forces

ISP: internet service provider

ISA: Islamic State of America; fictitious group

kaffiyeh: Arab male head covering

majnum: a demon

muezzin: the crier who calls Muslims to prayer five times a day

neodymium magnet: strongest permanent commercial magnet available

NPR910: fictitious nuclear power reactors that make up the propulsion system of the P2

NTSB: National Transportation Safety Board

PA: Patterson Aviation, a fictitious air frame manufacturing company

paella: a sausage and seafood dish

pollo escabeche: a savory chicken dish

R&D: research and development

shadeed: a Muslim who dies a martyr's death by blowing himself up or by other means

shia Muslim: believes Ali ibn Abi Talib, Muhammad's son-in-law, was first Caliph and successive rulers should come from this line. They also believe their messiah, the Mahdi, will come only after they have called for jihad and created world chaos

snafu: military slang indicating a mix-up

sunni Muslim: believes Muhammad's father-in-law, Abu Bakr, was first Caliph and that successive rulers should come from this line

SST: supersonic transport

CTOL: conventional take off and land

surah: chapter in the Quran

SUV: Sports utility vehicle

tambours: drums

tostadas: fried tortillas

VTOL: vertical take off and land

Yishuv: Jewish community in Palestine prior to the 1948 formation of the state of Israel

Author's Note

Many people look at what's going on in the world today and feel uneasy. Violence and uncertainty seem to mark the times, but no matter how unsettling things become, we, Christians, should remember that God is in control and more than able to protect us and guide us through these troubling waters.

While rewriting the novel which became *The Babel Conspiracy* I wanted redemption for my character, Audra Shields. After all, God is in the restoring, forgiving, and healing business, and He can do this for anyone. But try as I might, I couldn't make it fit with the story. That's when it hit me that, yes, God does forgive and restore, but He does so for only those who want it. He'll never violate anyone's free will. In addition, Audra is a reminder that not all those we love, pray for, or witness to will want to come to the Lord. This is a sad reality, but a reality nevertheless.

We are all sinners in need of a Savior, and God waits patiently for each of us to come to that realization. And salvation comes only through Jesus Christ who said, "I am the way, the truth and the life, no man cometh unto the Father but by me." (John 14:6) If you don't know

Him, won't you change that now by confessing to Him that you are a sinner, then ask Him into your life? It will change you forever.

Love and blessings,
Sylvia Bambola
Website: http://www.sylviabambola.com
Email: sylviabambola45@gmail.com

QUESTIONS FOR READERS GROUPS/BOOK CLUBS

- *The Babel Conspiracy* deals with the issue of adultery. As the world loses its moral compass, adultery seems to be on the rise. When men and women work together and share common interests at work, like Michael Patterson and Trisha Callahan, the temptation becomes even stronger. What are some of the things people can and should do at work to combat this?

- What does the Bible say about adultery?

- The Bible is full of types and shadows. Does physical adultery picture how God views spiritual adultery, when His bride, a member of His church, pursues other gods? Gods like money, pleasure, fame, etc.?

- Temptation is real. Christians aren't immune. As a Christian, how is it dealt with?

- Lord Acton said: "All power tends to corrupt and absolute power corrupts absolutely." Given the sin nature of man, could it be possible for even a future president of the United States to abuse his power? What abuse of power have you witnessed?

- The news is filled with stories of terrorists who tell their captives to either convert to Islam or die. What would you do if faced with this situation?

- Addiction is a destroyer. It destroys individuals, families, communities. And alcohol and drug addition are among the most common. In the novel, Audra Shields begins using alcohol to calm her fears. What are some of the other reasons people begin to abuse alcohol or drugs?

- If we are to turn to God for our security, identity, comfort, etc., doesn't that make using alcohol or drugs as a means of obtaining these things wrong? Aren't these things, then, like idols? Why? Or why not?